Kerry Langan will delight her readers with her comic eye, her honest heart, and her feats of characterization. These smart, lively stories are more than a pleasure to read. They are *fun* to read.

Joe David Bellamy, author of *Green Freedom* and *Atomic Love*

The characters in *Live Your Life*, Kerry Langan's masterful new collection of short stories, are you, me, and everybody: people navigating the ordinariness of life, and coming to terms with how often ordinary falls short of expectation. Her characters work in hair salons or in telemarketing call centers; they are aging soap opera actors with waning careers. They are also jilted lovers, divorcées, wounded children, and middle-aged women who remain invisible to the second-rate entertainers they hoped might have saved them from loneliness. With sharp eye and even sharper intuition, Langan captures every disappointment, every yearning, but also brings to light those fractional turns each person makes that signal a determination to continue on and lead lives of quiet dignity. Langan possesses a delicate yet assured touch and no tendency toward the sentimental. In her capable hands, characters make progress that is subtle, never mawkish, and every step is imbued with humanity.

Jane Ward, author of *Hunger* and *The Mosaic Artist*

Kerry Langan has an eye for the grace that sometimes comes as the unanticipated consequence of loneliness and loss. She transforms even the tokens of her characters' absurdities and failures—a pogo stick, a For Sale sign, an inexpensive ring—into unexpected instruments of grace. Each of her wonderful stories is a lesson in sympathy, delivered with gentle humor and a deep understanding of the human heart.

Rob Hardy, author of *The Collecting Jar*

LIVE YOUR LIFE
&
OTHER STORIES

LIVE YOUR LIFE
&
OTHER STORIES

KERRY LANGAN

Wising Up Press Collective
Wising Up Press
Decatur, Georgia

Wising Up Press
P.O. Box 2122
Decatur, GA 30031-2122
www.universaltable.org

Catalogue-in-Publication data is on file with the Library of Congress.
LCCN: 2012949505

Wising Up ISBN: 978-0-9827262-6-6

For Bob, Madeline, and Anna,
I love you so.

TABLE OF CONTENTS

LIVE YOUR LIFE

ORACLE HOUSE

Fourteen years after the Summer of Love, in 1981, I graduated from college with a marketless degree in philosophy. The buck stopped once I had that diploma in hand, my father, after the graduation ceremony, grunting "Philosophy," under his breath, like I'd just earned a degree in bottle capping.

It was all the challenge I needed to prove my self-sufficiency. After graduation, I went home to Oakland, but I spent all my waking hours in San Francisco looking for work and a place to live. In a coffee shop I saw an ad tacked on the wall about a room for rent on Waller Street so I went right over and found the place. It was a three-story Victorian house painted turquoise with lavender and pink trim. It stood out, even on that flower power street with one house after another painted a surreal mix of colors. On the front triangular peak of the house was a Delphic eye inside a pyramid. There was no eye lid, just a huge purple eye with the blackest pupil, a tunnel. I looked up at that eye and thought it was looking ahead, that it knew my future.

I knocked on the front door and a woman about my age, early twenties, opened it. I almost blurted, "I'll take it," before I even looked at the place, she was such a knockout. She had green eyes with blue flecks in them that flashed like a pinwheel. Her hair, red and down to her shoulders, looked like it hadn't been combed in a couple of days, like she had just gotten out of bed. She wore a dance leotard the color of red wine and a short faded jean skirt. She was barefoot, with tiny silver rings on both of her baby toes. I told her my name was Alan and I was there about the room.

"Oh," she said, looking over her shoulder. Then she called out, "Max, someone here about the room for rent." She stepped back to let me through the door and I walked in and sat in a sagging gray armchair in the front room. "He'll be right out," she said, and walked out of the room. It gave me a moment to look around. The place was wonderfully Spartan with dark wood floors and just a few pieces of furniture, nothing like my parents' cramped house with the fake paneling. The couch, a cushioned gray-brown thing, had one end missing. Some batik tapestry hung on the lavender walls, and in the open adjoining room I saw a mural of a woman's face with squiggly rainbow hair. That room was empty except for a battered upright piano. Somewhere in the house, sandalwood incense was burning.

Max stumbled into the room, stretching his arms as he walked through the entry way. He was older, maybe in his late twenties. Tall and skinny, his jaw threatened to poke right through his skin. He wore jeans and nothing, I mean nothing, else, as the tear in the seat of his pants showed. He shook my hand and sat down on the safe side of the couch, reaching under one of the cushions to pull out a crumpled pack of Marlboros and a Bic lighter.

"So, man, you got the dough to pay ninety bucks a month?"

"Ninety?" It was steeper than I was hoping.

"Ninety. You got a job?"

I wasn't expecting such an interview. I dug my hands in my pockets and said, "No, not yet. But I've got some money saved, enough to pay the rent through the summer, and I'll get a job."

"Cool," he said and stood. "Everyone pays me the first of the month and then I send a check to Bill."

"Bill?"

"The landlord. He lives in Berkeley. Sammy's moving out Friday. You can move in any time after that."

"I'll be here Saturday."

He nodded his head and left the room so I saw myself out. Standing on the porch of my new home, I felt complete, whole. I couldn't wait to tell my father I was moving out, that I would be a free agent. Walking around the neighborhood, I took it all in: the people, the shops, the music spilling out of the windows. There was a house on Frederick Street painted like a jungle in dappled greens, a mural of a tiger sprawled on the front. I thought, now *this* is a neighborhood for a philosophy major. Every street I walked down, I felt the Delphic eye following me, guiding me, telling me I had come to the right place. I was on the train back to my folks' house before I realized I hadn't asked to see the room.

That Saturday morning, my friend Joe drove me over in his van and I unloaded my stuff on the porch: a foam rubber mattress, clothes, and books.

My copy of Plato's *The Republic* was on the top of the stack. It was so worn, the corners of the pages curled up into little paper waves. The door was open so I just went in. Max was sleeping on his stomach on the couch, his feet hanging over the ghost end. A dark gray cat with huge ears was sleeping on his back. I was wondering how I could wake Max up when he opened just one of his eyes.

"Hi," he said, not moving.

"Hi." I relaxed. I was worried for a second he didn't remember me.

"Who are you?"

Right the first time. "I'm Alan," I said, crestfallen, "I'm moving in, remember?"

"Oh." He shut his eye and I thought he had fallen back asleep, but then he said, "Top of the stairs. Second door on your left."

Joe helped me lug the mattress up the stairs. We found the room, a large walk-in closet really, although there was a decent-sized window with a fat ledge. The room was about half the size of the dorm room I'd lived in the year before.

"You can paint it, hang some pictures, fix it up," Joe offered, as his finger traced one of many cracks in the plaster walls.

"Well, I'm only going to sleep here," I answered defensively; "I'm going to live in the whole house." But as I looked around at the pale green walls, I resolved to buy white paint that afternoon. And I would hang some posters over the really bad cracks. But still, it would just be a big closet.

I folded all my clothes and put them at one end of the room and lined my books up on the window sill. One of them kept flopping off and I finally laid it sideways. The sunlight fell on a black and white sketch of Thomas More, and the word *Utopia* seemed to make fun of me in my little room. Joe said he had to take off so I walked downstairs with him and thanked him for bringing me over. I went back in the house, the cat still on Max's back, both of them dead asleep.

For almost a week, I didn't know who was really living in the house and who was just a friend. Finally, I got everybody's name straight. In addition to Max, there were Garrett and John. Garrett was nice, always asked me how the job hunting was going and whether I was finding what I needed to in the neighborhood in the way of stores, banks, and what not. He had dropped out of college a year ago, said he got disillusioned studying political science, and had a good job waiting tables at a hot new restaurant in Pacific Heights. He was hoping to become a sous chef and then save his money to go to a culinary institute. John was okay, but he didn't talk much, just "Hey" whenever he entered a room. He didn't have a job as far as I could tell, but he said he had a degree in history from Occidental. He talked about becoming an actor, about moving to Los Angeles and making it big, but he seemed anchored to the house. He did have money, though, and was always sending out for pizza or shopping for beer. Max never seemed to wake up; I saw him sleeping all over the house, in different rooms. That cat, Merlin, was usually on top of him. Max didn't have a job but I guessed that he and John had some kind of arrangement. They were always handing bills back and forth to each other. One, or both of them, was probably dealing. Max had been there the longest and was something of a neighborhood fixture. When he sat out on the porch, anyone who walked by stopped to have a cigarette with him.

There were three women in the house when I moved in: Sierra (originally Sarah), who met me at the door that first day, Violet (originally Valerie), and Jennifer (who didn't feel inclined to change her name). Violet had a deep, sultry voice that melted my spine; she spoke each word as if it were a complete sentence. Jennifer, a petite woman with jet black hair always in a bun and a chalk-white face, was quiet. She was still going to school, studying dance at San Francisco State. She was really snobby and barely spoke to any of us. We heard her doing grand jetés in her room, a thud every now and then when she reached the wall too soon.

When Violet moved to New York to try her hand at modeling, Sierra and Jennifer quarreled over who would get her vacated room, the large circular room on the second floor with three enormous windows. Jennifer insisted that she needed the extra space for dancing, and Sierra countered that she had been there longer, and besides, what if Jennifer did one of her running leaps and went right out the window? The dispute was ultimately referred to Max, the groggy leader of the place by virtue of his seniority, who decided that he would take the room, although he continued to sleep any place he happened to be when he got tired. John moved into Max's vacated room and I got John's big room at the back of the house. It almost never got any sun, but at least I was out of the closet. We advertised my old room and a steady stream of people moved in and out. I didn't bother learning their names. Ninety bucks was too much for that closet and we all knew it.

I applied for jobs in book stores, libraries, and a meditation center. I drew the line at applying for work in fast food restaurants, imagining having to serve my father a Big Mac, hold the onions. I explained in interviews that I had a degree in philosophy, that I could read and communicate, that I was well-rounded, eager to try anything. One man told me, "I appreciate your enthusiasm, but we're looking for someone with experience handling cash." I guess he thought philosophers never got near money.

Then, a few things happened to give me the idea that I could use my college education after all. The restaurant Garrett worked at folded and he was out of a job. He scrambled to find another one but wasn't offered anything better than a part-time job in a restaurant that was really just a glorified bakery. He turned it down but then got desperate. A few days later, John came in the house agitated, mumbling things to Max and talking into the phone with his hand over the receiver. For a week, he never left the house. He laid on the floor in the front room for hours, lifting himself up just enough to look out the window and see if anyone was watching the house. I guess he was worried about getting busted, but no one ever showed up. But anyway, he too seemed to be without a job which meant Max was also. Sierra was employed; she worked part-time as a waitress at a sandwich shop, a job she said she was really good at because she had been a communications major at UCLA. Jennifer taught dance to kids on the weekends and babysat for a couple of families in the neighborhood.

Things came to a head when Bill, the landlord, showed up. He had never gotten the last month's rent and Max was evasive when we all started yelling at him about what he did with it.

"Max, we've been through this before," Bill said. He was maybe in his early forties, with a handlebar mustache, black and gray, and a Giants baseball cap over his mostly hairless head. I couldn't blame him for being pissed off, annoyed at having to come over and shake the money out of us. It turned out he owned several houses in Haight-Ashbury and was in the process of getting them painted. He offered us a deal: he'd overlook that month's rent if we painted our house.

That's when the light bulb over my head went on.

"Have you hired painters to do all your houses?" I asked him.

He looked at me curiously, twirling one end of his mustache. "Not yet. Why?"

"Well," I looked anxiously at the other guys. I hadn't been there long and I didn't know how it would go over, me making a suggestion. "What if you hired us, the four of us," I said waving my arm to include all the guys, "to paint the houses." I looked back and forth between Bill and my housemates, hoping my animated expression would bring them along.

Bill lifted his baseball cap slightly off and then pulled the bill back down. "You've got to be kidding." He looked at Max. "This one makes off with the rent and you think I'm going to trust him to paint my houses?"

"Sure," Garrett said loudly, surprising me. "I painted houses all through high school." He looked at me and we nodded our heads at each other.

"Give us a try," I said. "Hire us for a week. If you're not satisfied, fire us." I looked at John and Max to see if they were following the conversation. John cleared his throat and glanced nervously at Max, his eyes reaching out of their sockets. But Max ignored his look, yawning so his chin dropped to his chest, and said, "Whatever."

Bill looked at us silently for a few moments and then raised his eyebrows. He held up a rigid index finger. "One week." Then he jabbed the finger into each of our chests and said, "Get this house painted and I'll overlook this month's rent. If you don't mess up, you can paint four more houses. I'll pay you each three hundred bucks a house. Any screw-ups, you're out!" He pointed at the door, leaving his arm extended in mid-air as he swung his head to include each of us in his threat. Then he looked at Max directly, bringing his finger right between his eyes. "You hear me, Max? You're out. Off the job and out of the house. I mean it this time."

Max held up his hands limply, like someone was pointing a gun at him and he was surrendering. "Yeah, yeah," he said lazily.

Bill looked at Garrett. "You're the painter? Call me first thing tomorrow."

As soon as Bill left, John collapsed on a kitchen chair. "Painting houses. Can't wait." He put his head down on the table and covered it with his arms.

My chest tightened and I wondered if they were all going to turn on me and start yelling. John and Max weren't used to having to do anything for a living and I could tell that the thought of painting houses, of actual physical labor, was too much for them. I was relieved when Garrett yelled at John, "What the hell else are we going to do?"

Max sat down, bending his knee up to his chin; he looked like a Pez candy dispenser. Garrett glanced at him and then looked at me and John. "I think we should change the way we do rent," he said.

Immediately, Max jerked his head, his chin straining against the thin flesh of his jaw. "What are you trying to say, Chef Boyardee?"

"Max!" Garrett hollered, leaning over the table towards him, "what the fuck did you do with our money last month?"

Max stood and shouted, "I borrowed a few bucks, okay buddy? I was going to pay it back, all right?"

"Do you have any brains in your head, Max?" Garrett yelled. "Yeah, you were going to pay it back just like that time six months ago!"

I stood up and slipped my hands between their chests, trying to referee. "Okay, okay," I said quietly, trying to ward off more screaming. "Sit down. Let's discuss this intelligently. Fighting never solves anything." John rolled his eyes like he thought I was some asshole but Max and Garrett sat down.

"I have an idea," I said looking at each of them for a few seconds, trying to impress upon them the seriousness of what I was going to say.

John looked at me and curled his lips until they were as big as Mick Jagger's. "Better than your last one, I hope."

I ignored him and turned to look at Garrett, a friendly face, and out of the corner of my eye, Max, who was pulling dead skin off his arms, a remnant of a terrible sunburn from a careless nap on the porch.

"Why don't we live communally?" I extended my arms in an embracing gesture.

"I thought that's what we were doing, genius," John said.

"No, I mean *com-mun-al-ly. Co-op-er-a-tive-ly.*" I put my forearms on the table and bent my body forward to make eye contact with each of them. They all looked back at me; I had an audience! This is it, I thought, and I spouted lecture notes from a couple of years ago on one of my favorite subjects: utopian societies. For twenty minutes, I told them about groups of people coming together because they were dissatisfied with life in conventional society, how these people had new ideas about politics and economics, that they had banded together to be a model for society. I talked about Plato and Thomas More, Robert Owen and Charles Fourier. "We don't have to be just unemployed, temporary painters," I told them. "We could be practicing the ideals of some of the greatest thinkers, greatest visionaries ever!" Then I added, "And we could save a lot of money."

Garrett asked questions about where the communities were and how they sustained themselves; he was interested. Max was quiet, but he was nodding his head, like maybe he'd heard it all before or maybe he was just nodding off to sleep. John was the skeptic.

"So, where are these utopias today?" he asked, confident he was sticking the pin in my balloon.

I admitted that most of them didn't last that long, although some of the Shaker communities were still going strong. "But think," I said, "it was hard to keep so many people together, to reach consensus on so many different things. There are just four of us. It'll be so much easier to pool our money and share equally. We'll come out ahead. I'm not saying that we're going to come up with the answer to all of society's problems, but it could be an experiment for the summer, just until we're done painting the houses. Then the four of us can decide what to do next."

"What about Sierra and Jennifer?" John asked.

I paused. I had forgotten all about them. "Well," I said, "we can ask them if they want to participate. If they want to, fine. If not, they'll just be responsible for their share of the rent."

We sat at the table and discussed our guiding principles. I got a piece of paper and wrote it all down. I would open a checking account and deposit all of our money. Each month, I would send Bill a check for the rent and give money to Garrett to buy groceries. I would give money to Max and John to buy non-edibles, toilet paper, dish detergent, garbage bags, that sort of thing.

"Hey, why do you get to handle the money?" Max asked.

"Why do you think?" Garrett said sarcastically, and Max held up his middle finger but didn't say anything. I looked meaningfully at both of them and they seemed to relent, to follow my example. I continued jotting notes. We would keep lists of everything we bought and review it at the end of each pay period. I agreed to be our liaison with Bill; I wanted to show him that there was a responsible person heading up the arrangement. At first we thought we would take turns doing cooking and cleaning, but because Garrett was an aspiring chef, he offered to do most of the cooking if it got him off cleaning detail.

"Is that okay with everyone?" I said, looking around the table, directing the consensus-making process. Max nodded as he continued to pull what looked like withered plastic bags off his arms. John let his eyes go dazed, like if I asked him one more question, he'd slip off his chair onto the floor.

Max said he had one more rule he wanted to incorporate into the principles. He cleared his throat and tapped his finger on the table. He sat up a little straighter and looked at every one of us. Delighted that he wanted to contribute something, taking it as proof that I could reach anyone with my ideas, I looked at him expectantly. "No disco music in the house," he said. I started to laugh but then I realized he wasn't kidding. "Write it down," he said, motioning with his head to indicate the paper. I made a mental note to myself: take every suggestion seriously. With a flourish, I wrote the final sentence and announced, "They have but few laws, and such is their constitution that they need not many." None of them recognized the quote, but I sensed Thomas More's heavy nod of approval.

When Sierra and Jennifer came home, I explained the plan. Sierra thought it sounded like fun, like her older sister's experiences in a commune in Canada ten years earlier. She would contribute her waitress money to the community bank. "And I'll plant an organic vegetable garden," she said; "we can save even more money if we grow some of our own food."

"Terrific!" I told her, glad to see someone really grasp the concept of a utopian society.

Jennifer readjusted her bun and said, "Count me out."

I walked with her to her room, explaining it was an experiment, a great opportunity to explore an alternative living arrangement. "If we all work together, who knows?" I finished, raising my arms to indicate endless possibilities." I looked her square in the face, softened my voice, and quoted a little More, "The minds of the utopians, when fenced with a love for learning, are very ingenious in discovering all such arts as are necessary to carry it to perfection."

Her laugh, short and sharp, pierced my ear. "Do you have any idea what you're talking about? You read a few books on the subject in college and you think you're an expert. This is real life, Alan. Grow up."

Jennifer was a good six to eight inches shorter than me but now she seemed to loom larger than her form. I could imagine her with a pot belly like my father's. She seemed to have as much disgust for my ideas as he did. But I reminded myself that my biggest challenge could be my biggest victory. I took a long, slow breath and said, "First of all, I read more than a few books, and second—"

"Give it a rest," she said, shutting the door in my face.

That first week was bliss. We started painting our own house, each of us taking a different side. The only terrible argument came about because Max, in one of his sleepy stupors, painted over part of the Delphic eye. Now it looked more cartoon-like than spooky, with a turquoise glop just left of the pupil. John went nuts, calling Max a "blind jackass" and reminding him that everyone in the neighborhood referred to our house as "Oracle House." I mediated the fight, calming them both down, explaining we could re-paint it, but it did occur to me that we should have known better than to let Max do the front of the house.

Surprise, surprise, John and Max finished their sides first. I was certain that Max was going to slip through a window and sleep most of the afternoons away, and that I'd have to lecture him on equal labor, but that wasn't the case. And then I found out why: John and Max just slapped the paint on, letting it run and drip all over the place. Garrett was really careful, clean, even strokes, and I was improving. At dinner one night, I tried to launch a discussion about pride in workmanship, but I didn't press it when John scowled, "Look, we got the damn thing painted, didn't we?"

Bill stopped by mid-week when we were about half done and told us we were doing a good job. He didn't really care about the fine details, as long as the house got a fresh coat of paint. He took me aside and said "You know, I didn't think this was going to work out, but I got to hand it to you."

In a rush of pride, I started telling him about the utopians and how we were patterning ourselves after them. The Oneida community produced flatware, the Shakers made furniture, and here we were, the Oracle House Painters. I liked the sound of it; I thought how neat it would be for somebody to read about us in a book a hundred years from now.

"Fine, fine," Bill said, unimpressed. "Just stay on the job."

Sierra came out of the house and handed us each a glass of iced tea.

"Thanks!" I grinned at her, laying my hand gently on her shoulder. Sierra was really doing her part. She worked the afternoon shift at her coffee shop, so she was home in the mornings while we were painting, and cheerfully served us snacks and drinks. And she was busy in the backyard planting tomatoes and squash. A couple times, I talked about the utopians with her and she listened appreciatively. I offered to lend her my books and she said she might read them.

After I thanked her for the tea, she slipped her arm around my waist and kind of squeezed it. "You're welcome," she sang.

Bill watched her walk back into the house, a smile spreading out beneath his mustache. He looked at me appraisingly and there was new admiration in his eyes. "Say," he asked, "just how communal is she?"

Bill might have shown a bit more interest in my remarks on utopian societies if I had filled him in on John Humphrey Noyes, leader of the Oneida Community in which all male members were considered married to all female members. In college, that got a lot of discussion and gave new meaning to the phrase "free love." Ultimately, it was a failed experiment since a lot of the community's younger members got tired of being paired with older members. Anyway, I didn't plan on telling the other guys in the house about this part of utopia. Jennifer was strictly off limits to all of us, there was no doubt, but I had my eye on Sierra for just me, myself, and I.

Before the experiment, I didn't think I had a chance with her. She hung out with this guy, Dirk, a yoga teacher with a Dutch accent. But then she caught him at her friend's house with another woman and dumped him. I guessed Sierra wouldn't have made it in Oneida either.

After we quit painting each day, I walked down to Earthlight, the coffee shop she worked at, and drank herbal tea. Sierra usually served me, sitting down for a moment if her boss was in the back. Before she jumped up to serve another table, she always reached over and patted my hand.

What was I waiting for? I asked myself. Well, I was afraid of being shut down, that's for sure, but if I didn't do something soon, someone else would be Dirk's replacement. I worked on building up my nerve, planning my first move. In the meantime, I called my father to let him know that in a mere couple of weeks, I had not only become self-sufficient but I had organized a mini-society based on visionary principles.

"Painting!" he roared over the phone. "I break my back sending you to college and you call to tell me you're a painter?"

"Dad," I objected, "it's much more than that. We're a utopian community based on equal division of labor and the rewards of labor." He sighed loudly on the other end of the line. "I'm the founder," I emphasized, trying to make him understand the importance of what I'd accomplished. "I'm doing something Plato envisioned—"

"Congratulations," he cut me off. "I wonder if Plato ever painted the

Parthenon." *Click.*

Trouble started to brew at the start of the second week. The four of us went over to Belvedere Street to start work on this badly peeling salmon-colored house. It was in such bad shape that Bill told us to use heat plates to burn the old paint off before we put new paint on.

Talk about a dirty job. You had to hold the heat plate steady for a few seconds against the wood, take it off, then quickly scrape the charred paint off. Little flames burned into the wood and made it smell like an incinerator. Black flecks of burnt paint flew in my hair, down my shirt. I even had black flecks of burnt paint wedged into the corners of my teeth.

We had painted our own house so quickly, we expected every job to be that fast. But burning and scraping were painstakingly slow. We started at the top, on scaffolds, and by the end of the first day, only a tiny ridge around the top of the house was exposed to show the wood beneath the paint.

Max complained the loudest at dinner that night. "I feel like I smoked eight packs of cigarettes," he said.

"And it was so damn hot up there," John said looking at me. "Got any more bright ideas, Alan?"

It was time for a pep talk. People in Oneida probably complained too, I told myself. I got beers out of the fridge and passed them around. "I know, I know. It's hard work. But c'mon, we're doing it. We're doing a good job and we're getting paid for it."

No one said anything. I looked at Garrett and even he looked defeated, too exhausted to lift his beer.

"I don't know, Al," he said. "I think Bill should be using professionals to burn the paint. I think we should tell him we can't cut it."

"What?"

"Good idea," John pronounced, holding the cold beer against his face.

"Look," I said quickly, gesturing towards the cupboard. "The place is stocked with food. We're eating dinners fit for kings. The experiment is working!"

Actually, Garrett had gone a bit overboard with the cooking, fixing gourmet dishes that weren't always appreciated by our simple palates. We had enough leftover bouillabaisse to feed an army and it was starting to stink up the place. And he bought expensive gourmet ingredients; I was secretly worried that we weren't really saving any money yet.

Still, my point was we were living cooperatively, harmoniously. I couldn't remember the exact quote, but I fudged some thought of More's, saying, "How much may be done in those few hours in which we are obliged to labor . . ." Max burped in response, but I kept reasoning with them until they agreed to at least finish out the week burning the paint off the house on Belvedere Street. At that point, we'd see how far we were. If it was still hell, we'd ask for a house in better condition to paint, or, I tried to tempt them, we'd ask Bill to pay us more money to finish the job. "If we quit now," I warned them, "Bill will think we're a bunch of good-for-nothings and throw us out of the house."

They were grudgingly convinced but it really stung when Garrett, my ally, raised his finger at me, mimicking Bill, and said, "One week."

I had no other choice but to seek out Sierra and elicit her sympathy. She was the only one, I told myself as I walked up the stairs, who could appreciate the complexity of true cooperative living. She would reassure me, console me. I knocked on her bedroom door and she opened it just a little. All I could see were her blue-green eyes and part of her nose. When she saw it was me, she opened the door wider and I saw, my heart riding up a fast escalator, that she was wearing just a T-shirt that stopped at the top of her thighs. I stepped in and she shut the door behind me quickly. Before I knew it, she was nuzzling my neck. We rolled around and around the floor, over record albums, rumpled clothes, Merlin (we let him out), and a radio. She kept me up most of the night and I started to worry that I'd never be enough for her. Maybe that's why the Oneidans came up with the idea of multiple marriage.

When I woke up in the morning, the sun was storming through the windows, throwing light on last night's wreckage of intertwined sheets and the curtain that had been ripped down from the window somehow and now lay draped over the head of the bed. I looked at Sierra. Her hair was a fiery tangle on the pillow, even redder in the sun, and she was fast asleep. I looked at the little clock on her dresser and saw it was ten o'clock. Ten o'clock! Shit! I was an hour late to paint. Bill had mandated that we be on the job every morning at nine o'clock. He told us he'd check with the tenants to make sure we were showing up on time.

I ran to the guys' rooms shouting, "We're late! We're late!" but they weren't there. Incredible. They had actually gone to paint on their own. I dressed hurriedly and started over there. I planned what I'd say, how I'd apologize to them for being late. I decided I'd make a big deal of their coming over on their own, and I'd admire what they'd done so far. My mind raced as I tried to come up with an appropriate utopian quote, but maybe it was time for me to start quoting myself.

As I turned the corner on Belvedere Street, I saw it—a fire truck and lots of men in massive black coats and helmets. A number of them were standing on a lawn holding a hose, a fierce stream shooting up at a fire on the top of a house. I ran down the block trying to see which house, but was there any doubt?

Standing on the sidewalk, watching it all, were Max, Garrett, and John. They were quiet, awed by the flames that were searing the entire top half of the house. A woman wearing a bathrobe stood near; she held a small white dog that kept barking.

"What happened!" I stopped running and fought to catch my breath.

"The house caught on fire," Garrett said with no emotion in his voice, still looking up at the flames.

"How!"

Max looked at me like I was an idiot. "From the heat plates, how else?"

Garrett walked a few steps away and I followed him. "I think he fell asleep while he had the plate on the house," he said, glancing towards Max. "He's lucky he didn't fall off the ladder and break his neck."

At that moment, I wished he had.

I turned and watched the black smoke funneling into the sky. The firemen were shouting at each other and I heard a siren; another truck was rounding the corner. Up and down the street, everyone came out to watch. Garrett and I walked back over and joined Max and John.

"Did anyone call Bill?" I asked.

They looked at each other, terrified, and then at me.

"Maybe you should," John said.

"Why me?" I said, angry.

"Well, this is your utopia." He smirked and raised his hand towards the house. I looked up and saw wood falling to the ground, and someone yelled at us to back up.

Resigned, I went next door and called Bill, telling him there'd been something of an accident. "Accident! What are you trying to tell me?" he roared. When I finally revealed we were talking fire, he cursed for thirty seconds and then hung up on me. When he drove up about a half hour later, the flames were gone, but the house was still smoldering like a huge cauldron. The bottom half didn't look too bad, but the top of it was completely charred.

"Well, at least the paint's burnt off," Max said and I thought Bill was going to punch him.

He threw his baseball cap on the ground and screamed at us. "You morons! Get the hell out of here! Get the hell off of my property! Pack your stuff and get the hell out of my house!"

I tried to protest, tell him we were good painters, that it was just burning the paint that threw us off track. He waved his hand in my face and, desperate, I yelled, "Don't blame me! I wasn't even here when it happened!"

"GET THE FUCK OUT OF HERE!"

We took off running, not stopping until we got to Waller Street. John tripped once and none of us stopped to help him get up, our cooperative spirit gone up in smoke with the house.

John and Garrett started packing their stuff, making phone calls, trying to line up a place to sleep that night. Max plopped down on the couch and within moments was fast asleep. Just another morning as far as he was concerned.

I couldn't believe it. An hour earlier I had left the house feeling on top of the world. I was the founder of a successful utopia, just done with a raucous, sex-filled night, and now, here I was, homeless and jobless. My father would have savored the details of this mess. I climbed the stairs to the only bright spot left in my life, Sierra. Bill didn't say that she and Jennifer had to move out, and I was hoping to hide out in Sierra's room until I knew what I was doing. She didn't answer my knock so I turned the doorknob. I figured after last night, she'd hardly mind.

She was still in bed, but she was awake. She looked at me, startled, nervous, and said, "Hi, Alan. Um, do you know Dirk?" She gestured with her hand to the form laying beside her in bed, a big bony foot sticking out from under the sheet. Dirk grinned at me and managed to produce his hand, pulling it from God knows where, to give me a small wave. He said something in Dutch, hello or good-bye maybe.

I shut the door and went downstairs. Merlin came up and licked my leg, his tongue so scratchy it could probably remove paint. On the porch, I looked down the street and wondered what in the world I was going to do. My legs collapsed under me and I sat on the steps. I would have to go home until I found another job, there was no way around it. I could just hear it:

"What kind of unemployment benefits do founders of new societies collect?"

An old blue van pulled up to the curb and Bill got out. I braced myself, but where could I run to? Not back in the house. Down the street? He was already half-way up the walk, so I stayed put.

"Look," he said, sitting down next to me on the steps while he chewed on a cigar that wasn't lit, "I still need a couple painters. I can tell you're the responsible one. I've got another place on Beulah with an empty room. You want it?"

"Really?"

"Yeah, there's a couple guys there that owe me back rent too, and you can paint with them. No money this time, just a room to stay in until you pay off a percentage of the fire's damage."

"It was going so well. If it weren't for the heat plates . . . If only Max . . . I'm sure we could have kept the utopia going."

Bill knocked his elbow into my upper arm. "C'mon, get your stuff together. I'll give you a ride over."

I stood and started up the stairs. But then I walked back down them and went to the edge of the street, turning to look up at the Delphic eye, that purple circle in a black triangle that was still partly obscured by turquoise paint because of Max's absent mind. I wanted to paint over the whole thing now, blind the eye because it didn't know a damn thing about my future. Just like Max, it had fallen asleep.

Beneath the eye were two large windows on the third floor of the house. Through the glass on the left, I could see Jennifer in a black leotard bending and stretching, leaning over so her hands touched the floor. She picked up one of her feet and pulled her leg alongside her body until her foot was over her head. Then she did the same with her other leg. She looked so independent, so completely self-sufficient as she began to pirouette in a circle over and over again. If only Bill weren't yelling at me to hurry up, I could have continued to watch her. In fact, I could have stood there all day admiring this dancer who didn't need a partner.

BAG HEAD

Whoever coined the expression, "Easy as pie," never met my Aunt Martha. She served cherry pie, the pits still in the fruit, at a church picnic and was stunned when the minister cracked his front tooth and had to be rushed off for emergency dental surgery.

"*Cherries have pits?*" she marveled. "Well, the rest of you just eat around them."

That was how our family functioned, we did things *around* Aunt Martha. Although a single woman with lots of spare time, none of the relatives asked her to baby-sit. Mother instructed Martha to gather pine cones for the Thanksgiving centerpiece rather than cook anything. She was encouraged to give gift certificates at Christmas after the year she gave us all economy size versions of Mr. Clean. "Sniff it, Clare," she told me, "that's *real* cleaning power."

Mother was mystified as to how Martha managed to keep her job as a personal assistant to Marvin Genkins, an eccentric crime novelist who churned out a new potboiler every year. And Father, well, Father was just relieved that Aunt Martha had a job, period. I speculated Aunt Martha was the reason I was an only child. Father had spent the better part of his life bailing Aunt Martha out of self-concocted situations. When she was in first grade, she pulled the fire alarm in the school hallway because she thought the little red and white plaque was so pretty. While the fire trucks were at the school, the local diner caught on fire and burned to the ground. Once Martha climbed up a tree to rescue a cat, but Father ended up having to rescue both of them, breaking his collar bone in the process. Aunt Martha hit the same tree with a car some years later when Father was teaching her to drive.

We gathered that her duties for Marvin Genkins consisted of typing up his manuscripts, which he wrote in pencil, emptying ashtrays, and serving him coffee before 3 p.m. and bourbon after. We knew little else. When Aunt Martha visited us after work, she smelled of cigarettes and erasers. On one of these occasions, when I was about eleven, she was jubilant, announcing, "A new record! I typed nineteen pages today!"

Handing her a glass of sugary iced tea, Mother remarked, as she had so often, "That secretarial class you took has really paid off." Actually, we didn't know how much money Aunt Martha made. We only knew that since working for Mr. Genkins, going on five years now, Father had never had to pay her rent as he often did before when she worked as a waitress, a shoe store clerk and, finally, a perfume woman at a department store where she managed to squirt a customer in the eyes.

When she first went to work for Mr. Genkins, Mother suggested having him to dinner, but Aunt Martha said, "Oh, no! Marvin is a very private person. He never leaves the house. He even has his groceries delivered."

Father referred to him as a "reclusive agoraphobic" and Mother was simply fascinated by this man who was not a famous author but seemed to have something of a cult following. The two drug stores in our town always had his latest book on display in the window. Peering through the glass, Mother would shake her head and say, "And to think Martha knows him."

When I turned twelve, I grew four inches and lost my equilibrium. I became clumsy, bumping into furniture and tripping on the stairs. At school, my mind wandered and my grades fell from A's to C's in a few months.

"Clare is turning into Martha!" Mother wailed to Father one afternoon when they thought I was out of earshot.

"No, no," Father assured her. "Martha was always ditsy, from the day she was born. Clare was a normal child."

"Was! Was!" mother cried. "What's happened to her!"

I sensed them watching me. Nervous under scrutiny, I became even clumsier. I failed an eye exam and had to get glasses. Mother couldn't keep from blurting, "Now you even look like Martha!"

I lost friends. In seventh grade, who you hung around with could make or break you, and I was an asset to no one. I stayed home and read a lot. When I'd exhausted the young adult section of our library, I asked Aunt Martha to bring me some of Marvin Genkins books.

"He's so *pleased!*" she gushed, the first time she brought an armload over. "He thought the books might be too advanced for you, but I told him you started reading at three, just like me."

This approval, from a man I'd never met, meant too much to me. I stayed up late reading his books until the words danced on the page. My eyesight worsened and I had to get new glasses that magnified my eyes to an alarming degree. Mother all but took to her bed.

Mr. Genkins's books were formulaic, to say the least, and I took comfort in the predictability. The main character was Detective Hal Hittman, a gruff, burly detective in his forties, who "knew every dead end street in Milwaukee." With seemingly few clues, he found dead bodies, pointed his finger at the most unlikely, therefore the most likely, suspect, and concluded the case by sitting at his desk in the dark and musing about the "dame who seems to know a little too much about me." Although there was a different dame in every book, they were all shapely blondes with a pair of "baby blues" who needed rescuing of some kind. They were married to brute husbands or being blackmailed by former boyfriends. Hal Hittman never had a physical relationship with any of these women, but he gave every one of them "a long look that said it all."

Reading in my bed, my heavy glasses slipping down my nose, I squirmed at what I thought was an intimate statement. But why? I wasn't a shapely blonde; Hal Hittman would never give me a second glance. My baby blues moved like sluggish fish through a looking-glass bowl.

But I wanted to meet Marvin Genkins, tell him in person how much I loved his books.

"Clare, honey," Aunt Martha stammered, "it takes Marvin a while to warm up to an idea. It took me more than a year to convince him to let me sharpen his pencils each morning."

"Huh?"

"Sharpen his pencils. He used to throw them out when the point wore down. Well, he threw them on the floor and left them there. What a mess. Pencils everywhere." She took a breath, erasing the ugly sight from her mind, "But I convinced him my system was better. And now there are no pencils on the floor," she finished proudly.

I didn't ask to meet him again.

Mother was desperate to improve my poor social standing. She enrolled me in charm school and urged me to walk around the house with a book on my head.

"Stand up straight! Throw your shoulders back, for heaven's sake."

I tried to comply but was shocked at how far my new breasts stood out. A group of boys at school had started calling me "Bag Head." It started when Ronnie Lambert looked me up and down in the cafeteria one day and pronounced, "You wouldn't be half-bad if you wore a bag over your head." Horrified, I watched him slap his crotch as he growled, "Anytime. Any place."

As humiliating as this was, the backlash from the junior high girls was worse. Jealous that my breasts were eliciting male attention, they started a rumor that I stuffed my bra, a whole box of tissues in each cup. Then my face erupted with acne and I really did want to put a bag over my head.

To avoid school, I feigned illness as often as I could get away with it, re-reading Marvin Genkins's books until I knew entire chapters by heart. When Aunt Martha visited, we sat side by side on the couch and quoted favorite passages aloud:

"The sky was a furious purple when Hal Hittman reached the ocean. The waves crashed ferociously upon the calm sand. He listened to the roaring surf, knowing it had something to tell him. Be patient, he reminded himself, listen carefully. Then, with a brief nod of his head, he turned and walked to his car. He knew who the murderer was and he knew what he had to do to make the bastard hang himself with his own noose."

Aunt Martha and I giggled over "bastard." Such daring language! I asked her how Hal Hittman could drive to the ocean when he lived in Milwaukee, and Aunt Martha just blinked and said, "Why, I never thought of that."

"Maybe he drives to Lake Michigan?"

She nodded thoughtfully. "Maybe, maybe."

I asked her if she'd point this out to Marvin and tell him that it was me who noticed the error.

"No." She shook her head widely. "I never make suggestions. I tried once and Marvin didn't write for three whole weeks. Now I just type."

Mother went to visit her sister in Joliet for a week in late spring. On a Friday morning, after Father left for work, I dialed my school's number and affected my mother's breathy, girlish voice, saying, "My daughter, Clare Burnham, has strep throat and won't be at school today." The principal's secretary wished a speedy recovery and hung up.

Our whole family knew where Marvin Genkins lived, just a couple of miles from our house on a quiet, residential street. Occasionally, Mother drove by his house, a small bungalow with an overgrown lawn. She'd make a small sucking noise with her tongue and say, "You'd think he'd hire a gardener. He certainly can afford one."

On the bike ride over, I shivered with excitement although it was an unusually warm day. I parked my bike against the enormous tree on the curb lawn and hid behind the trunk. Peering out, I noticed that Marvin Genkins's lawn was as yellow as it was green because hundreds of dandelions dotted the grass. Aunt Martha's old Buick was parked crookedly in the driveway.

I took a deep breath and started to sprint toward the back of the house. Rounding the corner, I crouched low under a window and dared a peek. I found myself gazing at Marvin Genkins's kitchen. Through a narrow part in the curtains I could see a tall stack of pizza boxes on the table and a carafe of coffee simmering on the stove. But no sign of Marvin or Aunt Martha.

Bent over, I moved around the house until I was on one side, a large picture window over my head. There were no curtains, but the window was too high to look in. I heard music, a familiar melody. Frank Sinatra? Yes, that song he sang with his daughter about strangers in the night. Father had the album.

I ran to the garage and found the door locked, but then I noticed a small entrance on the side. I pushed the door open and stepped inside the garage. There was no car, but I found at least twenty large cardboard boxes filled with Girl Scout cookies, all of them Thin Mints. There were a few other boxes filled with the Hal Hittman books. Against the back wall were a few cans of unopened paint. I picked up two, surprised at how heavy they were, and carried them out of the garage and back to the window on the side of the house. I heard Frank Sinatra's voice again, this time a song I didn't know.

With a foot on each paint can, I stood carefully and slowly raised my head until just my eyes reached the bottom of the window. I was peering into a dark living room filled with books and papers stacked everywhere. Ghostly white cigarette smoke coiled up to the ceiling from at least three ash trays.

And there he was, Marvin Genkins. He seemed to be one size, extra large, from his neck to his ankles. His body was like some huge rectangle under that a massive black robe. He was mostly bald with gray hair striping either side of his head. He had a mustache beneath a dinky nose. He was wearing glasses with big black frames, but his eyes appeared to be closed.

More startling than his appearance, however, was that he was dancing with Marilyn Monroe or someone who looked just like her. An incarnation of one of Hal Hittman's dames. With big, broad steps, Marvin ushered this shapely platinum blonde in a black and pink polka dot dress around the room. Singing along with Sinatra, they bumped into furniture, knocked over a stack of books, and stepped on a cat's tail, the animal wailing as it fled the room. They never stopped dancing. Finally, they moved close enough to the window so I could see the woman's face. So beautiful and so strangely familiar. Too familiar, even with the blonde wig. I should have looked away.

Instead I watched their every move, this odd twosome clumsily dancing around the room together, out of step with the music. At the end of the song, Marvin opened his enormous robe and extended it to cover Aunt Martha, the two of them now one enormous terry cloth creature with two heads. Clouds moved overhead and the sunlight died. Marvin and Aunt Martha became shadow silhouettes. Then Aunt Martha's head disappeared beneath the robe, her body traveling down until she was kneeling on the floor. Instantly, Marvin threw his head back and opened his mouth, his large body swaying slowly at first and then faster with broad side to side movements. He started to moan, then holler loud enough so I could hear him clearly through the glass, "Oh, Oh, OH, OH, ATTA GIRL, MARTHA! YES, OH, OOHHHHHH!!"

I leaped off the paint cans and landed flat on my back in the soft overgrown grass. The clouds opened up and the light dropped onto my face. Slowly I turned myself over and then, on my hands and knees, I crawled around to the front of the house and got on my bike. My legs barely had the strength to turn the pedals but somehow the bicycle's wheels rotated over and over until I was home.

Our basement was big and drafty with damp spots in the corners.

My old baby doll stroller was down there along with a box of tap shoes in various sizes that I wore when Mother was convinced I could be the next Shirley Temple. Old lamps, rusted patio furniture, a broken television, all of this was stored in the cellar.

I put the stacks of Marvin Genkins's books under the stairwell. Climbing the stairs, I inhaled the dank basement air, the musty blanket covering our family's relics. I emerged blinking in the bright light of the kitchen where Mother sat sipping her creamy coffee. There was hope in her eyes these days. With minimal effort, I raised my grades to B's. My growth spurts were over and the clumsiness subsided. I saw a dermatologist regularly and my skin was greatly improved. My bathroom was now stocked with an arsenal of Bonne Bell cosmetics. The changes that could be wrought with concealer, blush, mascara and lip gloss were astonishing.

The biggest change was the contact lenses. They irritated my eyes and I dreaded putting them in and taking them out. Still, when I looked in the mirror, shyly at first but then with mounting eagerness, I saw someone who shocked me with her beauty. The deep blue of my irises was startling, and mother bought me a whole wardrobe of blouses and sweaters to play up the color.

A couple of girls in my class began sitting with me at lunch. Misfits who giggled at stupid jokes and stole glances at the boys on the basketball team. Then one morning when I was called up to the blackboard to solve a math problem, popular Ken Whitman whistled at me and some other boy said, "You ain't kidding." I dropped the chalk.

At lunch that day I stopped at the cheerleaders' table and said in a besieged little whine, "Can I *please* sit here? Cheryl and Judy are *so* strange." I glanced towards my usual table.

Susan Trimmer, prettiest of the bunch, stared at me as if she were appraising me. My heart stopped until she slid her tray down the table to make room for me and said, "Tell me about it. This morning Judy started crying in gym because she couldn't climb the rope."

That was all it took. I ate with the cheerleaders every day, and in eighth grade I was on the squad. I stood in the back row, but still, I got to wear the uniform. Mother took pictures of me with my pom poms and proudly included it with her annual Christmas letter.

Aunt Martha was disappointed that I stopped reading Marvin's books. "You won't learn anything from those *Seventeen* magazines," she admonished me. "Those models aren't real people, you know."

When Marvin Genkins died two years later of a massive heart attack, Aunt Martha inherited almost half a million dollars from his estate. But she was lost without the job, without him. She sat in a trance at family dinners or asked for a glass of bourbon which she only sniffed, never drank. For some reason her fingers were always smeared with typewriter ink. When someone at the zoo called us and asked us to come get the hysterical woman weeping in front of the gorilla cage, Father grudgingly insisted that she move in with us.

Aunt Martha tried to help Mother with the housework, but after smashing a crystal vase, Mother urged her to plant tulips in our backyard. For several days, Aunt Martha was enthusiastic about the project. She pulled weeds and constantly watered the yard. She bought at least thirty pairs of gardening gloves in bright floral prints. Martha got frustrated when she had difficulty digging six-inch holes for the bulbs, but later thought herself ingenious for getting out my old pogo stick and jumping through the back yard.

I was mortified one day when my friends witnessed Aunt Martha on one of her garden rampages, but I hid my embarrassment by rolling my eyes and shaking my head. "Father says every family has an odd ball and Aunt Martha is ours."

As she toppled off the pogo stick onto the lawn, I knew I should run over and help her up. But I was scared, scared of my friends seeing the two of us side by side. I averted my eyes as Aunt Martha stood. I knew she would jump back on the pogo stick and continue hopping until the yard was filled with holes. And for an all too brief period next spring, we would have the most beautiful yard in the neighborhood.

NO COST OR OBLIGATION

I met Millie that very first day of work at SRW Research, Inc. Don't ask me what the SRW stands for. They never told us. The job was to sit in a little cubicle with a phone and call people and ask them if they wanted a charge card with some department store. We called people all over the country for a zillion different stores.

Five of us were being trained together: me, Millie, and three other women. Everyone was over forty except me. I was nineteen and didn't know any better. My last job had been at the drug store working the cosmetics counter, but after six months of sorting the nail polish bottles by color and still no raise, I decided to move on.

Most of the women I trained with at SRW really needed the money, but one woman told us she was just dying to get out of the house. Her husband had retired recently and she said she was worried she'd put a bullet through his head if she was alone with him for too long. I almost jumped when she reached into her purse for a mint.

Millie was about five-feet, five-inches tall and very heavy. Her short, very frizzy blonde hair circled about her head like a ragged helmet. Her features were crammed into the middle of her face, a tiny nose and narrow eyes that disappeared altogether when she smiled, which was often. She had a million questions about the thirty-second spiel we were supposed to recite into the phone: "If they hang up on me, should I call them back? If they don't want the charge card, can I offer them a free store catalog? Can I talk to their kids? How old do you have to be to accept a charge card? What does no cost or obligation mean?"

The trainer, Sharon, was ready to lose it. She kept looking at her watch and saying how far behind we were. Before we finally left for the day, Millie raised her hand yet again and asked if it was possible to advance in the company, "Work my way up to trainer." Sharon looked at all of us and smiled encouragingly. Yes, it was possible, she said. She herself had worked the phones for two years before her promotion. Even though I had just met Millie, I knew she didn't have a shot in hell of being promoted. In fact, of the five of us, I knew I was the only one with trainer potential.

I took the bus home and told Jane, my apartment mate, about Millie. Jane's a hairdresser and I knew she'd especially love hearing about Millie's static-fro.

"Bring her in the shop, I'll do her hair for free," she laughed.

"She'd be your biggest challenge."

The next day was my first real day of work at SRW. The main office looked like a maze of stand-up white boxes on dark green carpeting. The boxes were actually adjoined cubicles. Each one had a tan phone and a computer print-out resting on the desk. Everywhere, women were setting their purses on the floor, chatting with one another while they cleaned the telephone receivers with rubbing alcohol. The place smelled like biology lab in high school.

A woman with long dark hair directed me to a cubicle across from a small office with mostly glass walls and no door, just an open entrance. A short man with circular glasses and a small, clipped black mustache stood behind the glass staring out at us. A buzzer sounded, and all over the room I heard the sound of fingers tapping telephone keys. The woman next to me pinched my thigh. "Start dialing," she said, "unless you want to get fired."

I looked at the print-out in my cubicle. It listed addresses and phone numbers in Syracuse, New York. Someone had written "Chancey's Department Store" in red magic marker at the top of the paper. I picked up the phone and dialed the first number. No answer. The second number was busy. On my third call, a woman answered. She sounded young, friendly. Nervous, I launched into my pitch. "Hello, Mrs. Lawson? I'm calling on behalf of Chancey's Department Store. You've been approved for a charge card at no cost or obligation. May I verify your address and mail it out to you?"

I spoke fast like Sharon taught us in training. The longer you talked, the less likely they were to hang up on you.

"Oh, I'm just the baby-sitter," the woman said. "Mrs. Lawson will be back after lunch."

"Oh," I said, disappointed. I told the baby-sitter I'd try back in the afternoon. The woman in the next cubicle leaned over and whispered to me to write a note on my print-out reminding myself what time to call back. I was surprised she had heard me talking on the phone; the noise from the voices of everyone on the phone was deafening. I tried to thank her for the tip, but she was already burrowed in her cubicle talking to her next customer.

For the next three hours I phoned neighborhoods all over Syracuse. Most people said no, a couple said no thank you, and countless people just hung up on me. I was starting to develop a sense as to how the conversation would go just from the sound of the person's "Hello." Some were already annoyed before they picked up the phone and others were probably dying of loneliness and waiting for someone, anyone, to call. I mostly talked to women and a couple of retired men who, all in all, were the nicest. One of them told me he didn't want or need the card, but he'd take it just to help me out. Another one flirted, asking me what time I got off work. When I laughed and explained I was calling from another state, he sounded sad. I felt bad saying good-bye to him, but they weren't paying me to make friends on the phone.

By noon, I had twelve people accept charges. It was only my first day, but I was handling the phone like a pro. Sharon came over and looked at my print-out while I tried not to look too proud.

"You're only averaging four an hour," she said. "Chancey's is an easy store. You've got to get it up to at least six an hour."

"What do you mean 'an easy store'?" I asked.

She sighed, irritated at having to take extra time with me to explain the obvious. I worried that she was already linking me in her mind with Millie. "It's a really nice store. They sell nice things. Lots of people want to shop there. Wait till you're calling for some bargain basement place no one wants to set foot in."

What did she know? I thought, walking out to the lunchroom. Easy for her to criticize since she wasn't on the phone all morning, having people slam the phone in your ear.

The lunchroom was a rectangular beige room with a couple of vending machines against one wall. Millie was seated at one of the long tables munching on an egg salad sandwich. It seemed inevitable that she didn't close her mouth while she chewed.

"Rosie, have a seat!" Millie called. She pointed excitedly to the chair across from her like I couldn't see for myself it was empty. I took out my salami sandwich and Pepsi from the crumpled brown lunch bag.

"How's it going?" she asked. "I don't mean to brag, but I got ten charges this morning."

I looked at her and nodded. "That's great." Whew. It would've killed me if I wasn't doing better than the worst person in my training group. Probably no one had looked at Millie's print-out yet, and she didn't know she was in trouble.

She stared back at me expectantly and then asked, "So? How did you do?"

"Twelve," I said, happy to burst her bubble. I avoided her face, looking down while I bit into my sandwich, the mustard sliding over the edges of the bread.

"You'll be the first in our group to be promoted!" she shouted. Embarrassed, I looked around the lunchroom to see if anyone heard her. A couple of women were punching the front of a vending machine, trying to get a pineapple Danish to come out. One of the women called the machine a goddamn money-eating hunk of junk. No one was paying any attention to us.

"Millie," I laughed, "there are, what, fifty of us? And three trainers and that guy who stands guard in the little office. There's not a lot of room for promotion." In my mind, though, I pictured myself as Sharon, going from cubicle to cubicle, telling the employees to get their averages up.

Millie bit her lower lip and tilted her head a bit to the left while she thought. She set her sandwich down on her napkin decorated with little hearts and licked the mayonnaise off her fingers. "Well, maybe they'll realize they need more trainers. Or," she moved her face in towards mine and leaned forward on the table, "maybe the ones already here will find new jobs!"

"You never know," I said, trying to sound hopeful, but thinking that she was an idiotic optimist.

Millie opened her purse and took out her wallet. She flipped through the photographs in the stiff plastic covers and pointed her finger at a picture of her sixteen-year-old daughter.

"Isn't she cute?" Millie asked.

Actually, she looked like Millie Jr. in the making except that her eyes weren't small; they popped out like she had a thyroid condition. Of course, I agreed she was cute.

Millie flipped through her wallet again and held up another picture. This one was of a handsome guy, maybe thirty-five, with very dark hair and blue eyes. He was wearing a blue shirt with a fisherman's knit sweater slung over his shoulder. He was supposed to look casual, but you could tell it was a posed shot. I was curious why Millie was carrying around some photo of a guy who looked like he could be on the cover of *GQ Magazine.*

"This . . . is the man . . . I love," she said slowly, dramatically. Then she ran her fingers lightly over the plastic, stroking it like it was velvet.

"Is he your husband?" I asked, startled beyond belief. Then I wondered if the picture came with the wallet; it had that commercial look.

"No!" she almost shouted at me. "I divorced my husband last year. He was a jerk who could never hold onto a job."

"I'm sorry." I didn't know what else to say.

But she waved her hand and smiled at the picture. "That's in the past. Now I'm focusing on marrying Wendell."

I pointed at the photo. "Wendell?"

"Wendell," she pronounced, a proud owner.

They must've made quite a couple. "How long have you been going out?"

"We're not really going out," Millie admitted. "But we know each other. We know each other very well. We're dear friends." Millie picked up an apple and inspected it for brown spots. She found one and, I swear to God, bit right into it.

"Where did you meet him?" I asked.

"I see him every Wednesday night at the Layover Lounge, you know, that club right by the airport? Wendell has the ten to ten-thirty gig. Oh, a gig is a show; it's show biz talk for an act or, or a performance," Millie explained as I tried not to roll my eyeballs. "He sings love songs and tells jokes. I knew from the moment I saw him that I loved him. I knew from that very first time last March."

"And that's when you decided you were going to marry him?"

Millie looked at me and nodded her head slowly. "When you know, you know," she said solemnly, like she was giving me the wisdom of the ages.

"Do you go out on dates with him?"

"No, not dates. But I see him every Wednesday night. He knows where I sit in the audience. Well, I sit right in front of the stage. I've never missed one of his shows since March, not one. Not even when I had a fever of a hundred and two."

I wondered what other accomplishments Millie was proud of. "That's loyalty," I said, as if I were impressed.

She asked me, "Do you have a boyfriend?"

I shook my head no. I didn't want to talk about it. Joe, my ex, had given me the heave-ho the previous week because I beat him at bowling every time. And when we played Monopoly, I never lent him any money. I really liked him, but it killed me to lose at anything. I was swallowing the last of my soda when Millie looked at her watch and stood up slowly. "I'm going back in early. I want to make a good impression."

"Okay. Have a good afternoon," I said.

"You too," she said smiling so I could see her little teeth shaped like niblet corn with spaces in between them. She walked to the door, her nylons rubbing against each other and making a *kshh-kshh* sound.

I had five minutes before I had to be back, so I walked into the ladies room. Both stalls were being used, so I looked in the mirror and brushed my hair. Jane was always after me to cut it in a bob, but I liked it long and loose. One of the women in one of the stalls started talking to the other, saying, "I've got a real rookie sitting next to me. Doesn't know her ass from a hole in the ground." I recognized her voice as the woman who pinched my thigh that morning. The woman in the other stall answered, "We ought to get paid for breaking in the new ones. After eight years, I can't be bothered. I've been passed over for promotion to trainer so many times, it's just not fair."

I bolted out of the restroom and ran to my cubicle. My head down, I started dialing and never looked up. If the person on the phone sounded doubtful, I thanked them for their time while I scanned my list for the next number to call. I had to pee so bad, I thought my bladder would burst, but I never went to the bathroom. I just kept dialing. When Sharon walked up to me at 4:30 to check my list, I was averaging eight charges an hour, double what I got in the morning.

"You're in the lead!" she told me. "That *never* happens to anyone on their first day." Then she said, and I loved it, "Watch your back, Madge" to the woman in the cubicle next to mine. I heard Madge mutter, "Beginner's luck" under her breath, and I thought, don't count on it, lady. I leaned around her cubicle and said innocently, "Thanks for the tip this morning. It *really* helped." She looked like she wanted to slap me.

Jane was already there when I got home. We sat on the couch eating leftover pizza and watching Phil Donahue while I told her about my day. She thought Millie's crush on Wendell was hysterical.

"I've got to meet this woman! She's crazier than Mrs. Packson." Mrs. Packson was an infamous customer of Jane's who always had her hair done in a beehive the day before Publisher's Clearinghouse announced its million-dollar winner. She wanted to look nice when they presented her with the check on television. She and Millie were probably two peas in a pod.

With each day, I got to know Millie better. She started bringing *Bride Magazine* to work with her. She folded down the corners of the pages with pictures of the dresses she liked. She had plans for a three-tiered wedding cake with lemon and chocolate filling. Her cousin's band would play at the reception, and she and Wendell would go on a Caribbean honeymoon cruise. Since Wendell wasn't in on any of her plans, it was pathetic. But Millie was undaunted. In her mind it was just a question of time before Wendell, singing to the crowd at the Layover Lounge, would be thunderstruck by her. He'd set down his microphone and propose marriage as the band gave a drum roll and the audience waited on pins and needles for her answer. Dream on, Millie.

Work itself couldn't have been going better. Almost every day, I had the most charge card acceptances. The little guy in the glass office, Russell Thompson, announced that I was the "girl to beat" and he congratulated me in front of everyone on my "meteoric job performance." Madge was so jealous, she was practically hissing at me. I knew she was listening to me when I talked on the phone, waiting for me to make a mistake so she could report me. Fine; it slowed her own calls down and I thrived on the competition. Every day I pressured myself to dial faster, to coax more people into accepting the charges. Every morning I sweated that I wouldn't be able to do it, but at the end of each day, I was in the top three, usually numero uno.

When I walked into the lunchroom each day, things got quiet and I could tell that the old-timers had been talking about me. Madge was probably feeding them all some line about how I was cheating. I couldn't care less. I had already gotten two raises and I wasn't interested in being friends with any of them. And besides, I had Millie if I wanted to talk to someone. In a strange way, I looked forward to our lunches, egg salad sandwiches and all. They were comic relief after a morning of racing to tap the phone buttons with Madge on my tail.

One Wednesday after work, I found Jane adjusting a curly red wig over her own chin-length dark hair.

"Um, let me guess, you're practicing for Halloween. You're Little Orphan Annie."

Jane started putting on makeup, almost purple lipstick and black mascara. We had loads of cosmetic samples from my days at the drugstore.

"Don't laugh," she said. "Yours is in the bag." She motioned to a white plastic bag on the coffee table.

"What do you mean?"

"Your wig. It's in the bag."

"What?" I emptied the bag and a furry ball of yellow ringlets fell onto the table.

"Careful!" Jane yelled. "I have to return them tomorrow. If anyone finds out I took them, I'll be in deep shit."

Jane continued putting on makeup.

"This may be a dumb question," I started, "but why would I possibly want to wear a wig?"

"So," Jane said, smacking her lips together to even her lipstick, "so Millie won't recognize you."

I looked at her, started to talk, but she got up, picked up the blonde wig and hoisted it on my head. The ringlets hung in front of my face like tentacles on an octopus.

"Nooo waay," I said, sniffing the plastic-smelling hair.

"Guess again." Jane was already moving in to fix my wig. "Tonight," she said jerking the wig right, then left, "we meet Wendell."

The Layover Lounge was best seen in the dark, and it pretty much was except for the tacky mood lighting from cheap fluorescent lamps. Black Formica tables were sticky with drink spills and the blood red carpet was shedding everywhere. Every time I touched anything, I got a shock. We were sitting on what were really just wooden folding chairs painted black. Each table had a miniature plastic airplane holding a card advertising drink specials. "Clear Skies" was a blend of citrus juices and rum, and "Fasten Your Seat Belt" was something your waitress would set on fire for you. I would never have ordered that because I didn't trust the waitresses who were dressed as stewardesses except that they wore stilettos and mini-skirts.

The stage was just a little wooden platform with a microphone at the front of the room. A piano stood against the back wall. I wanted to sit way in the back, but Jane insisted we sit near the front. I kept my eyes down, terrified Millie was going to recognize me despite the wig and heavy makeup.

"Is that her?" Jane whispered loudly, jabbing me in the side. I looked up and saw Millie sitting at the front center table by herself. I could just make out the left side of her face. She was drinking a glass of white wine and smoking a cigarette. She had tried to do something with her hair; a little piece of it wrapped around her ear and came out in a spit curl on her cheek. She wore a yellow sequined nightmare of a dress with straps made out of braided gold chains that pressed deep into her shoulders.

Talk about a mistake. Instead of laughing, I wanted to go and sit at Millie's table and order her an egg salad sandwich. Or convince her to leave with me and catch a late movie. I knew Millie thought she looked sultry in her sequins as she inhaled a cigarette, tilting her head back so the smoke blew up and away from her face, but she looked ridiculous. Ridiculous in a sad, heartbreaking way. And here I was, a spectator to her delusions.

Jane kept poking at me. "That's her, right?" she asked.

I nodded. "That's her."

"Is she for real!" Jane laughed as I put my finger over my lips to tell her to be quiet.

"Oh, come on," I whispered back, "she doesn't look that bad." I sounded hopeful, like I was trying to believe it myself.

Jane looked at me like I had lost my mind and asked, "Do you need glasses?"

We had to stop talking because the piano player started to introduce Wendell. "Ladies and Gentleman, the Layover Lounge is honored once again to welcome that velvet-voiced gent from Toledo, *Wennndelll Schuuulller!*" There was some clapping and this guy in a vest and too tight jeans walked up to the mike. He didn't look as good as his picture, you could see that in a second. He was actually a little pudgy and his hairline was receding. The photo must've been touched up a lot. But still, he was handsome in a certain way for an older guy.

I looked at Millie. She was entranced, beaming up at him like he was Frank Sinatra, giving him a small, private wave with her right hand. Wendell thanked the audience for that warm welcome and started singing "Lay Lady Lay." It was immediately obvious why he had the Wednesday night gig. He sounded like my Uncle Stan after a couple beers, slobbery with one word sliding into the next, jumping and losing octaves at a time. And he kept waving the microphone around. Sometimes we couldn't hear anything, and the next instant we were covering our ears to keep from being blasted out of the place. It did kind of sound like a plane taking off, so maybe that's why they hired him. Then Wendell told some bad jokes about drunk pilots and tried to talk to the audience, mainly people waiting for a flight. There were only about fifteen of us in the room and I was scared to death he was going to say something to me and Jane. I couldn't believe it when Jane asked him to sing "Rolling on the River." I kicked her under the table, but she just laughed and snapped her fingers in time to the music.

Finally, 10:30 came and Wendell introduced the next performer. He started to leave the stage and I watched Millie stand up and motion to him. He walked right past her. *Bastard*, I thought. You're really no prize yourself, buddy. But then, the unbelievable happened. Wendell walked straight to our table and stood grinning down at us. Dentures, I thought.

"So, *ladies*," he said, way too loud, "did you enjoy the show?"

I couldn't talk. I picked up my Clear Skies and started gulping. Then I heard Jane say, "Loved it. Won't you sit down?" Jane floated her hand to the empty chair. It shouldn't have surprised me. She was probably thinking this was a riot. I looked over at Millie again. Her face was a round orange ball and her mouth hung open in a perfect little circle, like the opening of a birdhouse. She didn't even try to hide that she was staring at us. I worried that she was going to burst into tears. I wanted to run over and tell her that we weren't really interested in Wendell, that it was a game, Jane was pulling his leg. *It's a joke, Millie!* I silently screamed. *It's all a joke!* Of course, I couldn't, so I stood up to go the ladies room instead.

"Excuse me," I said, with a murderous look at Jane, and walked to the restroom at the back of the room. I stayed in there a long time. The wig was itchy, but I didn't dare take it off for fear Millie would walk in. Finally, the door opened and Jane entered. She looked at me and cracked up laughing, doubling over at her waist.

"What a *loser!*" she screamed. She kept talking, but it was hard to make out what she was saying. She kept breaking into fits of giggles and grabbing her stomach like it hurt. Something about dandruff on the collar of Wendell's shirt, bad breath, and a toupee that slid. "Actually, Rosie," she choked out, "I think," and she cracked up again, "I think," she tried once more, "Wendell and Millie make a beautiful couple!" she spit out.

"Can we go now?" I'd had enough. I knew that for days I would be haunted by the memory of Millie's orange face.

"What's the matter with you? Don't you think this is funny?"

"Look at us, Jane." I pushed her in front of the mirror. "We look like hookers. No, I do not think this is funny."

Jane looked at my reflection in the mirror and started laughing again. "*You* look like a hooker," she said, "*I* look hot." Then she added, "Ask Wendell," and started to laugh all over again, working herself up so much that she was snorting to catch her breath.

"Jane, can we *please*," I started, but she cut me off.

"Okay, okay, we can go now. But you got to admit, it was too much. Millie thinks she's going to *marry* this guy and he makes a pass at me."

"What do you mean? He made a pass at you? What kind of pass?" I spoke as fast as I did on the phone at work.

"Yeah, he was real subtle and suave-like. He asked me if I'd ever done it in a Jacuzzi. Told me I hadn't *lived* until I did it in a Jacuzzi." Jane ran her fingers through her red wig, fluffing it up on top near the front. "He asked me to meet him after the last act," she said, giving me a fake, seductive wink.

"*Jane!* What did you say?" This was going too far. I didn't put it past Jane to go out with him and play this game a little longer. Soon she'd be taking his toupee to her salon for shampoos or whatever they do to toupees.

"Relax, would you? Like I'm going to be interested in some tacky lounge lizard. I told him I had a boyfriend who was a professional wrestler and I had to go meet him at his gym."

Well, thank God for that much. Then I asked, "Was Millie still there when you left?"

"Millie? She ain't going nowhere. She kept waving to him and then she sent a drink over to our table for him. That woman needs professional help." Still laughing, Jane cupped her hands under the faucet and drank some water.

I didn't say anything more. I thought of poor Millie sitting there in her chain dress trying to look seductive while her heart was being smashed to bits by some no class jerk. She didn't deserve that humiliation. No one did.

Millie didn't show up for work on Thursday. She'll be here tomorrow, I told myself, but she was a no show on Friday. I started to worry that she did something desperate. Took a bottle of pills and left Wendell some broken-hearted suicide note. Jane kept joking that she'd probably run off with Wendell and they were munching on wedding cake on some beach in the Bahamas.

On Monday, though, Millie walked in like nothing had happened. During lunch, she took out her wallet and showed me the empty plastic casing where Wendell's picture used to be. "You think . . . you know . . . a person," she said, in her pausing, dramatic way.

My heart felt like a basketball being dribbled all over a court. "What do you mean?"

"He was playing games with me," Millie said matter of factly. "I was the other woman. His girlfriend, this redhead, showed up at the club Wednesday night. She took one look at me and left him alone at their table." Millie sounded almost normal. If I didn't know the real story, I might have believed her.

"Did Wendell admit that this redhead was his girlfriend?" I asked, starting to wonder if Wendell had as active a fantasy life as Millie.

"He didn't have to. I sent a drink over to his table and she got so jealous, she walked out on him." Millie grinned widely and said, "Serves him right."

"Good for you, Millie!" I said, genuinely impressed. "What now?"

Millie leaned forward like she was letting me in on something really big. "I stayed for the last gig," she said, trying to draw it out and keep me in suspense.

"And?" I said, trying to play along like I was dying to know.

"There's a new singer from Toledo. His name is Mike Kellman. Cuter than a bug's ear."

"Really?" I said, amazed that Millie was already on the rebound.

"Say, Rosie, maybe you'd like to go with me some Wednesday night and hear his act? He's on from twelve-thirty to one."

That meant he was worse than Wendell, impossible to believe.

"Millie," I said, trying to flatter her, "I go to bed about eleven o'clock on weeknights; I'm not the swinger you are. But keep me posted."

"You bet."

Rumors were flying at work that one of the trainers was leaving. There would be interviews. Madge and a woman named Lucille were thought to have the inside track. That is, until Mr. Thompson came up to me and asked if I wanted to interview for the position. I had only been there four months, but my record, as he said, was outstanding. I said sure, I'd interview, what did I have to lose? It was another chance to rub Madge's face in it.

But Madge got the trainer's job, seniority and all, no big surprise. A rookie was placed next to me, a girl about my age who just couldn't catch on. I tried to help her, coached her between calls, but she didn't improve. And to my surprise, I missed having Madge next to me. I floundered without the competition. I didn't race to dial the phone numbers and I started to sound like a robot on the phone, a recorded message. People started hanging up on me right and left. Then I got desperate and begged people to take the charge cards. I took it personally when they told me to buzz off. After one really depressing day when I was way under average, the whole office heard me shouting into the phone, *"Why won't you just take it! Just take the damn charge card!"*

Madge had her moment in the sun when she gave me the company spiel about severance pay. I stood and said, "I really enjoyed working with you." She thought I was being sarcastic, but it was the God's honest truth.

The only other person I said good-bye to was Millie. "Good luck, Rosie," she told me as she pulled me into her for a hug. "I know you'll find a great job."

I thanked her and then asked how things were going with Mike. Millie lifted a new copy of *Bride Magazine* and opened to a mermaid-style wedding gown. I swallowed hard and said, "You'll be beautiful in that."

Maybe I liked being the receptionist at Jane's hair salon because people called me instead of me calling them. And the customers, the old women, were so nice. They were friendly and smiled when they came in, and I smiled back and offered them coffee and a fashion magazine while they waited for their beautician.

The only drawback to the job was that Jane and I spent too much time together and we started to get on each other's nerves. It was to be expected, I guess. I didn't like the way she made fun of the customers when they were barely two steps out the door or, worse, under the hair dryer. True, many of them were deaf, but still. And Jane thought I had turned into a killjoy. She had gotten me the job so she didn't appreciate my no-nonsense attitude. After work, she started hanging out with a couple of the other beauticians, and I usually went home to watch television alone. When the phone rang, it was almost always for Jane. I took messages for her and posted them on the refrigerator.

From time to time, I thought about Millie and wondered if she was still going to the Layover Lounge. Was she still pursuing Mike or was there a new singer who had caught her eye? When it was quiet in the shop, I went through the pile of worn journals and pulled out a *Bride's Magazine*. Folding open the satiny pages one at a time, I ran my fingers over the elegant, romantic photos. I studied each picture carefully, noting the dress, the flowers, the face of the model. As the months went by and the magazines became more creased and tattered, I continued to look at the brides, smiling at the pictures as though these women were my friends, or at least people I recognized.

COMPROMISE

This neighborhood is big and sunny. New. The yards are a full half-acre and the trees are these spindly little things planted last year. Directly across the street is a colonial two-story with a ridiculously wide driveway. The pudgy woman who still lives at home with her parents is washing her blue Prius again. Every time I sit on my porch, she runs out with a bucket and a sponge and lathers up the car. It has crossed my mind that she's trying to place herself in my field of vision, as if I could miss her. Still, she's more subtle than Mrs. Genoa, my next door neighbor, who has told me six times already about her niece, a graphic artist who's "a proper girl, a real lady."

I was supposed to get married last weekend. No way I would have moved out to suburbia on my own. Beth and I picked this house out together six months ago, five months before she walked out on me because her former fiancé, Brad, called and she was having second thoughts. Second thoughts? About me or him? Crying, she buried her face in her hands and sniffled, "Second thoughts about *ev-ev-everything.*"

So here I am driving home from work every day to Butternut Estates, a wonderful neighborhood "to raise a family in," just ask our real estate agent. I'm living alone in a place five times as large as the apartment I gave up in Boston. What I'd give to be back in that cramped place with the cracked plaster walls and a dinky view of the Charles River. Here, my voice could echo off the cathedral ceilings, that is, if there was someone around to talk to.

This house was not my favorite. It was the compromise house. Beth liked an even bigger place in an even newer development, and I wanted to get a townhouse in the city. But we were planning on kids fairly soon and the school district here is supposed to be tops.

I was able to cancel a bunch of the furniture we ordered, but the kitchen set and bedroom suite were already paid for and delivered. Every other room in the house is empty except for the television in the living room. Beth convinced me to get rid of all my bachelor furniture, the couch I got at a garage sale and my wobbly bookcases. The only familiar thing in this house is me, but lately when I stare at my reflection, I don't know who the hell is looking back at me. I look shell-shocked, like I've just come out of some bloody battle.

My plan is to sell the house and get the hell out of here. Move back to the city and rent an apartment. My parents, my friends, they tell me I'll feel so much better when I'm out of the suburbs, that it will help put Beth out of my mind. As if anything could.

The woman who still lives with her parents is named Diane. When I was reading the paper on the porch last night after dinner, she came over and introduced herself. I shook her hand and said, "Mark." I didn't even add, "Nice to meet you." She coughed and said, "Want to go for a ride sometime? I have a new car." She turned her head and gazed with pride at her Prius.

I closed the paper. "Where's there to go around here?"

Clearly she had rehearsed this before she came over because right away she blurted, "Have you been to Braemar's for ice cream yet?"

"Ice cream?"

"They have the best!" She started talking about the creamery attached to the shop, how you can watch them make the ice cream, about the special flavors of the day. What the heck? I climbed into her Prius and away we went. She played light rock on the radio and I ate a double Rocky Road. Yeah, these suburbanites are real party animals. And, yet, it was the best night I've had in the neighborhood so far. Sad.

For once in my life, I'm glad I'm an accountant. Numbers are a great distraction. During the day I'm fine. I'm working on a big audit that'll take a couple of weeks and my mind is busy every second. My co-workers were tentative around me when I first told them about Beth bolting, but they took their cue from me and now it's business as usual. My office-mate, Don, who got divorced last year, tells me I'm lucky. "Better you got out now," he says, "before you had to hire lawyers to split everything up and take your last dime." He's bitter, and who can blame him?

At night, though, I'm not fine. I don't sleep and I end up getting up at dawn every morning and driving to Dunkin Donuts. That's where I met Alice.

She's great. Like those girls in college who are perfectly comfortable hanging out with the guys and don't expect any special treatment. She was at the doughnut shop with her two boys, and just came up to me and said, "Hi. I'm Alice Sommers. I'm on the street behind yours; our back lawns are kitty corner."

She had on jeans and sneakers, no makeup. I'll bet she was hot ten years ago, but now she looks like a mom. A nice one. Laugh lines around her eyes and mouth.

Her two sons, Jason and Ben, are ten and twelve. Noisy, nice kids. We talked about sports while I dipped my doughnut in coffee. I waved my hand when Alice asked if they were bothering me.

Ben said, "My dad's going to put a basketball hoop on the back of the garage the next time he picks us up for the weekend." I wondered if Alice dumped her husband or if it was the other way around. She talked basketball with me, a true Celtics fan. Josh knocked her coffee over and she just grabbed a stack of napkins and kept talking. After they stood to leave, she said, "Well, feel free to stop over any time." But she said it casual, no come on.

Wedding presents are still arriving. Not everyone got the word on time. I get home from work and there's a bundle of UPS packages on my doorstep. The way I see it, this stuff isn't my problem. Beth should be in charge of getting it back to people. I would tell her that if she'd call or drop by. We're having a stand-off, I guess. All I know is that when the woman you've been sleeping with for two years makes an exit, the ball's in her court.

And apparently Diane is pissed at me. She hasn't washed her car in five days and she doesn't even wave when she comes out to get the paper. I guess she expected our little ice cream excursion to be the first of many. She's nice, cute, I guess, if you like that type. Her hair is kind of non-descript brown and she doesn't wear too much makeup. She's a little on the chunky side and she wears what my mother would call sensible shoes. She gives piano lessons to kids and teaches a class in music theory at the community college. Like I said, she's nice. Safe. Predictable. She'd never pull out of a wedding in the eleventh hour.

One night I get a call from Mrs. Genoa's niece, Andrea. She sounds out of breath on the phone, like she's just come in from jogging, and says, "Aunt Kathy says you could use an ear. Want to grab a sandwich?" Like me, she works downtown, so we meet that Friday at a café with outdoor seating.

Andrea has a beer with her burger and clearly doesn't mind that I eat French fries with my fingers. She laughs easily and gets me laughing too. Her eyes, dark as Oreo cookies and almost as big, could pin me to a wall. She's at ease with herself, with her body. She moves when she talks, her breasts sliding under her silk blouse. And she's smart. She runs her own graphic arts studio and tells me that business is going well and she's moving to a larger location.

"So, Andrea, when can I see you again?"

I like that even though her mouth is full of food, she gives me a goofy smile before she swallows. "Don't get me wrong," she said, "I think you're a hottie—"

"A what?"

"A hottie. Well, maybe you're not up on the lingo, but you're cute, okay? Very cute."

That's always nice to hear, but I know she's going to turn me down. She takes another swallow of beer and continues, "I just don't want to be your transition person. Been there, done that. Too many times."

I nod. Before Beth, I used to know how to play it cool. "You want me to work out my latent anger toward females before we get involved."

"Latent anger?" Her eyebrows lift comically. "Yeah, whatever, I just don't want to fall for you and a couple of months into it have you tell me that you're going back to Beth. When you're over her, and I mean *way* over her, give me a call."

Grinning, I ask, "You're not worried I might fall for the transition person, never get around to calling you?"

She slaps the table and gives me a long look, the corners of her lips curling up. "That, Mark, is a chance I have to take."

I insist on paying the bill. For the first time in weeks I feel almost human. When I get back to my office, though, I check my messages first thing, still hoping Beth called. No such luck.

A few times a day while I'm at work, I slip into a stall in the men's room and open my wallet to look at our engagement photo. Yeah, I still carry it. Beth's head is leaning against my shoulder and my arm is proudly wrapped around her. Her hand is resting on my chest so the photographer could get a good shot of the diamond, a full carat. Beth has strawberry blond hair, not too red, and freckles across her cheeks. One of her front teeth turns in a just a little; it gives her a flawed, friendly smile.

We met at a softball game. One of her girlfriends was dating our pitcher. I played first base. Afterwards, when we were drinking beers at the team's usual bar, Beth walked up to me and said, "Nice double-play in the third inning. I never saw anyone run that fast."

An hour later we were still talking. Beth's just a couple inches over five feet. I had a crick in my neck from leaning over to hear her talk over the bar music. When she told me she'd downed two beers to get up the nerve to speak to me, I tried not to smile too big. At the end of the night, she only kissed me on my cheek, standing on her tiptoes to reach me. My heart punched back and forth against my chest, and I knew I was going to fall hard.

Now I look at the ring she gave back to me and wonder if her feelings for me are as hard and cold as the diamond. And what am I supposed to do with the thing? Sell it back? Let the jeweler who talked me into the pricey ring give me a look of sympathy as he offers me a third of what I paid for it? I stick it in the medicine cabinet since just thinking about the damn thing makes me sick.

One Monday morning, as soon as I get to work, I call Beth's office. She's a copywriter for a publisher. When she picks up, I say, "Beth. It's me. You've got to do something about the gifts piling up in our, I mean my living room."

Her sigh is tired, exhausted, and she waits before she says anything. Finally, with strain in her voice, she says, "Mark, I just can't deal with it now. It's too . . . difficult."

"Difficult?" I can feel the follicles of my hair tingle with my anger. "How do you think I feel? I want that stuff out of the house!"

"Okay, okay," she almost whispers. Then, as an afterthought, she asks, "How are you?"

I focus on my computer screen and say, "Busy, really busy."

"Oh?" There's surprise in her voice and maybe something else. Hope? Yeah, hope. If I don't tell her I'm miserable she gets to lower her guilt a notch. "Why are you so busy?" she asks.

I cough lightly. "Work. And everything else."

"Oh?" That word again.

"Look, what do you want to do with all those gifts?"

Her fingers are tapping against the phone when she growls low, "AAaaarrrrrgggghhh! I hate this!"

She hates this. How ironic since she engineered the whole situation.

Well, with a little help from Brad, that dick. "It ain't a picnic for me," I say.

"I know, I know. Look, I guess I'll come over with my mother sometime and we'll clear everything out. Maybe I'll take off this Friday."

"If you come on Saturday, I can help. There's a bunch of heavy boxes. I've got a client coming in Friday, so Friday's no good."

She hesitates then says quietly, "I think it would be better to do it on Friday."

I wait a few seconds and then repeat, "Better." She doesn't want to see me.

"Could you leave the key under the mat?"

"There is no mat."

"Oh, I thought there was a mat. Well, it's a safe neighborhood. Just leave the house open."

"Right."

Mrs. Genoa has made me an entire pan of lasagna. I'm standing at the front door and she makes me put on her oven mitts before I take it.

"She was here with her mother. In a van," she says deadly quiet, like she's giving me top secret CIA information.

"Yeah."

"You knew they were coming?"

"Yup."

"They took the gifts?"

The lasagna is heavy and I'm so hungry, I want to sit down and devour it. "Cleaned the place out," I say.

She shakes her head and pulls her lips inward. "A nice boy like you. You don't deserve to be treated like that." She does wait at least two seconds before asking, "You had lunch with my niece?"

"I did. She's terrific. Really great. She wants to make sure I'm over Beth before she goes out with me again."

"Pfft," Mrs. Genoa answers, spitting a little air through her teeth. "Andrea doesn't know what's good for her. Give her a call and take her to a movie."

Smiling, I answer, "Maybe. Thanks for the lasagna." After she leaves I notice that Diane is out washing her car again. She looks so alone while inspecting the windows for dirt. I almost want to cross the street and offer to help her, but that would be a mess. She'd think it meant something and it would be all over the neighborhood that I buffed her chrome. When she looks up and sees me watching her, she waves, a shy little girl wave with her fingers opening and closing. I'd wave back but I don't want to drop the lasagna.

Alice's mother is in the hospital with heart trouble, and she calls and asks if I could watch Jason and Ben for an hour or so. "I'm so sorry," she says when I get there. "My regular sitter is watching other kids and their father is out of town this weekend." She scribbles a phone number on a piece of paper and hands it to me. "If you need me, just call my cell. Now, where are the boys? Jason! Ben! Get down here! Now!" There's a monumental crash over our heads but it doesn't register on Alice's face. Then I hear the boys running down the steps. "This is so kind of you," Alice says. "I can't thank you enough."

"No problem. Happy to help."

"I just found out. My sister called and said they had to take my mother in an ambulance because she started having these awful chest pains. Where are my keys?" She starts fishing through stuff on the kitchen counter and wails, "Why can't I ever find them when I need them? Ah, ha!" She slips the keys into her purse.

The boys come into the kitchen. "Hey, I remember you," Ben says. Jason nods and says, "Yeah, you're that guy from the doughnut shop. Hey, we've got a basketball hoop now. Want to play?"

"You bet."

"Both of you, be good," Alice says in a commanding voice. "You do whatever Mark tells you. I want a full report when I get back."

When the boys hear the car pull out of the driveway, they dash over to the kitchen table and open a canister. "Chocolate chip!" Josh yells and they pull out fistfuls of cookies.

Ben asks, "Would you tell Mom you ate the cookies?"

Joining them, I put an entire cookie on my tongue and start chewing. "I'll tell her I helped." We eat more than we should and go through a carton of milk. Then it's basketball, two on one, and I don't have to try super hard to let the guys win game after game. Ben is very good, always focused. Jason isn't a natural, but I know what it's like to have an athletic older brother, so I compliment him often. Just moving around feels great and I realize it's been weeks since I've done anything but sit on my ass. The endorphins must be kicking in because I'm feeling pretty good. Later, we turn on the TV and watch a comical martial arts film. We try to imitate the karate moves while screaming out "Hee-yah!"

Alice calls all apologetic, asking if I can stay longer, and I tell her sure. Her mother's got to have an EKG and she wants to stay with her. The guys and I go out for pizza and then I take them to the ice cream place I went to with Diane. After more basketball, I turn on the television and we watch professional wrestling. Eventually, both of the kids fall asleep on the living room floor and I turn off the TV. While they're sleeping, I sit on the couch in the dark room and listen to the boys' breath rising and falling. Jason snores loud even though he's just a kid.

Beth and I wanted to have two kids, boys, girls, it didn't matter. Sitting here, it occurs to me for the first time that she and Brad might have kids together. This moment has been building for a long time and I give into it, just start crying like the insides of me are going to spill out onto the floor. When I can't muffle my sobs, I go into the bathroom and cry until I'm spent. There's nothing left. Avoiding the mirror, I wash my face and go back to the living room.

I hear the key in the lock and Alice comes in. Meeting her in the kitchen, I tell her, "The guys are asleep on the living room floor. Hope that's okay."

Nodding, she answers, "They do that all the time on the weekends. That's fine. Did they give you any trouble?"

I tell her how great they were, how much fun it was hanging out with them. "They invited me to come over and shoot hoops again tomorrow. Is that okay?"

She looks shocked and she gives me that terrific smile. Something's wrong, though, and I realize that she's shaking a little, and then the tears start coming down her cheeks. "Sorry," she says, pressing her hands against her face to blot her crying. "It's just that I'm at my wits end with my job, my kids, and now my mother. You offering to help is just so damn *nice!*" The tears start again, but she gets up, blows her nose and says, "That's enough of that. Let's have a drink."

I noticed beers in the fridge earlier, but I didn't think I should knock any back while watching the kids. But Alice opens an upper cupboard and takes out a bottle of Scotch. Like I said, I like this lady. She pours a double for each of us and we just sit at the kitchen table talking. She likes hearing about what I did with the kids and interrupts me too often to thank me. We plan that I'll watch the kids tomorrow afternoon while she goes back to the hospital.

I ask her about her ex-husband, telling her not to answer me if it's none of my business, but she just shrugs her shoulders and says, "The usual story. We met in college. Used to have a blast partying together. Then we got married but he never stopped partying. After the second affair, I threw him out."

"Must have been rough."

She takes a slow swallow of her Scotch. "By the time it ended, I'd had enough. But the boys were devastated." Her face is pinched and her mouth is set in a firm straight line. "I promised myself I'd never get married again and risk putting them through another break-up."

"How old were they when you got divorced?"

"It was two years ago. Jason was eight and Ben was ten. The thing is, they worship Kevin, their dad. And Kevin's the life of the party." She shakes her head. "It's just that he's nothing else."

"Nothing else?"

"Yeah, he's not responsible, he's not conscientious, he's not reliable. He says he's going to come to the school play, the ball game, whatever, and nine times out of ten, he's a no show." She shakes her head. "It just kills them. And it kills me to see it happen over and over."

It's hard to hear this. "They're great kids," I say, because I can't think of anything else.

Alice's face relaxes again and she smiles. "Thanks. I think so too."

By the time I finally walk home, it's dawn. Alice and I worked our way down the bottle and I'm feeling no pain. Well, that's not true. I'm thinking about Alice and the boys and their pain. But not my own for once. I'm just about to enter my back door when I look across the yard and see Mrs. Genoa glaring at me from her kitchen window. Instantly, she pulls down the shade and I know that before I wake up from the long snooze I intend to take, it will be all over the neighborhood that I spent the night with Alice.

A few days later I'm at work and the phone rings. Andrea. I can't keep the smile out of my voice when I ask her why she called.

"Hear you had your transition person. That qualifies you for a date with me."

"What?"

"Don't deny it. Aunt Kathy called me and gave me this speech about how it was a good thing I didn't get involved with you since you were spending time with that divorced woman and coming home in broad daylight for the whole neighborhood to see."

I chuckle. "So, you consider one night with someone, a night when *nothing* happened, I might add, transition enough?"

I hear a little sigh on the other end of the phone. "Nothing happened? Oh, shit, you haven't had your transition person yet."

Shaking my head, I say, "Sorry to disappoint you. The lady in question is just a friend. I watch her kids sometimes because her mother's in the hospital."

Disappointed silence. Then, "Well, shoot, why didn't you set Aunt Kathy straight?"

I laugh out loud and Don looks up. "Because Alice and I like being the gossip targets in the neighborhood. Livens things up."

"I bet. Well, call me after you've broken a heart or two."

"Wait! Andrea, don't hang up. You're the one breaking my heart. Have dinner with me."

"No way," she says flatly but there's a bit of a challenge in her voice.

"C'mon. Let's go out on Newbury Street. Get a fancy bite."

She's quiet but I sense a semi-surrender. "Do you like tapas?" she asks.

"Tap what?"

"Tapas. Spanish appetizers. There's a place on Newbury where you can order a bunch with a bottle of wine."

"We're there. Make a reservation for two for Friday night, eight o'clock. Give me directions to your place."

No sooner do I hang up than Don's at my desk. "Back in the game?" he asks.

Tapping a pencil against my coffee mug, I half-smile and say, "Maybe, maybe."

He slaps my back and says, "Nice going. What's she like?"

This is the first time anyone's asked me to describe Andrea and I assess her thoughtfully. "Beautiful brown eyes. Always smiling. Killer shape. Sultry laugh. Real smart." There. That about does it.

"She sounds too good to be true."

"Yeah." I lift my eyebrows. "I'm sure she has her pick of guys. I'm a little surprised she's giving me the time of day."

Don turns to leave but then says, "Be careful. Don't get your heart bashed in again. Next time around, I'm going for one of those quiet girls. Someone who wants to have kids and stay married for the rest of her life."

His words play in my mind a bit and I say, "Hey, Don. Why don't you come home with me tonight. We can grill a couple of steaks."

Andrea, Andrea, Andrea. No, I'm not in love, but I am in lust. This woman is funny, smart, tough. She's helping me tunnel up out of my grief from the center of the earth. With each level I pass out of, I know the sun's up ahead and one of these days I'll see it.

Thinking about Beth still makes my heart stop. But I'm not thinking about her as much. But then one Saturday Andrea and I are having lunch in Beacon Hill and in walks Brad, the bastard himself. I lift my head and stare right at him. When he notices me, I nod my head and then turn my attention back to Andrea.

"You know that guy?"

"Not really. Beth's old fiancée. Maybe her new one."

Andrea gives him a glance. "He ought to work out. He looks like the guy who gets sand kicked in his face at the beach."

Not true, but this woman always knows just what to say.

"So," she continues, "Aunt Kathy loves you again."

"She does?"

"Yeah. I told her how you were babysitting Alice's kids so she could be with her poor mother in the hospital and now you're Saint Mark."

"That ought to earn me some good food."

"Say, how is Alice's mother?"

I set my burger down. "She's been through a lot. Angioplasty and a triple by-pass."

"That's it. I'm quitting smoking."

"You said that last week."

"I mean it. I'm going to get one of those patches. Put it in a sexy spot and make you look for it."

"You're on. Hey, guess what? Alice's mother's doctor asked her out."

"He asked out Alice's mother? He's got a thing for women with chest scars?"

"No! He asked out Alice."

"Oh. Ohh! Go, Alice! Did she say yes?"

"I think she will. She couldn't believe he asked her to have dinner because she says she's looked like a wreck every time she's been at the hospital. And this is no flunkie doctor. He's one of the top heart surgeons in Boston."

"Sounds like you like him."

"Never met him, but if he likes Alice, he's got good taste."

She leans over and plants a kiss hard on my mouth. "You taste pretty good yourself," she says.

Two days later Beth calls me at work. This time when she asks me how I am, I say, "Not bad. Good. How about you?"

She doesn't answer. I hear muffled crying and my stomach lurches. "Beth? What is it, honey?" Honey. What a slip. I haven't called her that in months.

In a small voice, she says, "Oh, Mark. I'm so sorry. You have to believe me. I am just so very, very sorry."

I've been waiting to hear this. Oh, she's said it before, but now it's with feeling. In her voice I hear some of the pain I've been feeling. But my next question is, "How's Brad?"

There's a faltering sigh at the other end of the line. "I don't know what's up with Brad these days," she finally says.

"You don't say."

"Mark, please don't be sarcastic. I've been through so much."

"Tell me about it."

The sigh again. "Okay, I know I deserve that. I deserve it all." Her voice gets stronger as she continues, "But have you ever just been *so* confused that nothing in your life makes sense?"

"What are you confused about?"

Now I hear the sniffling. "Beth, don't cry. Tell me what you're confused about."

"Well, Brad wants to move in together," she says, sobbing.

My lungs stop working. I've forgotten how to breathe. Then the air comes back in a rush, and I feel like I'm going to drop to the floor. What the hell am I listening to this for? I need to hear about Beth and Brad like I need a hole in the head.

"Mark, are you there?"

I grunt. Clenching my fist, I say quickly, "Brad wants to play house. What's so confusing?"

Now her voice has this accusatory icing on it: "Well, I guess none of this bothers you."

"What the hell am I supposed to say! You walk out on me, the wedding, the house, everything. What do you think? I'm just sitting here waiting for you to call me and tell me the latest about you and dickhead?"

There's an irate gasp at the other end. "Well, what about you! Brad says he saw you in a restaurant with some girl who was acting all slutty."

Slutty? I could kill that little bastard. "Brad doesn't know shit," I spit into the phone.

My brain is a jigsaw puzzle but none of the pieces fit. Part of me is pissed off at Brad, part of me wants to defend Andrea, part of me wants to holler at Beth that my personal life is none of her goddamn business, but there's another part. The mystery piece in the puzzle. The part that's hoping that Beth really is jealous. That she's come to her senses. That maybe life will go on the way we thought it would before she gave me the heave ho. I wait. I say nothing. But then Beth whispers, "I have to go."

Damn. How many times will this woman say good-bye to me?

Saturday night in suburbia. I'm watching Andrea pound a make-shift sign that says "For Sale" into my front lawn. She brought the poster board home from work and wrote the words with her lipstick.

"This isn't just any lipstick," she informs me. "This is top of the line Clinique."

"Then what are you wasting it on the sign for?"

She laughs. "A discriminating buyer will recognize the shade and make a good offer."

"You're a genius."

"I keep telling you."

I didn't have a hammer but she's pounding the thing into the ground with her beer bottle. From her window, Mrs. Genoa is looking alarmed. Andrea sees her and waves hello with the bottle.

Across the street, Don and Diane are sudsing up the Prius. We'll be joining them for an ice cream run later tonight. Jason and Ben are over because Alice is out again with the doctor. The sun is going down and the clouds have pink and orange streaks running through them. A few people on the block must be barbecuing because there's a nice, smoky scent all over the street.

The boys and Andrea start a game of running across the lawn and leaping over the "For Sale" sign. Ben is able to sail over it head first and roll into a summersault. Jason can just barely make it over, but he manages. Then Andrea tries a flying Russian over it, her legs stretched out straight in front of her, and she dares me to try one. My ass hits the sign as I tumble over, Clinique all over the seat of my pants. Everyone starts laughing and Jason begs me to try another one.

I'm rolling around on the ground, freshly cut grass in my hair, when I notice a red Honda turn the corner and come barreling down the street. I could swear it's Beth's car, but red Hondas are everywhere these days. Wait, it is her car. I can see her through the windshield. There's a ringing in my ears like a five-alarm fire as she parks in front of the house. She just sits there for the longest time, and I'm wondering if she's just going to take off again. Ben asks loudly, "Who's that?" and Andrea says, "I've got a good idea who is is."

Finally, Beth opens the car door and I see a figure in white emerge. She keeps climbing out and this flow of white keeps dragging out behind her. Then she's on the sidewalk, arranging the dress so the train comes from the back and circles around her feet. She's not wearing a veil but some little hat that looks like a miniature Frisbee. And she's holding a bouquet full of white lilies with long green stems.

She stands like a statue on the sidewalk as if posing for a picture. She doesn't move; she's waiting for me. I walk over and stand in front of her. She's gorgeous, more beautiful than I've ever seen her. With a shy smile, she looks up at me and says, "I do."

I feel everyone's eyes on me. Jason and Ben are standing at the edge of the lawn, Andrea between them with her arms around their shoulders. A screen door slams and Mrs. Genoa is on her porch. Diane and Don put down their sponges.

Beth waits, the little smile giving way to a pout, then a frown.

"Mark?"

"What?"

"Isn't this what you want?" She smiles fully, that sweet little curved front tooth that I've missed so much. "I'm ready now, Mark. I'm ready to be your wife." When I still say nothing, simply stare at her, she announces loudly, "I DO."

Shaking my head, I look away. When I face her again, she looks confident, ready to throw her arms around me.

"Sorry, Beth. I don't." I realize I'm stepping on part of her dress and take a big step backwards. The imprint of the bottom of my sneaker is fully etched on the white material.

Beth is stunned. She starts to speak several times and finally gets out, "What's wrong with you? What about all our plans?"

I wait to answer. She is so beautiful standing here. I can imagine what it would have felt like to stand beside her in a church, to have kissed her as my wife for the very first time. Resting a hand on her shoulder, I hear myself say, "I'm sorry. I've moved on."

The slap on my arm is so abrupt, so unexpected, I start to stumble. For such a small woman, she really packs a punch. Andrea starts to come toward me but I shake my head at her. She hesitates but she stays put.

"Mark!" Beth screams, "I'm the best thing that ever happened to you and *you know it!* You're going to be sorry for the rest of your life." She tosses the flowers on the ground and turns around, pulling the train of the dress with her.

She gets back in the car a lot faster than she got out. A good portion of the wedding dress is hanging out the door when she slams it. It looks like a huge dollop of whipped cream as Beth screeches down the street, out of suburbia, out of my life.

Andrea comes over and circles her arm around my waist. "The dress wasn't bad. A little too poofy, but I liked the neckline."

I swoop up the flowers and make a show of presenting her with them but she grabs them and says, "Pee Eeww. Lilies stink." She turns to Ben and Jason and calls out, "Hey, guys, run out for a pass."

As the flowers sail through the air, I look around and admire my girlfriend, my neighbors, my friends. Hell, I even admire my house with its front bay window and the extended porch. It just looks so nice with that "For Sale" sign in front of it.

ONE DAY, SOMEDAY

The light had a distilled quality, as if any dull rays had been removed and what was left to flow down was pure and hard and white. Joanna stood at the window of the beauty salon and looked up at the sky. Closing her eyes, she felt the warmth in two wide bands across her cheeks, at the tip of her nose. By noon, some customers would be complaining about the glare, asking that the ugly, semi-sheer black shade be pulled down so they could read their magazines while sitting under the hair dryers.

She was readying the shop for opening, a chore that fell to her every second Friday. She had just left the considerable clutter of the cramped home she shared with her two daughters, and the salon was equally unkempt. It was eight o'clock; she had forty-five minutes to clean before the other beauticians arrived. At nine o'clock on the dot, the receptionist would hang the sign on the door that read, "No Appointment Necessary."

The air in the salon was rank from aerosol hair products. Smoking wasn't allowed but the gray odor of tobacco that clung to smoking customers never left the shop. Joanna hadn't smoked in almost a year and found it repugnant and seductive. Spraying Windex on the mirrors, she then rubbed the glass vigorously until there wasn't a trace of a smudge. She couldn't avoid her reflection in the glass. Her hair, hastily tied back in a ponytail after her morning shower, looked too simple for a beautician. Most of the women in the shop were always experimenting with new colors and styles, but after fussing over other people's hair all day, Joanna viewed anything she did to her own as work.

The supply closet was always a mess although each shelf was supposed to be arranged by product and brand name. Joanna began to sort the cans and boxes, mentally taking note of what they were low on and needed to order. The phone rang, startling her, and she dropped a heavy can of hair spray on her foot. "Damn!" She hobbled to the front desk and picked up the phone.

"Good morning. Hair Fair," she said crossly into the receiver.

"Mom, it's me."

Joanna paused and looked at her watch. "You're up early." Kayla, seventeen and always evasive, didn't answer readily. Joanna told her, "Put out the cigarette."

A pause and then her daughter said, "I'm not smoking!"

"You are too. I can tell by the way you take too long to answer. You're inhaling." She heard an insulted sigh at the other end of the phone and imagined Kayla resting her cigarette on the edge of the kitchen counter.

"Is your sister out of bed?" Joanna's younger daughter, Mandy, had just turned ten.

"She and her little friends are already off on their bikes. Listen, the reason I called, I need to go to the mall. Can I come over to the shop and borrow the car?"

"What do you need to go to the mall for?" When there was no answer, Joanna commanded, "Kayla, put that cigarette out!"

"I'm *not* smoking, okay! Chill, why don't you. I just don't want you to go ballistic if I tell you why I'm going to the mall."

Joanna understood that her daughter wanted her to ask, was in fact challenging her to. Neither spoke for several seconds.

"Promise me you won't go ballistic."

Joanna opened the desk drawer and pulled out the order pad. Leaning over, she wrote "two" next to *Vitacare Shampoo* and "four" next to *Curl and Spray.*

"Mom?"

"I'm here," Joanna said evenly while she studied the pad.

"Did you hear what I said? About not going ballistic?"

"I'm not deaf." She wrote "seven" next to *Earthmud Henna* and wrote in parenthesis: "two brown, two dark brown, two auburn."

"Great, Mom. I hate it when you're like this."

"I've got to get back to work. Did Mandy remember to put on sunscreen before she left?"

"How do I know? She left a mess in the bathroom like always. Can I borrow the car? I could pick it up at ten and have it back by noon in case you need it over lunch."

Joanna tore the order slip from the pad and pinned it to a small corkboard hung on the wall next to the desk. Also on the board was a photo of the receptionist's family. The four figures, the receptionist and her husband and their twin sons, stood in front of an imitation backdrop, an absurdly blue sky with a garish rainbow arching over their heads. "You may as well tell me what I'm going to go ballistic about." She heard dry coughing on the other end of the line and said wryly, "Smoker's cough."

"Enough, Mom. Okay, here goes: Keith gave me a ring last night and I want to take it to the jeweler to get it sized. It's too big."

Joanna gasped, swallowing what felt like solid air, oxygen turning to stone in her lungs. She felt movement somewhere in her abdomen, her kidneys maybe, and sat down. She pounded the desk lightly with her open palm to steady herself. "Too big isn't the only problem. You give that ring back." She was surprised her voice sounded as calm as it did.

Her daughter's sigh, a swift strong breeze, foamed with static. "I knew you'd be like this. Look, it's my ring and I'm going to keep it."

Joanna, in a deeper tone, pronounced, "You're not getting married, young lady. You're seventeen."

"You can't make me give it back. It's mine."

"*It's mii-ne,*" Joanne mimicked, making her voice whine. "You're not even through high school. And you just met this Keith."

"No I didn't," Linda protested, her words sliding together. "We just had our six-month anniversary. Besides, it's a *pre*-engagement ring, Mom, so relax." Her daughter's voice dropped as she continued, hesitantly, "But you're the one who got married at eighteen, so I don't know why you're yelling at me."

Joanna knocked the desk with her tightly coiled hand. "That's exactly *why* I'm yelling. You think I want to see you—"

"Save it. I don't want to hear it. I've been hearing about your lousy marriage since Dad walked out the door."

Joanna took a moment to inhale, feeling the swell of her stomach before she exhaled with a weak sigh. Tapping her nail against the mouthpiece of the receiver, she yearned for a cigarette. God, she needed one. If she couldn't push her finger through the phone and into her insolent daughter's ear, poking her hard, she had to have a cigarette. In a clipped voice, she said, "Well, my *lousy* marriage, as you say, obviously didn't make an impression on you."

"I'm not you, Mom, okay? I have my own life."

"You could've fooled me." Joanna laid her head on the desk. *I'm too tired for this.* Pre-engaged, what nonsense. It means, what? That they're in training to get engaged? Was that something like a training bra? Training wheels on a bicycle?

"Look, you never even had an engagement ring, you just got married. Keith and I are taking our time: This just means that, you know, that we're serious about each other. That we plan on getting engaged someday."

Joanna stared through the window at the empty parking lot. The asphalt would get so hot today that the teenagers who went barefoot would have to run for shade. "What does the ring look like?" she asked and then hit her forehead. She shouldn't show any interest.

"Oh, it's *so* beautiful," Kayla's voice sparkled. "It's an opal with little diamond chips in a circle around it. The band is gold and—Why are you laughing?"

"An opal?" Joanna held her forehead with her hand and shook slightly as she chuckled. "Oh, I can see Keith is really serious about you. He must have saved up a week for that beauty."

"Opals are precious stones," Linda insisted, obviously wounded. "Look, can I have the car? If I don't get the ring sized, I can't wear it."

"Exactly," Joanna said. "I'm hanging up now. Don't forget to empty the dishwasher."

"What about the car?"

"No. I don't want to hear another word about it."

Slowly, Joanna put the phone in its receiver. She checked her watch again, twenty to nine. The job she hated the most was sweeping the floor. Each beautician was supposed to keep the area around her own chair clean throughout the day, but there were always mounds of hair lying here and there. Joanna turned on the radio to a country station while she swung the broom about, trying to hear lyrics through the crackling static. She amassed a pile of hair of every possible shade, a small mountain of dead protein. As she swept it into the dust pan she wondered, as she often had before, how many people were represented in the waste, how many people came in the shop each day and let part of themselves be clipped off and thrown away. Hair had no nerves, no feelings, yet Joanna always felt there was something very real about it, something harshly honest. When you cut it off, you could see exactly how much you'd lost.

The salon had toys for kids. There were a couple of coloring books and a box of ninety-six broken Crayola crayons. The plastic train was missing one wheel and most of the puzzles were absent a piece or two. There were a couple of trucks in fairly good shape and a xylophone with all its colorful slats intact, but the mallet was missing. Joanna scooped these things up and put them in the large wicker basket next to the magazine table. There was also a dollhouse, a surprising donation from elderly Mrs. Martell, a widow and regular customer who said that she'd bought it on sale and saved it for a granddaughter, but after five grandsons, she'd given up hope.

It was a Victorian-style house, white plastic with turquoise and pink trim. Joanna knelt in front of it and examined its rooms. The furniture was never in the right place. She took the couch out of an upper room and placed it in the living room behind the coffee table. The Victorian bathtub, missing one of its clawed feet, was upside down on the roof. Surprisingly, the rocking chair was where it should be, in the living room on the rug that was actually just a large sticker with a floral pattern. Joanna searched for the grand piano, an elaborately carved oak piece with sheet music painted above the keys. It was the only piece of furniture that wasn't plastic; Mrs. Martell must have purchased it separately. But where was it? She examined each room, beginning with the first floor, a slight tremor in her hands. Had some child stolen it? Slipped it under her shirt while walking out of the store with her mother?

Joanna had taken piano lessons for two years beginning when she was six years old. "It's something no one can take away from you," her mother had told her. "Knowing how to play an instrument says something about a person." But then there was a hike in fees and her family couldn't afford the lessons. Sometimes, when she heard a familiar children's song, her fingers still moved, searching for the keys.

She found the piano in the attic on the third floor. Relieved, she picked it up carefully with her thumb and middle finger. She blew on it and watched the small particles of airborne dust reflect the sunlight in hues of green and violet. Funny how even dust could look beautiful when spun out into the light. With the bottom of her cotton smock, she wiped the wood and gently set the piano in the parlor. She arranged the inhabitants of the doll house in various rooms. She put the baby in its crib and the little girl figure in the bath tub. The mother figure had movable arms and legs and Joanna normally settled her into the rocking chair. Today, however, she placed her on a bed and said, "You get to sleep. Lucky you." She located the father figure in the den and, as she had for the last year, tossed him into the wicker basket with the other toys.

"Are you playing with that thing again?"

Startled, Joanna looked up and saw Bonnie, the receptionist, closing the door behind her. "I swear you should just take it home and fix it up to your heart's content." Bonnie walked behind the desk and put her purse in a drawer.

Joanna stood slowly, tapping her left foot slightly because her leg had fallen asleep. "Mrs. Martell would miss it."

"Oh, that old bat. I'll be happy when she kicks. She gives me the old prune every time she comes in." Bonnie turned her lower lip inside out and squinted her eyes in imitation. "She acts like she's royalty when I tell her she'll have to wait a few minutes, like she expects us to wait on her hand and foot."

Joanna motioned to the corkboard and said, "Not too many supplies today."

Bonnie nodded and unpinned the list. Joanna walked to the back of the room and started to set up her station. She arranged hair rollers, lined up combs on the counter, loosened the lids on hair gel pots. The best thing about being the first beautician in the store was having your pick of smocks. Joanna was embarrassed when she laid a smock full of tears and holes around a customer. She once had a woman threaten to sue when a permanent hair dye dripped through a rip and stained her shirt collar. Joanna went to the very back of the store and selected a brand new adult-sized smock, brown plastic, and a bright orange one for children. Back at her station, she sat on her high stool and waited for her first customer.

The other beauticians were arriving, calling out good morning to each other and asking Bonnie if she'd brewed the first pot of coffee yet.

"Morning, Joanna!" Ashley, the young woman who worked to the left of Joanna, opened the bottom drawer beneath her section of the counter and deposited her purse. "How are you today?"

"Fine." Joanna forced herself to ask, "And you?"

The young woman leaned back her head, rolled it between her shoulders and said, "*Exhausted*. Justin and I went out for drinks after the movie last night and ended up staying at this bar until two. I keep telling him I need my beauty sleep. After all, we've got to look good for the customers." She looked at Joanna, expecting confirmation, and then said, "Oh, you poor thing. You had to open today. So you really had to get up early."

Joanna felt the corner of her mouth tug at the implicit remark about her appearance. She pretended to yawn and said, "I'm ready for eight hours sleep."

She tried not to stare at Ashley. The girl had worked at Hair Fair for two months. At twenty, she was the youngest operator by years. The salon had a hard time retaining young stylists who always set their sights on trendier shops. Sherry, the manager, was hopeful that Ashley would stay and attract the young clientele, single women from eighteen to twenty-five. "That's the demographic we need to build up," Sherry told the stylists whenever they had a staff meeting. She went out of her way to keep Ashley happy, letting her leave early and take personal days.

Joanna stood and caught sight of her reflection. Well, maybe she should put some effort into how she looked. A little makeup. Maybe put her hair in a chignon and wear earrings. Ashley looked as if she had permed her hair one too many times, dyed it platinum too frequently. It had the overly bleached, dry quality of a swimmer's, but it was long and loose, hanging about her face in sultry loops. Despite her youth, there was something nostalgic about her appearance. With white patent leather boots, she'd look like Nancy Sinatra back in the sixties, Joanna thought. She wore perfumes that smelled like synthetic fruits: cherry, grape, lime, apricot, watermelon—a different one for every day of the week. Joanna had to admit that her fragrances were nicer than those of hair products, but they added to the riot of scents that invaded her lungs.

It was the consensus of the older beauticians that Ashley spent too much time talking to the customers, asking their opinion about styling as she cut their hair. Joanna and the other beauticians knew that the majority of their customers didn't care about styling; they just needed a good trim. Most of the cuts involved simply following the lines and waves of the last haircut. After all, what could a person expect from a salon that didn't require appointments and only charged twelve dollars for a cut?

The morning wore on, the radio station changing frequently from country to rock to country again. Bonnie switched it every half hour to keep everyone happy. Joanna had lots of regulars, people willing to wait if she already had someone in her chair. She gave a pixie cut to two little girls and a long, layered look for a teen-age girl who was going to her first prom later in the week. Mrs. Tytle came in for her weekly shampoo and blow dry, making a big show of sneaking a dollar tip into the pocket of Joanna's smock. She had only one male customer so far, a middle-aged man wearing a short-sleeved plaid shirt with a pocket protector. He seemed terribly embarrassed when he told her he wanted "a younger look." Looking down at his shoes, he asked, "Can you do that?"

Joanna said, "Sure," even though she wasn't certain what he meant or if he even had enough hair to style. After she sprayed his hair with water, she felt even more challenged as she saw how little she had to work with. "I won't take much off since longer looks younger." He nodded heavily, relieved that she seemed to understand him. "And I think we'll part it a little higher so there's more on your forehead." As she combed and clipped his hair, he stared hopefully into the mirror. Joanna noticed he wore his wedding ring on his right finger. After blow drying his hair, she was happy to see that he did look a bit more youthful, and he was less nervous. He thanked her and asked where he should buy his own hair dryer. Joanna chatted with him about stores for a minute, surprised at how pleased she felt with herself for having won his confidence. She watched him exit the store, walking through the parking lot and getting into an old blue van.

"He was a lost cause," Ashley said, startling Joanna.

"What?"

"*Please.* I almost started laughing when he told you he wanted to look more youthful. He looks like he should get an AARP discount." Ashley started removing curlers from the hair of a woman who appeared to have fallen asleep.

Joanna blinked. "He was nice. Just a little sad."

With a roll brush, Ashley began working the underside of the woman's short curls, brushing them with an upward raking motion. "You're too nice, Joanna. That guy is going to go hit on some woman who's going to be repulsed by him." She shuddered. "I know that type, quiet and needy, can't take a hint."

Joanna felt the pulse of her blood in her cheekbones as she bent over to sweep hair into a dustbin. "Well, you know the old saying," Joanna said, straining to sound nonchalant, "if you can't think of anything nice to say —" She couldn't finish the phrase. She stood slowly and emptied the hair into the garbage can.

Ashley turned abruptly to look at Joanna while continuing to brush her customer's hair. "Well, *excuse me*," she said under her breath.

"Ow!" the customer screamed. "Watch it! That was my ear you just brushed." Ashley tossed the brush onto her counter and turned suddenly. "I was just making conversation, Joanna. You don't have to act all high and mighty."

"Let's keep it polite, okay?" Joanna smiled tightly, imagining how she'd relay her side of this if Ashley complained to Sherry. She had complained a couple of times before about what she referred to as Joanna's "superiority complex." Last month she'd gotten in a snit when Joanna had asked her not to swear at her station. Ashley had retorted, "The worst I say is 'shit' or 'damn.' Give me a break."

Sherry was no help. "I'm in a bind," she told Joanna. "We really need to keep her. So try to get along, okay?"

Shrugging now, Ashley said, "Fine. From now on, I'll keep my opinions to myself."

"Like I said, let's just keep it polite."

Ashley's customer grimaced, her reflection in the mirror brimming with dissatisfaction. "I'm not sure I like it." She turned her head from left to right. "It makes me look like Betty White."

Joanna listened as Ashley insisted to the woman that she looked just like Jane Fonda. "It's just a question of the right accessories. Get some hoop earrings and a great lipstick."

When Joanna checked her watch, it was twenty minutes after ten, almost time for her morning break. She imagined taking her coffee outside, sitting on the curb and enjoying the shade beneath the salon's awning.

Bonnie called back to her, "Jo, can you take Mrs. Martell before your break?"

Noooo, she moaned internally. She saw that Bonnie was standing in front of the customer, skewering her face as she had earlier to imitate the older woman's expression.

"Sure. Come on back Mrs. Martell." Joanna walked forwards a few steps to greet the petite woman. "How have you been?"

"The same. The same." She stepped up into the chair and said, "My hair grows faster in the summer. I wasn't planning on coming in until next week."

Joanna arranged the smock over her and tied it loosely behind her neck.

"This looks new." Mrs. Martell raised her arms beneath the smock and looked down approvingly.

"Mm hmm. So, I'll just trim the ends?

"Yes. I know I was just here but it will look shaggy before I know it."

As she began combing the woman's fine gray hair, Joanna said, "Someday you'll surprise me and tell me you're going to let it grow out."

Mrs. Martell smiled briefly and said, "Not likely."

Joanna knew the shape of this customer's head as well as she knew her own. Mrs. Martell was sensitive about a cowlick in the back, and Joanna knew to cut it as short as possible and then weave in the hair around it. The elderly woman had a slight depression on the left side of her head where, twenty years ago, she had struck the corner of a kitchen cabinet when she had stood up abruptly while scrubbing the floor.

"How are those girls of yours? Where are their pictures?" Mrs. Martell nodded slightly towards the mirror.

"Oh, fine. I took down those pictures because they were so old. I'll have to get new ones. Kayla turned seventeen last month."

"Really. Did she have a party?"

Joanna began to clip the front of Mrs. Martell's hair, clasping the bangs between her fingers. "Um, not a party, exactly. We had cake and ice cream, but she wanted to spend the day hanging out with her friends."

"Hanging out?"

Joanna moved to one side of the chair and fingered the hair over the woman's ear. "That's what they call it." If the sides were even a smidge off, Mrs. Martell would notice. They had to angle back over her ear lobes so that her pearl earrings showed.

"Spend as much time as you can with her. Pretty soon she'll be off on her own and you'll wonder how time could have gone by so quickly. It's lonely when the kids are gone."

Mrs. Martell always sat as straight as a soldier in the chair, never flinching, even when tiny hairs fell on her nose and cheeks. When Joanna moved behind her, Mrs. Martell instinctively knew to lower her head. "Does your daughter have a beau?"

Joanna smiled at the old-fashioned term for boyfriend. She brushed away the hairs on the woman's neck with a damp washcloth and began to snip in vertical rows. "I'm afraid so. In fact, he gave her a ring."

"At seventeen?" She sounded aghast.

"That's what I said. I told her to give it back."

"Well, what kind of ring is it?"

"An opal."

"No, I mean is it an engagement ring or a friendship ring? One of my nieces exchanged friendship rings with a classmate when they were only in high school."

"Oh, it's a *pre*-engagement ring."

Mrs. Martell laughed, surprising Joanna. "Then I wouldn't worry. Don't make a fuss over it and the whole thing will die down. If you forbid her to wear it, she'll only dig her heels in."

"Spoken by someone who's raised a few daughters herself."

"I certainly have. Being determined to wear a ring isn't any different than being determined to wear lipstick or pierce your ears or whatever the rage is."

Joanna decided not to mention the white hairs that were mixing in with the gray ones around Mrs. Martell's ears. "You're right, Mrs. Martell. Teenage girls can be so stubborn. And a ring isn't as bad as a tattoo."

"A tattoo! That's barbaric. But you know, it's considered bad luck to wear an opal unless your birthday is in October."

"Oh? Why is that?"

"Foolish superstition, I guess."

There was really nothing more to cut. Joanna turned the chair around and gave Mrs. Martell a hand mirror. "Is the back okay?"

The elderly woman studied the reflection for several moments before nodding slightly. "Fine, fine." She pushed her small hand from beneath the smock and whispered, "But maybe you could just touch it here and here."

Joanna was surprised. Mrs. Martell had never asked for further styling. Joanna turned the chair front again and picked up her shears. Mrs. Martell shook her head. "Just touch my head," she whispered.

Carefully, Joanna placed her hands on either side of the woman's head. Her fingers funneled beneath the dampened hair to the old woman's scalp. Slowly, Joanna began to knead small circles. When Mrs. Martell closed her eyes and lowered her chin, Joanna widened the circles. Moving her entire hands up and down, over and back of the woman's head. She increased her pressure and found a rhythm, watching as Mrs. Martell started to sway slightly in the chair. Suddenly, the woman was erect again, reaching up and taking Joanna's hands off her head. "That's fine," she said, "just fine." Joanna untied the smock and held Mrs. Martell's arm while she stepped down.

"The usual rate?" She pulled a wallet from the pocket of her dress and began to count bills.

Joanna washed and re-washed her hands, the soapsuds thick and bubbly. She held her hands under the warm water until they felt free of styling gel and invisible pieces of hair. She headed out to her station to collect her mug and get a fresh refill of coffee. But then she saw Kayla standing behind her chair and she stopped walking.

Her daughter had always been tall for her age and now she was five feet, ten inches. Self-conscious about her height, her posture was poor. Since forever, Joanna had been telling her to stand up straight, to stop slouching. She waited for Kayla to emerge as a graceful swan, carrying herself with confidence, but today she looked as hunchbacked as some of the old customers. Kayla crouched on the arm of the chair, one leg lazily crossed over the other. Her jeans were too tight but all the girls wore them like that. Kayla's hair, however, was beautiful, thick and golden, bound in a simple fat braid that rested on her shoulder. When she saw her mother, she held up her hands as if she were praying: "Please, Mom, say yes, please."

Joanna picked up her mug from the counter. "I thought I made my feelings on the matter perfectly clear."

"Oh, Mom," she whined, "I walked all the way down here."

"You could have saved yourself a trip." Joanna curled her fingers and placed them on her daughter's cheek. "You're flushed. It's hot outside, huh?"

Kayla didn't answer. She lowered her chin and looked at the floor.

"All right. If you're determined to wear this ring, go ahead, but—"

"Thank you, Mom!" Kayla jumped up and leaned over to hug her mother. She jumped again, jostling Joanna.

"Wait, wait," Joanna said, holding her arm out as if she were trying to stop an oncoming car, "I'm not finished," she said, anchoring each word. "I want to talk to Keith and make sure he understands that you are *not* engaged, not anywhere near being engaged."

"Thank you, thank you, Mommy!" Kayla squeezed hard one more time and finally let go. Joanna was momentarily stunned that her grown daughter had called her "Mommy," and even more surprised to feel an unexpected rush of gratitude flood her.

"Engaged? Are you engaged?"

Joanna turned and realized that Ashley had been watching them. "No," she said, "she's pre-engaged. This is my daughter, Kayla."

"Hi." Ashley stepped forward. "Congratulations. Pre-engaged, that's really neat. I was pre-engaged a couple of times in high school. It's cool."

"Yeah," Kayla said, lifting a skinny chain necklace from beneath her T-shirt. Joanna parted her lips slightly as she watched her daughter produce the ring on the end of the chain. The way she held it between her thumb and forefinger, her face glowing with pride, caused Joanna to remember when Kayla had lost her first tooth and held it the same way. She had wanted to bring the tooth to school for show and tell.

Ashley lifted the ring, saying, "Can I see?"

Joanna felt a stab of remorse watching the two young women stand side-by-side. Ashley wasn't much older than her daughter, and Kayla certainly said inappropriate things from time to time. In the afternoon, Joanna would make some overture, offer to fetch Ashley coffee, buy her a ladyfinger at the bakery next door.

Leaning forward, Joanna peered at the ring, a milky-pink stone in a gold setting, and said, "It's very pretty, honey."

"I told you!" Kayla beamed down at the ring. Joanna wished she had a camera, her daughter looked so happy.

Ashley continued to appraise the ring, lifting and turning it in every direction. "You won't be able to get it sized, though."

Kayla looked down at the ring and stepped back, causing Ashley to finally let go of it. Clasping her hand around the ring, Kayla said, "What do you mean?"

Tilting her head, Ashley glanced sympathetically at Joanna before saying in a soft, smug voice, "The setting is only gold-plate, not real gold. A jeweler will tell you it's not worth it to cut and seal gold-plate."

Cupping the ring, Kayla looked at it. "I think it's gold," she challenged. She looked at Ashley and asked, "Why would an opal with diamonds have a gold-plate setting?"

Placing her hand around Kayla's shoulders, Joanna tried to make her daughter walk away with her, but Kayla's legs were locked. "It doesn't matter—" Joanna started, wondering how she'd finish. What would she say? It's the thought that counts?

Kayla repeated, "Why would a ring with diamonds have a gold-plate setting?"

Glancing towards the front of the shop to make sure a customer wasn't waiting, Ashley said, "Those aren't diamonds, they're zircons. You know, fake diamonds. And I'm afraid the opal is poor quality, maybe not even real. It might be what's called a "common opal," one that doesn't flash colors. Do you want to know how I can tell?"

"No," Kayla said immediately, clutching the ring and sliding it beneath her T-shirt.

Ashley picked up the small broom beneath the counter and began to sweep around her chair. Without looking at Joanna or Kayla, she said, "I'm sorry. I just thought you should know in case the jeweler tells you just to get a couple of ring guards for the back. They work really well."

Kayla, her head hanging over her chest, bolted forward, walking to the front of the store with long strides. Her shoulders were upright as she pushed open the door with both hands.

"I didn't mean to upset her."

Joanna looked blankly at Ashley for several seconds and said, "What did you mean to do?" She ran to catch up with Kayla.

It was hot in the car, but the air conditioner was broken. Beside Joanna, in the passenger's seat, Kayla sat with her eyes closed, two tears, replaced over and over, moving silently down her cheeks.

"Honey, what does it matter what the ring cost? It's the thought that counts, remember?"

Kayla sniffled noisily and whisked the back of her hand under her nose. "Oh, God, Mom, I can't believe *you're* saying that."

Joanna stroked her daughter's forehead. "Neither can I." She spread open her hand and rubbed Kayla's temples with her thumb and little finger. Her skin was so young, so taut.

"I wanted the ring. I asked Keith to get it for me," Kayla blurted. She lifted her mother's hand from her face.

"Why?" Joanna moved her eyes from her daughter's face to the dashboard. The sun made the dust look like nasty dandruff. "Why?"

"*Because!*" Kayla wailed, as if the answer were obvious. "I wanted to feel like I mattered to him." Shaking her head, she continued, "Then, even if he broke up with me, I'd always have this ring as proof, proof that I mattered to someone."

Sighing, Joanna leaned back in her seat. She opened her purse and put on her sunglasses. They barely helped; the light was merciless. "You matter," she told her daughter quietly. "You matter to me. You matter to lots of people."

Kayla reached behind her neck and unclasped the chain. Slowly, she lowered the necklace into her palm, closing her fingers around it. "Keith must've gotten a good laugh over this. He probably told his buddies. He probably said something like, 'She's so dumb she'll never know the difference.'"

"Then you don't want to be with him anyway," Joanna said too quickly, wincing when she saw how her daughter cupped her hands over her eyes and shook with fresh sobs. "What I mean," she said, reaching out her arm to rest her hand on Linda's shoulder, "is that he doesn't deserve you."

Kayla opened her eyes briefly, the light swimming in her blue irises, then closed them again. "I used to wake up really early in the morning," she said.

"What?"

"I know you think I sleep all day long, but I used to wake up as soon as it got light out."

"You did?"

Kayla lifted her legs and bent them against the dashboard. Joanna didn't normally allow this. "Why? Why did you wake up early?" Several moments passed. Joanna realized that she was afraid to ask again. She could only watch her daughter and wait. Perspiration pooled on her upper lip and her underarms were damp. Her break was almost over. She couldn't leave her daughter like this, though.

Finally, Kayla said, "I had this idea that Dad was going to slip back into our lives again. That one day, someday, I'd wake up and he'd be back. He would come back early, while we were sleeping, so he'd be in the kitchen when we came down for breakfast. And we wouldn't talk about where he'd been or how long he'd been gone. He'd just be standing next to the table mixing a bowl of pancake batter."

"Put your feet down, honey." When Kayla didn't, Joanna put her hand on her daughter's knee. "Come on now, put your feet down."

Slowly, one at a time, Kayla lowered her legs. She opened her eyes and stared directly in front of her. "Am I going to end up like you?"

Joanna put her hands on the staring wheel, moving them until she felt the bump of the grips between her fingers. "I don't know." The sun was ambushing the windows now with hot, wavering streaks. "I don't know what the future holds."

Rolling her head to one side, Kayla said, "God, Mom, I don't know how you can stand this life. I mean, don't you feel just *stuck*?"

Joanna's pulse quickened. That was exactly how she felt, how she'd felt for months. To hear her daughter describe the sensation so aptly disturbed her. She swallowed the anger, the rage she felt toward her husband, and felt it lodge heavily and deeply within her chest. With an even voice, she managed to say, "I have two beautiful daughters I love so much. I'm lucky."

"Really?" Kayla looked at her mother. "Is that *really* how you feel?"

Joanna exhaled slowly, feeling the stone in her chest loosen into small stones, then tiny pebbles that seemed to pop as gently as soap bubbles. "Of course that's how I feel."

"Oh, Mommy!" Kayla began to cry loudly as she leaned across the gearshift, her head finding a place on Joanna's chest.

It was broiling in the car now. Kayla's tears felt as hot as soup as they soaked Joanna's shirt. She needed to go back in the shop and stand next to Ashley for the duration of the day. But why? Why couldn't she just sit here and let the heat of the sun burn her cheeks as hot as love could burn the soul? Joanna marveled at how easy it was to breathe now, to feel lighter than feathers despite the weight of her daughter pressed up against her.

THE HISTORY OF PREJUDICE

People were looking more and more like animals, Ken Onis decided. The woman who worked in the next office was a dead ringer for Miss Piggy. And why did he never notice before that his law partner had a sheep's snout, the center and bottom of his face protruding like an enormous tumor? His wife, Lisa, he sadly acknowledged, had the jaw and teeth of a horse, a backside large enough to merit her own stable.

Sometimes a person's likeness to a particular animal was uncanny and should have been embarrassing. If the mailman had any idea how much he looked like a beagle, his long ears flapping along the sides of his face, those squinty little dark eyes, he'd never come out of his house. But still he delivered the mail every day, whistling as he dropped the envelopes through the slot.

Ken studied his own face in the mirror, running his hand over his narrow face, his jutting but skinny chin, and declared with conviction, "Goat." Not bad. Some people resembled rodents, reptiles, even insects. He thought of his daughter, Jasmine, only six years old and not a care in the world. Like all children, she was beautiful, but for how long? When would her peaches and cream complexion start to resemble a goat or a horse, or perhaps some hybrid animal? Only time would tell.

On the morning train into the office, Ken read news magazines. One day, he became engrossed in an article titled, "The New Animal Bioethics." Animal organs were being transplanted into humans. Animal cloning would allow more harvesting of organs. Some people were upset; was it moral, ethical? One nurse was quoted as saying, "Forget morality; it's disgusting!" A doctor who had performed several transplants, however, was quoted as saying, "Look, we share about 99% of our DNA with chimps. We're not that different." Ken studied a photograph in the article of a pig's liver, an amorphous shape that looked like some kind of raw meat. He placed his hand over his abdomen and imagined his own liver hard at work, endlessly vacuuming the toxins from his body. In a pig, in a person, the liver had the same function. This struck Ken as revelatory.

He read further, staring at lists of all sorts of life-sustaining possibilities reaped from animal intervention in human life. We're *mutating*, he thought excitedly. We're slowly but surely evolving into another *species*. Looking around the train, he stared at the other passengers. We're not going to look like this, like people look now, forever. Maybe during his lifetime there'd be significant changes in the appearance of humans. Maybe there'd be animal to human nose and ear transplants, limb transplants. At what point was a man more animal than person? What percentage of his body parts would have to be his own to be considered a member of the human race? He was startled from his thoughts by the sound of sneezing from the man seated next to him. With each snatch of air released from his body, the man gave a soft utterance that sounded to Ken like "hoink." He tried not to stare, but he couldn't resist staring at the man's abdomen and wondering if a pig's organ wasn't lodged somewhere inside of him.

At lunch, he tried to share his thoughts with Barney, another lawyer at his firm. "What I think," he said, "is we're going to see the whole history of prejudice repeated as we start getting more and more body stuff from the animals."

"Don't follow." Barney was slapping the bottom of a ketchup bottle over his cheeseburger. He gave up and inserted his finger in the bottle and flung the sauce onto his plate.

Ken was too animated to eat and rushed his words into windy statements: "Well, just think about it. I can imagine people getting snooty, saying things like, '*We* have horse blood in our family.' Or, 'There's not a *single* drop of pig blood in my family going back to the twentieth century."

"You think everyone will want horse blood?" Barney always played devil's advocate; it made him a wickedly good litigator.

"Of course! Wouldn't that be better than pig blood?"

"If you say so, buddy. Although they say pigs are very intelligent. Say, can I have your dill pickle? It's just sitting there."

"Take it." Ken dropped his lower jaw and stretched his mouth until he felt his throat muscles relax. Sometimes he had trouble swallowing. His secretary told him it was anxiety and recommended yoga, told him that the rooster and camel positions would do him wonders. He watched Barney scraping his teeth up and down on one end of the pickle and said, "Really, can't you just imagine some teenager saying something like, 'Well, if you must know, Mother, I'm dating a partial cow. But I'm not as prejudiced as some people about these things.' And the mother will say, 'Well I don't want cow grandchildren!'"

Barney looked up quickly. "And then the cows will say to each other, when they're sitting in a restaurant like this, 'Just think, it used to be that the only time we could be in here was when we were on the menu.'" He laughed and picked up his sandwich, eating a fourth of it in one bite. He chewed vigorously and noisily, taking another bite before he swallowed. Gagging, he grasped his throat until a portion of the food returned to his mouth. Horrified, Ken watched as Barney re-chewed it and swallowed again. But Barney was still amused when he said, "And the pigs will take umbrage about having been a mere side dish to the eggs. Mmm, bacon. Maybe I should've got the club sandwich."

Ken's gaze locked abstractly on the ketchup bottle, he blinked and slowly looked up at Barney. "Why, I bet you're right! That *will* happen. People who are part animals are going to be very angry about how their ancestor animals have been treated all this time. So, the history of prejudice will repeat itself, but we'll also have another kind of animal rights movement."

Barney picked up his napkin, blew his nose, balled the napkin and threw it under the table. "Do you think the ASPCA will take their cases? Hey, maybe we should get into this on the ground floor." He laughed, a small piece of meat flying from the space between his front teeth. "How much do you think we could rake in representing cow people who got kicked out of their apartment or weren't hired because of their, um, *cowness*?"

"You're laughing, but that's exactly what will happen."

Snapping his fingers, Barney caught the waitress's attention and mouthed, "Check." He licked the ball of skin on the back of his index finger and rubbed it clockwise on his plate through the remnants of ketchup and salt.

Ken said, "At some point, no restaurant will serve meat dishes because it will be considered cannabilistic. You follow what I'm saying, Barney?"

"This is awfully interesting, Ken, but what's your point? Where is all of this leading?"

"I don't know." He pulled bills from his wallet, counted them and laid them on the check. Ken tilted his head, squinted, and said excitedly, "Wait a minute. Yes, I do. I do! I think we should learn from history and prevent centuries of prejudice from happening. I think we should embrace the cows. Embrace them now!" He slammed his hand on the table. "Partial people, partial animals, whatever, are all living creatures. Pretty soon we'll all be partials. It's inevitable. It's evolution." He lifted his water glass and toasted, "To the future of our species."

Drumming his fingers on the table, Barney shook his head lazily and said, "You're nuts, Ken. I hope you know that."

Once he realized how much Lisa looked like a horse, Ken stopped having sex with her. He knew Lisa was concerned. She had made some tentative queries about a mid-life crisis, and Ken found her once going through the pockets of his suits looking for evidence of an affair. One Friday night, after Jasmine was asleep, she came out of the bathroom wearing a jade green negligee trimmed in fluffy white fur. Noting the embarrassed flush on her face, Ken felt sorry for her. Still, he couldn't keep himself from laughing. He had never seen a horse in lingerie before, let alone those ridiculous stiletto slippers with the feathery puffs across the top. Lisa let out a startled sob and locked herself in the bathroom. Ken pleaded with her to come out, promised he wouldn't laugh again, but secretly felt pleased when she stayed put and he was free to doze off.

He had to be honest with himself; Lisa wasn't a thoroughbred. No, she was more of a quarter horse, large, loyal, hard-working. He didn't mean to offend her but he didn't want to make love to her either. They'd graze through life's meadow together side by side, but no more rolling in the hay. He grew a goatee, the scruff on his chin longer than was fashionable, and installed a climbing wall in his office.

The first real change came that sweaty afternoon in June when he was mowing the backyard. Rain had pounded the grass for days and finally stopped long enough for Ken to get the mower out. As he pushed the machine up and down his yard, the shorn grass called to him with its sweet, dewy fragrance. Normally the smell of grass made his eyes water and itch, but today he couldn't escape the infused scent of dandelions and clover. His head felt light, and a giddy sensation traveled up and down his limbs. He looked back at his empty house. Lisa had taken Jasmine to the library and wasn't expected back until almost dinner. Swinging his head left and right, he felt protected by the tall hedges bordering each of his neighbors' yards.

When he knelt, he felt as if he were about to do something sacred. He paused for a minute to experience what he knew would be a private ritual, one he hadn't yet performed but was eager to do over and over. Finally, lowering his hands, he allowed them to fondle the grass before he gently lowered his head and ate his fill.

He vomited after his first feast of grass but then learned to swallow and re-swallow the regurgitated feed until the nausea passed. Every Saturday afternoon, he grazed on all fours in the backyard. Lisa found him once with his nose in the dirt and he told her he was checking for mole holes. She seemed to accept that explanation, and he was then emboldened to spend most summer evenings pretending he was concerned about lawn care. Lisa wanted to hire a professional because she couldn't understand why the grass grew so unevenly. Ken told her it was a problem with the fertilizer and he was going to switch brands.

And he did. Each night, about two or three in the morning, he began sneaking out of the house and moving his bowels in the yard, visiting a different spot each time. Lisa suspected the neighbor's dog and complained, but Ken said, "Relax, honey, a little dog poop never hurt anything."

"A little? That damned mutt has crapped all over the lawn! What the hell are they feeding that animal? She shook her head and breathed noisily through her flapping lips.

"But you have to admit, dear, the grass *is* a lot greener."

Lisa narrowed her eyes at him and tapped her foot on the floor. "What's with you, Ken, anyway? You're preoccupied all the time. You never eat. You don't sleep. I hear you get up at night. Maybe you should see the doctor. I'm going to make you an appointment."

Doctor Sincus was a hairless white ape, no doubt about it. His broad forehead was a portico over his small sunken eyes. His nose was nicely rounded, as were his cheeks and chin. He was barrel-chested but stooped, and he walked with a thumping, heavy stride.

Ken was amiable while the doctor took his blood pressure and felt his abdomen. He breathed with extra gusto when he felt the cool, clinical pressure of the stethoscope on his back. When asked about stress at the office, Ken answered, "Oh, I guess there's some tension, but I don't let it affect me too much."

"Your wife seems to think you've been acting a bit oddly for a few months now."

Yeah, what would she know, she's a horse, he wanted to say. Instead he answered, striving not to sound irritated, "Lisa worries too much. You know how women are."

Peering into his ears with a tiny light, Doctor Sincus said nonchalantly, "She told me that the two of you haven't had intercourse in quite some time. Open up." As the doctor slipped a wooden dipstick into his mouth, Ken bit down on the man's hand until he tasted blood and the doctor began to screech. Ken said, "I'm so sorry! Forgive me! The stick made me gag and I had an involuntary reaction."

Shocked, the doctor glared at him for several long moments. Finally, he said, "I've been practicing medicine for over twenty-five years and nothing like this has ever happened to me."

"Again, I'm so sorry. I feel just terrible." Ken blinked innocently, his expression vacant.

"I have to disinfect this. I'll be back in a moment."

When the doctor returned to the examining room, a large gauze bandage taped around his hand, he said, accusingly, "Do you think it's physical or emotional, this hiatus from sex? Are you simply uninterested or are you not able to sustain an erection?"

Not able to sustain an erection? Who was this man kidding! Ken's libido was a force of nature, a true animal lust. Why, he was a buck ready to spawn a whole herd! He just needed to find the right mate, or mates, he reasoned. A buck had his pick of females, didn't he?

When he didn't answer, the doctor assumed Ken was embarrassed and said, "Would you like me to write you a prescription for Viagra?"

"Viagra?"

Doctor Sincus nodded. "Yes, you've heard of it, surely?"

Sliding off the examining table, Ken slipped his loafers on and said, "Sure, I've heard of it, but it's not for me, Doc." He walked out of the office, giving the door a good kick with the back of his heel.

That night Ken had the same dream he'd had since the first day he ate grass. He was a buck with huge curved horns wandering the rugged steppes of some pastoral country. He ripped the sparse grass from the ground and chewed it contentedly. Circling him, the female goats vied for his attention. He especially fancied the young one with the prancing walk, but he didn't want to show favoritism. Bad for herd morale. After satisfying his hunger, he bellowed, "MAA-aaaaaaa," his thunderous call echoing through the mountains. With some pushing and shoving, the girls lined up, youngest to oldest and one by one, he heaved himself into them, never leaving one until he was sure she'd had a tremulous orgasm. His herd was different from the others on the mountain. Much more content. He knew how to please a goat.

"Friday is Jasmine's class trip to the zoo," Lisa announced one evening. "I volunteered when they went to the museum. It's your turn."

Immediately Ken started to protest, saying something about a deposition, but then he thought, *why, of course, the zoo!* Yes, that's where he needed to go. Why hadn't he thought of it sooner!

When the day came, he sat in the back of the bus with the other parent volunteers and watched as Jasmine's teacher, Miss Pursonne, led the children in song. She stood in the aisle and grasped the back of a seat in each hand. Transfixed, Ken watched her turn her head from side to side to make eye contact with children on both sides of the bus. Miss Pursonne, wearing an above-the-knee denim skirt and striped T-shirt, radiated a wholesome, natural beauty. There wasn't a speck of makeup on her face, and yet her skin was radiance itself. She was of medium stature, with long, coltish legs composed of lean muscles that flexed when the bus came to an abrupt stop at a red light. Her eyes were as open as a doe's, a dreamy brown as dark as tree bark. And that nose! No one had as tiny and inoffensive a nose as Miss Pursonne! Could she actually breathe through those kitten-sized nostrils? She smiled as she sang, her luminous teeth framed by full pink lips. She wasn't married, but she should procreate, Ken thought. She must! She was the fittest of the species!

He lost sight of her periodically at the zoo. As a parent volunteer, he supervised five children, including Jasmine, through the fish pavilion and a temporary exhibit of Malaysian butterflies. Although Jasmine and her classmates protested it was too babyish, Ken insisted on visiting the petting zoo. Once there, the children ran off to the bunny house while he opened a gate and walked up a small hill to pet a baby goat. He approached it with fatherly pride, calling out, "Here, little fella, right here!"

The kid studied him as he chewed and cocked his head to one side.

"You're a handsome little fella, aren't you?"

As Ken reached to touch his forelock, the goat jerked his head upward, knocking his hand to his side. "Hey, that's not nice. I just wanted to pet you, little fella."

"Open the gate."

Incredulous, Ken lowered his head and stared at the kid's mouth. "What did you say?"

"OPEN THE GATE!" The small goat pushed against him now, butting his narrow head into Ken's thigh. Ken started to protest, but the animal reared and struck again. Running, Ken ran to the gate, leaping over it and stumbling into a gravel path. His daughter and friends were congregated now several yards away and cheered him on.

"Some jump, Mr. Onis!" one of the girls called.

Could the children hear the goat? He still heard the bleating, "OPEN THE GATE! OPEN THE GATE!" He didn't know if his mind were echoing it or if the goat was still yelling. He looked at the oblivious faces of the children; they hadn't heard a thing. Jamine was laughing, "Daddy, that goat was chasing you."

Trembling, he tried to assess what had happened. *I spoke to a goat!* The damn thing had no manners, but it's just a baby. Still, we *communicated!*

This is wonderful, this is wonderful! Ken thrilled over and over as he walked with the girls through the zoo. His mind was still reeling when he looked up and saw his grandfather sitting in a tree in an area supposedly fashioned as an Australian outback. Why, Grandpa Bill, he said to himself, what are you doing here? He stopped walking. Wait a minute; Grandpa Bill died when I was in college. What's going on?

"He's soooo cute!" he heard Jasmine say as the other girls agreed with her. They were standing in a group staring at Grandpa Bill who was starting to shift on the tree branch.

"Ohhhhhh!" Ken shouted. "It's a koala bear!"

Embarrassed, Jasmine turned quickly and said, "Shhh! We know that, Dad! We're not stupid, you know."

Transfixed, Ken took note of the bear's flat nose that spread over most of his face, the tufts of fur emerging from the friendly-looking ears. Gosh, he looked so much like Grandpa. That stout little body. *The resemblance is unbelievable*, Ken thought. *All this time I've been thinking about how people look like animals but I never considered how much animals look like people!* He wanted to stay and watch the bear, but the girls were ready to move on. Ken walked with them, pleasurably flustered, and decided he'd return to the zoo alone the next day.

In the monkey house, Ken caught sight of Miss Pursonne standing in front of a panoramic glass cage of lemurs. She appeared engrossed as she watched the exotic, athletic creatures swinging on an intricate web of ropes. Their long tails, so sleek and muscular, twisted and twirled as the animals flung themselves back and forth, back and forth. The lemurs stopped playing occasionally to peer back at the human spectators, their glassy eyes reflecting the light from a large window at the back of the cage.

Ken took his place beside Miss Pursonne and heard her murmur, "So beautiful, and they look so intelligent, like they understand everything about us." She sighed. "It would be so wonderful to swing like that, to feel like you're flying."

Ah! She understands! Ken felt exultant. He turned to her and studied her exquisite profile, the pleasing curve of her forehead and the miniscule slope of her nose. Her lips were slightly parted as she watched the animals, her head moving to follow their movements. Ken's blood throbbed with elation. If anyone deserved to hear about his verbal exchange with the goat, it was Miss Pursonne. Yes, she was worthy to hear his wondrous announcement, she alone. Ken opened his mouth and was shocked to hear himself utter, "MAA-aaaaa!"

Frightened, she jumped, her hand flying out and hitting his chest. Miss Pursonne said, "Oh, sorry Mr. Onis. I thought I heard something. I was startled."

Touched that she was so apologetic, he rushed to say, "No problem," but again, louder this time, said, "MAAA—A—A—AHH!" The children began to laugh. A little boy said to Jasmine, "Your daddy talks like a goat."

But Miss Pursonne was horrified, her eyebrows lifted to her hairline as she looked disbelievingly at him. Then, with a teacher's authority, she said, "Come with me, children," and began to lead them hurriedly away.

"But I'm in Mr. Onis's group," one of the girls said, but Miss Pursonne grasped her hand and pulled her. "You too, Jasmine," she said, "come with me. Your father, well, he's not feeling well and we should leave him alone for awhile."

No, no, no! She didn't understand! He tried to protest: "MMAA—AH—AH—AHHHHH! MMAAH—AH—HHHH!" Miss Pursonne began running with the children, all of them frightened now, his daughter's face a palette of fear and embarrassment. He chased the group as they ran to the exit, calling no, let me explain, but with each word a chorus of goat cries rang out. Now everyone was watching him, but he couldn't be concerned about them. He had to get to Miss Pursonne! He had to explain! "MMMMMMMMMAAAAAAAHHHHHH!" His sound trumpeted through the building.

Outside, in the bright light, Miss Pursonne stumbled, falling to her knees, her skirt riding up over her backside. She continued to stumble forward, one of her elbows scraping against the pavement. She called to the children, "Keep going! Find another group from our school and stay with them!" She tried to stand, but one of her ankles was unsteady and she fell into a crouched position.

Ken emerged from the building and beheld Miss Pursonne on all fours, the back of her exposed, panties the color of summer grass. Before Miss Pursonne could attempt again to rise, he rushed to mount her, yanking down his pants to his knees. As he fell upon her, his groin straining against her underwear, Ken heard screaming all around him as the ignorant began to slap at him, to try to knock him from his perch. A man hit him squarely in both shoulders and toppled him to the ground. Ken tried to stand but the man sat heavily on his back. Turning his head, he saw that Miss Pursonne was still on all fours, but she was wailing, "*Help! Help!*" An older woman helped Miss Pursonne up and led her away. Several other people followed them while Ken butted helplessly under the weight of the man who toppled him. Pinned, he still cried out for Mrs. Pursonne, "*Maaaaa! Maaaaaa! Maaaaaa!*" until his throat hurt and he could bleat no more.

They fed him three meals a day and began removing the straight jacket at bedtime. Some sedative was in his food, he suspected, because he fell asleep immediately each night. Sleep was a release. All day, the doctors questioned him, the same questions over and over: Do you want to be a goat?

Are you afraid to be human? Do you understand you did that teacher physical harm? Do you want to see your family?

He never answered. They wouldn't understand. He hadn't spoken since that day at the zoo when he at last found his true tongue. But at night, when he shut his eyes from the gazes of all the people with clipboards, he frolicked with the other goats on the mountain. He was no longer the only buck, but he was content to share the herd with others. Together the goats grazed and nuzzled, crapped in the grassy steppes and climbed the mountain. From a great height, Ken looked down at a small village, at the tiny creatures going about their lives. He strained his eyes to see her. She was still dressed in her denim skirt and T-shirt, and she walked on two legs, not four. Ken lived for the day when he would see her start to climb the mountain. Her supple legs would allow her to climb higher and higher until at last she would stand before him, her hand fondling his forelock. This time she would understand. This time she would get on his back and together they would travel to the highest peak. Together they would share every pleasure known to man, to woman, and to beast. Their days would be filled with endless contentment and she would never descend the hill.

LIVE YOUR LIFE

David Tetlow had been portraying Dr. David Hammond on *Live Your Life*, a daytime soap opera, for thirty years. More than that, he had quite literally become his character. Affecting an authority on medical matters, he called his relatives each year and reminded them to get flu shots. Whenever he boarded an airplane, he carried a copy of *The New England Journal of Medicine*. He watched medical information shows on cable television, gravely nodding his head as a disease was explained, concurring with the prognosis. David was meticulously groomed, the cuticles on his fingernails never visible, the edges of the nails hygienically short. He ate a balanced diet and took brisk walks about Bayfinch, his hometown in upstate New York, an hour's drive from the soap's Manhattan studio.

His education had not included medical school, college, or even much elementary science to speak of. He graduated from Sycamore High School in Dayton where he had dabbled in the drama club, playing the role of the doctor in *Our Town*. But the theater teacher, Miss Scummer, thought he had a classic profile, chiseled Gregory Peckish features, and a voice that could fill Sycamore High's auditorium. It was the only encouragement he'd gotten from any teacher, and he headed for New York a few days after graduation. He had trouble getting auditions and hid his nerves by acting overly confident at the few he went to. He did voice ads on the radio for several years before finally landing a role on *Live Your Life*, at the time a fledgling soap. Playing Dr. Hammond gave him, he felt, hard-earned respect. He didn't realize how hungry he was for it after years of rejection until he put a stethoscope around his neck for the first time, feeling the metal tubes solid and official against his skin. When people asked him where he studied, he assumed they meant medical rather than drama school, and answered evasively "Ohio." He scoffed at younger actors arriving in New York with drama degrees from

Yale and other prestigious institutions. All that money spent for what? There was nothing to acting. You simply became the character. He and Dr. David Hammond had been one and the same since he was twenty-nine, more than half his life.

When he first joined the soap's cast, his character had just graduated from medical school and was an intern at Loveland Hospital. He was quite the catch in those days, every nurse throwing herself at David Hammond *and* David Tetlow. In real life, he married Lucy, a fellow actress who left him when she got a part in *Hair* on Broadway. On the show, David married Jenna, a sweet-faced nurse with lips as thick as bricks. She was thought to be too bland a character, however, despite the lips, so the writers made her a mercy killer, stabbing patients with lethal injections during the night shift. Doctor David divorced her and married the angelic Alicia, the social worker with pre-Raphaelite hair and altruistic eyes. David didn't like that phase of the show; Alicia upstaged him with all of her benevolence and self-sacrifice. Luckily, she died during childbirth, and he became the grieving, stoical parent raising a daughter who bore such a resemblance to her mother, it was almost painful for Dr. Hammond to look at her. In fact, David developed a wince of which he was inordinately proud. It came to be known as the "Hammond wince" and was regularly written into the script as a direction.

In the course of thirty years, Dr. Hammond had been married four times, had nine extramarital affairs, had three children, had been held hostage twice, had switched a pair of babies at birth, had delivered triplets in a subway car, had performed plastic surgery (even though he was a general practitioner) on a mobster, and had suffered three gunshot wounds on separate occasions. David Tetlow's life was not nearly as colorful, but he strove to make it as similar as possible, exchanging spouses and lovers with nearly the same frequency. He divorced one wife because she had slept with her gynecologist, something he absolutely couldn't forgive, and two others because they, like the charitable Alicia, had upstaged him. Eleanor and Grace were well-intended women, but he had felt that all eyes were on them, when they should have been on him. Eleanor starred on a rival soap, *The Power of Passion*, known as "PP" in the trade, and Grace was a housewife with a gift for gardening. She made the most stubborn plants bloom with a verdant zealousness, and Bayfinch residents called the house constantly seeking her advice on a gamut of horticultural problems. David had observed Grace examining plants, touching their leaves, kneading their soil, and it had been too much; she had the life-saving skills of a physician and there was room for only one doctor in the house. Presently, he was married to Caroline, a divorcée with two children in college. Ten years younger than David, she was very charming, and dressed and acted with the flair of a doctor's wife. He approved of her, but this marriage too seemed ill-fated since her son, Greg, was considering majoring in pre-med.

For the past year or so, Dr. David Hammond's role on the show had been drastically cut. For several months, David was unconcerned. He thought they couldn't survive without him. Yes, younger actors perhaps gave the show its sex, its drama, but he fancied himself the *soul* of the show. He was the main patriarchal figure of Loveland, the soap's fictional town, and his picture was still featured prominently in the opening credits. More than that, at midpoint in the show, in between commercials, it was his voice that announced, "Live Your Life will be right back." That, more than anything, convinced him that his future was secure.

One day, however, while he was watching the show in his dressing room, he heard a different voice at the commercial break, a woman's voice, English, saucy, with a come hither timbre. It belonged to Kate Heckles, the woman who played the newly arrived health club owner. This rankled David more than he could admit to himself because the woman had made outright cracks about his obsession with his character. Most of the cast referred to him as "Doc," a friendly, respectful address, but Kate, who exhibited herself in a rainbow of spandex outfits on and off the show, greeted him with "What's up, Doc?" in an absurd Bugs Bunny voice. She was in her mid-twenties, an aspiring stage actress. She made it clear that her work on the soap was just a brief stint before Broadway called. When she voiced this in rehearsal once, David had thought he charmed her with his response: "My dear," he bellowed, summoning his own stage training on volume and inflection from high school, "we all thought that at one time and . . . here we are!" He waved his hand with a flourish to take in the set. Kate had extended her own arm, mimicking him, and said in her wisecracking voice, "No . . . there *you* are!"

Most disturbing was her influence with the head writers. Margaret and Bill were notorious for turning down suggestions flat. They viewed the cast as jealous, vain robots who could be trained to recite a few sentences each show without stammering. Any more than that was gravy. Several actors had quit over disagreements with them, but Bill and Margaret had the backing of the executive producer and loved telling an indignant actor where to shove it. Kate, however, was not put off by their reputation and went to them freely, even in her first weeks on the set. David watched her attempts at camaraderie with them with a simmering smile, hoping he'd be present when they really shut her down, told her to stop whining and memorize her lines, or go back to England and get a bit part in a BBC drama. When David saw the three of them having lunch at the commissary, however, even overhearing Bill ask Kate's opinion on a recent re-write, he swallowed a radish whole and decided it was time to take action.

But what was he worried about, after all? He had worked with Margaret nearly the entire time he'd been on the show, and Bill for the last ten years. He simply had to confront them, he told himself. And he did. On the telephone. At night. He called Margaret at home and told her he was overdue for a major story line.

"Overdue?" she said bluntly, irritated at being interrupted at home for such a common complaint. Margaret's personal life was something of a mystery; there were rumors of younger men, aspiring soap actors. As he held the phone to his ear now, David thought he heard bullfighting music in the background.

"Yes," he said quickly. "The last time I was on screen for more than a mere minute was two years ago when I—"

"Had that seizure," Margaret finished. "Well, what can I say, Dave? Doctors used to be everything on soaps, but people are sick of them now."

Had he heard her correctly? Sick of doctors? "Don't be insane, Margaret; we're the most important of occupations. I suppose you think aerobics instructors are important? That they make a valuable contribution to society?"

Margaret laughed her characteristic, "*Ah ha!*" enjoying having caught David in an openly jealous moment. "Well, since you put it that way, Dave," she said, "doctors and aerobics instructors do have a couple things in common; I mean, they both get the blood pumping, am I right?"

"Rubbish." David felt particularly learned at the moment, disdainful of such ignorance. He had a high card he knew he could play only once. He had played it many times as a young man, but he knew better than to wave it wildly about now. But this was such a moment. "I will demand to be released from my contract if I am not given fifteen minutes air time in a single episode by next month."

He let his statement hang over the wire, waiting for Margaret's astonished breath. He did hear something, but it sounded more like a man's voice calling out, "Olé! Olé!" Margaret partially covered the receiver and hollered, "I told you to leave that tablecloth alone!" She spoke into the phone, "I'll talk with Bill," and hung up.

David rejected the first script, a ludicrous story about his joining Kate's spa and having a heart attack while Jazzercising. The scene would culminate with Kate performing CPR on him while people in exercise clothes would stand around screaming "Save him! Save him!"

"I'm the doctor, I'm the one who saves people!" he railed at Margaret and Bill, irritated that they were eager to profile Kate at his expense. "And besides," he continued, "I would never Jazzercise. I'm a doctor, for Christ's sake."

The second script was worse, much worse. He and Kate were to meet at a cocktail party, leave together and go back to her house, make mad, passionate love until he had a heart attack. Kate wouldn't perform CPR, but she would lift him and carry him to her car in an audacious display of female strength.

"No one would believe I'd be interested in that woman!" David said, throwing the script on Bill's desk. "She has no class. She's just a loud-mouthed bully."

Bill looked up, giving Margaret an obvious *I told you so* look, but then said, "Dave, the older man, younger woman thing is very hot right now. We think you and Kate could be the stars of the trend."

"Then why are you so damn determined that I have a heart attack! We can't very well be hot if I'm about to expire, now can we!" David stood between the two writers and witnessed the guilty shadow eclipsing Bill's face. Margaret normally had a poker face, but he noticed the twitch on the left side of her mouth.

"All right," David said, waving a finger at both of them. "I know what's going on here!" He drew himself up and spoke to the imaginary back row, charging his voice so that Margaret covered her ears. "You're trying to get me to quit the show! You can't fire me before my contract is up, so you're trying to humiliate me into leaving. Well, forget it! Give me a heart attack, throw me together with that loathsome woman, I don't care! Write some cockamamie story about her being my sex therapist . . ."

He stopped shouting because he noticed Margaret was starting to jot notes.

He lowered his voice but spoke with seething confidence, "You can never get rid of me until I say so!"

He strode out of their office as if he were exiting a stage and went to his dressing room, pouring glasses of bourbon until it was time to go home. Once there, he didn't tell Caroline what happened. They had a routine where she would rub his neck and his shoulders as he sat reading the paper, and she would say, "Rough day at the hospital, darling?" and he would respond with details of Lois Medford's recurrence of amnesia or little Charlie's broken arm. If he wasn't in the show that day, he made something up.

They sat on the patio and drank gin and tonics. Looking at her, David admitted to himself that she was not his prettiest wife; her nose was too long and her chin was creased too severely, bending in and out as she chewed her food. When she spoke, only her bottom teeth showed, lovely teeth, straight and white, but nonetheless, just the bottoms. But Caroline knew her lines; she deferred to him, she entertained well, throwing the most elegant dinner parties in Bayfinch. If she were a bit loose with money, it was worth it to see her looking so consistently well-groomed in designer apparel. Really, if her son would just drop the pre-med major, she had potential to be the one David would stay with. The events at the studio that day made him see her in a very fond light. She was so gracious and receptive to all his remarks, even when he complained that her hair color needed a touch-up. They retired early that evening, making love with an energy that surprised both of them. Why, there's nothing wrong with my heart! David told himself victoriously.

When he arrived on the set the next day, Sally, one of the production assistants, reminded him that he wasn't needed that day. This was often the case. Most actors were called at home well in advance, but David came in regardless. A set needed a doctor, he reasoned, so the crew thought nothing of waiting until he arrived each day to tell him.

In his dressing room, he contemplated his future. He had three years left in his contract, and then he would be sixty-four, a respectable retirement age. In a way, he welcomed the thought of not having to come here each day, not having to work so hard at convincing people he was a doctor. It would be much easier, David thought, to be a retired doctor. He and Caroline would travel and entertain at home, attending their children's graduations and weddings, their grandchildren's christenings. So many events at which he'd be the admired and respected retired doctor. Yes, it was a role he would welcome, but only when he decided to take it.

At one o'clock he turned on the large-screen television in his dressing room. David didn't bother reading scripts unless he had lines, but he hadn't missed a show since the day his daughter was born twenty-three years ago. During the opening credits, he admired his face on the screen. The photo had been taken fifteen years ago, but he thought it was still a good likeness.

The opening scene took place at the health spa. Kate was directing an exercise class, standing on a little stage in a neon yellow one-piece body-suit, her red hair clipped up into a tight assemblage of curls. She was bouncing about the platform, calling out to the members of the class. "Push it! Move it!" she yelled, grunting as she kicked her feet out behind her.

"Oh, move it yourself, lady," David said to the screen. He was irked that Kate was the lead story in today's episode. She began doing a ridiculous exercise, thrusting her pelvis forward while she waved her arms over her head. David started laughing, thinking that Kate looked like she was doing a poor imitation of a Hawaiian dance. He stood and began doing the exercise in an exaggerated fashion, shaking his hips from side to side, punching his arms up in the air.

"Push it! Move it!" he repeated, mocking her instructions. He caught sight of himself in the mirror and stopped moving. For a moment, he looked like an aging man struggling to catch his breath, and he composed himself, sweeping a piece of hair back from his face. He was just about to sit down when he felt a pinching in his chest, like a clothespin clamping down just left of his breastbone, but then it was gone, released, and he wondered if he had imagined it. He got a glass of water and sat in front of the television, assuring himself that it must have been just the start of a pulled muscle.

The second scene began at Sushi Soy, the restaurant secretly owned by the illegitimate heir to the Sheridan family fortune. David had trouble remembering all the particulars of the Sheridan family. They'd been rich, then poor, then rich again so many times over the last fifteen years, he couldn't keep up. The camera panned the diners who were dressed in extravagant clothes, and David was alarmed to see nearly the entire cast there. This was unusual. The whole cast was normally only brought together for big events, a wedding or a murder trial. Why, I could easily be sitting at one of those tables, he thought. There was Millicent, his present wife, sipping coffee with his stepson. David was outraged. He planned to go to Bill and Margaret directly after the show and complain. The camera stopped moving and focused on a table of women, Kate the focus of the shot although he barely recognized her because she was wearing a white linen suit instead of a leotard in some obnoxious color. The women at the table were leaning in around her. At first David thought they were studying her dessert, not real, he guessed, from the sheen of the frosting, but then Kate said, "You heard what I said; he's a fake!"

A woman wearing an enormous rhinestone necklace said, "You're mistaken. Why, he removed my daughter's gall bladder last year, and she's absolutely fine."

"It's just a miracle she's all right," Kate said, "because word is all over town that Dr. Hammond faked his medical credentials and God knows what else." Kate looked out across the room and continued to speak. "Poor Millicent. She doesn't have a clue. She thinks she's married to a legitimate doctor."

David toppled sideways out of his chair, his left shoulder colliding with the floor with such force, he wondered if he dislocated his collar bone. But his eyes never left the camera, now showing Millicent who was daintily wiping the corners of her mouth with her napkin.

"Millicent!" David called. "Help me!" He couldn't even remember what the woman's real name was; they had only recently married and he always called his wives by their characters' names. The camera came in close on Kate's face. David noticed that she lowered her chin, making her eyes and lips appear bigger.

"He got some medical training in Korea, but he never went to med school. He's been passing himself off as a doctor for years, pulling the wool over your eyes." Kate looked meaningfully at each of her luncheon companions, reprimanding them for their blind trust.

David sputtered, trying to find his voice. He raised himself to his feet and picked up a newspaper, hurling it at the TV as he screamed, "Liar! Slanderer! I'll sue the leotard right off your back, lady!"

Another woman at the table clutched her water glass, shaking it melodramatically so that some of the water spilled onto the table. She began to weep pathetically, her eyebrows becoming one although no tears actually fell down her face. "When my second baby died in delivery," she sobbed, "they blamed it on a lack of oxygen. Now I know," she said, trembling, "I know . . . *Dr. Hammond killed my baby!*"

Everyone stopped eating and looked at the woman as she stood and waved her arms at them. "Everyone!" she shouted. "Listen to me!"

Forks and knives were dropped and the restaurant became deadly quiet. The woman trembled as she held onto the back of her chair. David didn't recognize her; she must have been an extra. "We've been had! We've been used," she said. "We've been lied to!" she yelled, her voice growing louder with each word. "Dr. David Hammond isn't really a doctor! He's been lying to us for years. He's nothing but a *fraud! An imposter!*"

The woman continued screaming until she collapsed. Kate was at her side immediately, ordering a waiter to get an ambulance while she made sure no one crowded the woman. She leaned her head over the woman's chest and cupped her hand around the woman's wrist. The woman was carried out of the restaurant on a stretcher while stunned, hushed onlookers affected a collective look of terror.

David was befuddled. "But, but . . . I don't even know that woman! What baby is she talking about? I never killed her baby. Why, she's mad, she's insane." He could clear it up, all of it, he told himself. He would simply tell Bill and Margaret that it was all false, every word. How could it be true when he'd never seen the woman before? And since when did extras get to make such pronouncements?

He walked to the television and stabbed the power button. His feet seemed to sink into the carpet; it was an effort to move. They've done it, he thought, and he felt the pinching sensation in his chest return. They've come up with the one thing they knew would make me leave. He sat before his mirror and looked at himself, at his face that for years looked back at him with such confidence, with such unquestioned faith. Now his expression seemed that of a petty thief, a shoplifter who loitered about discount stores. He put his hand over his chest, as if he were about to recite the Pledge of Allegiance, and held it there until the pain stopped. He picked up his Emmy, the only trophy he had ever won. He received it in 1978, the year he was on camera for sixty-three shows in a row. That year, he had convinced a patient not to jump from a tenth story window and diagnosed his own wife with spotted yellow fever. Now he packed the trophy along with a few other things in his duffel bag and left the set, walking out the back door to avoid the cluster of autograph seekers who usually hovered by out front.

He walked uptown, wondering how long he'd have to wait for his train at the station. He always caught the 5:45 but it was only mid-afternoon.

He stepped slowly along the sidewalk, his head down.

That's the thanks I get, he thought, his heel chewing into the pavement. Thirty-two years of service and that's how they thank me. No gold watch, no party, just complete and utter humiliation. He felt a thrust on his shoulder and looked up. A dark-haired man with aviator sunglasses barked at him, "Hey, watch it! Look where you're going, old man."

Old man? He had half a mind to follow him and give him a piece of his mind, but the pinching was back and his breath felt as if it were in a vise, struggling to be released. Looking about, David saw a small grocery at the end of the block. Water, he thought; I just need some water.

Inside, the pinching subsided and his breathing eased. Indigestion, he told himself. The broccoli in my lunch salad. Cruciferous vegetables can cause gas; gas can manifest as chest pains. Doctor, heal thyself, he thought with a smile. They'll never take my medical knowledge from me.

Still, some water would be refreshing, make the remainder of the journey to the station easier. David walked to the back of the store and found the Evian in the glass refrigerator. As he removed a bottle, he heard someone, a woman, cry, "Doc-tor Ham-mond! Doc-tor Ham-mond!"

He turned to find a very short, pudgy woman with gray braids crisscrossing the front of her head. She grasped his wrist and said, "Doc-tor Ham-mond! Shame on you! Shame on you! You kill that lady's baby. You fool all those people. You not a doc-tor! You fake doc-tor!"

Closing the refrigerator door, David said, "No. That wasn't me. The writers did that. I'm a good doctor." He patted his chest and repeated, "Good."

Stamping her foot, the little woman insisted, "No good! You no good! You no doc-tor. You fake! *Fake!*" She raised her index finger and pointed it at him over and over.

David was appalled. "Madame, I assure you, you are confused."

Affronted, the tiny woman took a step backwards. "I not confused! You fool everyone but you no fool me!" Crossing her arms, she shook her head with wide, exaggerated swings.

"It's just a show," David began, but the little woman was eager to speak.

"*Live Your Life*. Ever since I come to this country, I watch. I learn English. I see you be doc-tor long time. But you no doc-tor. You *fake* doctor." She clasped her hand and raised her arm, punching David twice in the shoulder.

"Ow! Madame, you can't do that! I don't deserve that. Listen. I am an *actor*. Dr. Hammond is a *character*. He's *not real*. He's a character on a TV show." Rubbing his shoulder, he lowered his voice. "The show isn't real. I'm . . . not real."

The little woman sniffed and raised her chin. "You made him real! Real!"

Nodding, David said, "That's my job. I'm an actor."

Looking up, she seemed to consider this. She turned her head and looked at him sideways. "You good actor. I believe Doc-tor Ham-mond. He best. Best on show."

Immediately, David smiled. Good actor. This woman knows what she's talking about! She's the type of person the writers should hear from.

The little woman started to walk away but then stopped. She smiled fully and David saw she was missing several teeth. "You do the face," she told him.

"Face?"

She frowned, her face becoming a maze of wrinkles, and then moved her head back as if she had seen something horrible beyond words.

The wince! She liked the wince! David bent down so he was peering directly into her face. "Let's do it together. You do it very well."

"I do? I do face good?"

"*Very* good. Now let's do it together."

David crouched and set the bottle on the floor. With their chins touching, he made the face, watching as the little woman mimicked him. She laughed as if she were being relentlessly tickled.

"Again," the little woman said.

"Take two," David said, and he winced with all his might.

A LONELY VIRTUE

PROSPECTIVE

Howard Leister found it easier to make eye contact with the waitress than his son who was seated across the table from him at Bidwell's Cafe. Howard asked the young woman for more coffee and then said to Jeremy, "Would you like anything else?" His son continued biting a hangnail on his thumb.

"Jeremy," his father said, not loudly, but the utterance was like a firecracker, and his son looked up immediately and said, "What?"

"I asked if you'd like anything else. Let's not keep the lady waiting."

He shook his head no, turning slightly to look at the waitress, a college student with her hair cut so it sprouted like a willowy shrub from the top of her head. Her chipped black fingernail polish revealed a shade of lavender beneath.

"Just a refill on the coffee, and the check when you get a chance," Howard told the woman.

"I'll have another raisin bagel," Jeremy said suddenly.

"No problem." She walked away from the table, her Doc Martens scuffling against the linoleum.

With his thumbnail already in place against his front teeth, Jeremy swiveled and watched as the girl went behind the counter. Howard lifted one eyebrow and smiled. "Do you think she's pretty?"

Jeremy turned his head instantly and said, "*Da-ad*," in a muffled tone.

Clasping the back of his neck with his hands, Howard said, "Fill me in. What counts for pretty these days?"

It was the type of conversation he wanted to have with his son, something that would give birth to camaraderie, rapport. So far his expectations for this trip, touring colleges with his only son who would be a freshman this time next year, hadn't been met. Jeremy had spent most of his time calling his mother and stepfather on the phone.

Howard tried again, "Is the waitress what I would have called 'a looker'?"

Jeremy made his habitual scowl, a vertical crease running the length of his forehead. "I don't know."

Leaning over, his forearms taking up most of the small table, Howard said, "In my day it was a pair of baby blues, a cashmere sweater and a string of pearls. And it helped if she talked a lot because then you didn't have to."

The waitress returned with an urn of coffee and poured the steaming liquid into Howard's cup. She set Jeremy's bagel in front of him.

"Thank you," Howard said, and Jeremy softly echoed, "Thank you."

The girl hesitated for a second and then asked Jeremy brightly, "Are you a prospective student?"

Jeremy nodded, looking directly at the waitress. "But I don't want to go to Hancock. I want to go to Brown. I applied early admissions there."

"Oh," she said, tossing her hair so the bush flounced up and down. "A lot of students here wanted to go to Brown. I wanted to go to Brown too, but I didn't get in."

"What were your SAT scores?" Jeremy asked with an animation that surprised Howard.

She laughed. "They were good, but not good enough. Don't feel bad if you don't get in there. Hancock is a great place. A lot less snobby than Brown."

As she walked away, Howard said, "See? An unsolicited testimonial."

Jeremy removed the top half of the bagel and began to coat cream cheese on its underside. "I still want to go to Brown."

Howard looked at the ceiling and stifled a heavy sigh. Trying to sound casual, he said, "Brown doesn't have as good a swim team as Hancock. You could get a scholarship here." Howard took a small swallow of coffee, smiled, and said, not really joking, "but you'll have to cut that hair if you want to improve your times."

His ex-wife, Bernice, had instructed Howard not to "upset," that was the word she used, Jeremy about his hair, but it rankled him to see his son looking like an ugly girl. Jeremy parted his hopelessly straight brown hair in the center and it lay lank on each side of his face like a pair of limp curtains.

"I don't know if I want to swim in college," Jeremy said.

Howard set his cup down too heavily; small splashes of very hot coffee escaped and landed on the back of his hand. "That's news. When did you decide that?"

Jeremy barely shrugged his shoulders.

"It's a tremendous sport," Howard said encouragingly, "you've put a lot into it; you shouldn't give it up." Wiping the coffee off his hand with a napkin, he continued, "I swam in college. It was good for me. Taught me discipline." When Jeremy didn't respond, Howard said, hope leaking from his voice, "You could be a chip off the old block." He playfully punched his son in the shoulder, exasperated when Jeremy rubbed his arm as if he had been hurt.

"Mike and I shoot hoops."

Close-mouthed, Howard stared steadily at his son, determined not to let his expression change. Jeremy's stepfather was forty, younger than Bernice, and more than twenty years younger than Howard. Jeremy didn't mention him often, but when he did, there was always something of a challenge in his voice. Gripping his mug, Howard said, "I didn't know you played basketball."

"I don't. Just with Mike at the gym. He thinks I should have gone out for the team."

The light over their table flickered for a few moments before settling into a dim yellow hue. "Never too late to pick up a sport," Howard conceded, "but I say, if you're going to go out for something, be the best at it. A lot of guys are just average and they're wasting their time. Sure, it's good exercise, but at your age it's all about competition. I remember my swim coach—"

"Dad, that was about a hundred years ago, when you were in college."

Howard pretended to laugh. "I'm sure that's the way it seems to you. Sometimes that's how it seems to me too."

The age thing. Howard couldn't deny it was a factor. Jeremy's mother had been his second wife. Bernice was thirty when they married and eager for children. At forty-five with two teenage daughters from his first marriage, Howard had been adamant that they wouldn't have children. He remembered that morning when Bernice had looked at him coyly, slyly he thought now, and told him she was pregnant. The pregnancy made her so happy, so solicitous of him, that he forgot he didn't want more children. And when Jeremy was born, a cleft in his chin just like his own, Howard was glad, proud, to have a son. But he and Bernice divorced six years later and she remarried almost immediately, causing gossip. Howard was stung. He stayed away, didn't dispute the every other weekend visitation with Jeremy his ex-wife offered him. Later he realized his error, but he also sensed that Jeremy hadn't wanted more time with him. He should have insisted, Howard knew that now, but his son was still young; there was time for them to become close.

This was the fifth and last day of their journey. Howard had insisted that they visit Hancock College, his alma mater, last. He wanted this campus to leave the final impression on Jeremy's mind. Tonight they would fly back to Boston and this father-son experience would be over. But it couldn't end without the breakthrough Howard was hoping for, something that would set their relationship on a new course.

"All ready for your interview?" Howard asked.

Jeremy continued to chew his bagel as if his teeth hurt and finally swallowed. "They all ask you the same thing. All you have to do is remember where you are. Don't say, 'I really want to go to Amherst when you're at Williams." Jeremy frowned. "Where are we again? Oh, yeah, Hancock."

Appalled, Howard all but shouted, "*Hancock!* We're at Hancock College. Don't forget."

"What time is our flight tonight?"

"It's around nine. I have to check the tickets. We transfer in Pittsburgh again."

"Will there be anything else?"

Howard and Jeremy both turned to see the waitress.

"No. No, thank you," Howard said, "just the check." He would leave this girl who had managed to catch Jeremy's attention a big tip.

Alone, Howard walked around Hancock Park, a circular mass of green and trees in the center of campus. He looked at his watch and guessed that Jeremy was just beginning his interview. Howard's last words to him were, "Sit up straight in the chair and look the person dead in the eye." Jeremy had groaned at this advice, but Howard ushered him into the office, his hand heavily on his son's shoulder. "He's all yours," he'd said with a wink to the receptionist. "Don't let him give you any trouble." He watched as the woman opened a door and led Jeremy into an inner office.

Walking out of the building, he'd thought, well, it's out of my hands. It's up to Jeremy now. Howard felt he had done his part in the application process. He had reviewed his son's essay repeatedly, advising rewrites until it was perfect. Last month, he had spoken to the teachers who were writing Jeremy's letters of recommendation, urging them to emphasize his year on the debate team and his math skills. And he had contacted an old classmate who was on the Board of Trustees at Hancock and asked him to speak to the swim coach about a scholarship. Howard would have no trouble footing the tuition, but he hoped that Jeremy would be so flattered by a scholarship that he might accept it. If there was anything more to be done to get his son into Hancock, Howard didn't know what it was. Getting him in was one thing, getting him to go was quite another.

Taking one of the brick paths that led to the center of the park, Howard ambled leisurely. He sat on one of the many benches that ringed the heart of the park and wondered whether he had time to go back to Bidwell's and get a cup of coffee to go. It would be nice sitting here, he thought, sipping coffee and watching campus life all around him. Across the park, students were sprawled on the grass. They played Frisbee and some funny game of skill that involved bouncing a small ball off the side of your foot. There were also several clusters of students playing backgammon and chess, or just sitting and talking.

Howard imagined coming back to campus next fall to visit Jeremy during Parents' Weekend. Hancock was beautiful in the fall, the maple trees blazing with color. He and his friends used to gather the fallen chestnuts and roast them in a big bonfire on the Park. He remembered his father had complained about the poor taste of the roasted chestnuts, and Howard had replied, "Dad, that's not really the point. It's an excuse for a party." His father had laughed in agreement and slapped him on the back. When he left campus, he'd told Howard, "I can't wait for next year's trip to Hancock." But then a tumor was discovered in his pancreas and he died the following summer. Howard felt his eyes mist, but he forced himself to think of him and Jeremy at the bonfire. He would protest that the chestnuts were less than haute cuisine and Jeremy would be amused. Parents' Weekend, it would be wonderful. And there would be other weekends too, homecoming and the important swim meets. Howard was only a year away from retirement. He'd be able to spend lots of time at Hancock. This was his turf. He couldn't imagine Bernice and Mike coming here that often. For one thing, Bernice hated to fly. And the fact that she had agreed to Jeremy's taking this trip with Howard might be evidence that she understood it was time for him to play a greater role in their son's life.

Howard inhaled deeply and stretched his legs out, crossing them at the ankles. If Jeremy went to Hancock, he'd receive his diploma at the graduation ceremony held annually in this park. Howard chuckled. Forty-five years, he thought, shaking his head at the thought, forty-five years since I got my college diploma right . . . where? He searched the park to mentally place the commencement stage on the eastern edge of the circle and thought, right *there*. His eyes took him to a female student sitting on a bench reading. In the midst of the entire park, she was the only person, except Howard, who was alone. As she turned a page, she briefly lifted her book up, and Howard saw that she was reading *Lord of the Rings*. Periodically, she glanced about the park, pausing to gaze at the students playing Frisbee. Howard thought she looked wistful as she resumed reading. Poor kid, he thought, she's probably just a freshman, hasn't found her way yet.

During his own first semester at Hancock, Howard had been lonely. He didn't know anyone, and some students found his Boston accent amusing. What was the name of that guy? he asked himself, that guy in his freshman dorm who always hollered, "*Paa-hk the caa-ah in Haa-vaad Yaa-ad*," whenever he saw Howard. Swimming had saved him. He had gotten to know the guys on the team and they liked him, especially after he broke a division record in backstroke. Academics, girlfriends, everything else had fallen into place after that. By his junior year, he was captain of the swim team and vice-president of his fraternity; life was grand. If Jeremy just had enough guts to strike out on his own, Howard thought, he'd have the time of his life here.

The young woman shut her book and looked about the park. Howard considered talking to her, asking her how she liked going to school here, telling her that he was an alum, that his son would probably be enrolled next year. But there was something about her expression that inhibited him, a furtive tremor behind her glasses as she surveyed the park. She stood, and Howard noticed how petite she was, not a hint of muscle anywhere. She won't be able to go out for sports, he thought. He watched as she walked through the park with tentative strides, as if she had nowhere else to go. Howard's heart lifted as she paused to observe a trio of students arranged like a triangle playing Frisbee. *Ask her to play*, he willed them silently.

As if in response, the boy at the apex did aim the Frisbee at her, but she made no effort to catch it. With her hands at her sides, the disc whirled towards her, hitting her in the temple and bouncing her glasses from her face and onto the brick path. She dropped the book. As she bent to pick both up, the other students ran to her.

"I'm sorry," the boy who had aimed the Frisbee at her said, "I thought you saw it coming."

Her voice trembled, "It's all right. It was my fault." She barely glanced up at him.

"Are your glasses broken?"

The girl backed away, a hand on her forehead presumably to shield her eyes from the sun, but it seemed to Howard that she couldn't bear to look at the students trying to help her. "No, they're okay." Turning, she took small quick steps out of the park. Howard considered following her, asking if she needed a ride to an eye doctor's office. Would she think he was odd for asking? If it were Jeremy, would he want a parent to intervene? God, he thought, I hope that will never be Jeremy. He watched the girl until she reached the edge of the park and began to cross a street.

Howard checked his watch and guessed Jeremy would be done with his interview by the time he got to the admissions office. He took his time, knowing his son would be annoyed if he were standing at the door the moment he walked out. Just past the library, he stopped to watch a makeshift volleyball game. There was no net, just a line of books on the ground separating the teams. Earning points didn't seem to be the goal. The students were batting the ball wildly back and forth, laughing when a player on either side stepped over the line of books. Howard watched intently, asking silently, what's the point? No side will ever win. Sure, it was fine to have a bit of fun, but any time there were teams, there had to be a winner. A tall boy in cut off jeans noticed Howard and called out to him, "Hey, man, want to play?" Amused, Howard smiled briefly and shook his head. For a moment, he allowed himself to think about Jeremy finding him here tossing a ball around with these students. Would his son die of embarrassment? Or maybe Jeremy would be impressed? Is that the type of thing Mike would do? Hell, I don't know the kid! Howard exclaimed to himself. I'm walking on eggshells around him. He slipped his hands into his pockets and walked away from the game.

There were no chairs in the hallway outside the admissions office. Howard leaned one shoulder into the wall and waited, his arms crossed. He heard bells somewhere on campus chime twelve times and soon the corridor was bustling with staff members leaving for lunch. A few minutes later, he was alone again in the corridor and was surprised when he saw Jeremy come up the steps outside the building and walk through the glass entry door.

"Where've you been?" his son accused.

"I was in the park. Sorry. How'd the interview go?"

Jeremy shrugged his shoulders and turned. "Let's get out of here." He started to walk towards the door, but Howard exclaimed, "Wait a minute! Wait just a goddamned minute!" He looked around to make sure no one else was present. He did not feel like lowering his voice or extracting every word from his son with tweezers.

"Chill, all right?" Jeremy said.

Howard seized his son's shoulders and backed him against the wall. His voice was low and furious as he said, "You show me a little respect, you hear me? You hear me!"

Jeremy deposited his chin on his chest and said, "Yeah."

Howard dropped his hands and said, "That's better." He smoothed the wrinkles on his son's jacket where his hands had bunched the fabric. "Now, tell me how the interview went. What did they ask you? What did you say?"

"The usual." Jeremy's eyes glistened. He blinked and teardrops spilled down his cheeks and hugged the curve of his chin. Howard was astonished at how young his son suddenly looked, like a child. He had a sudden memory of Jeremy at six, crying in frustration because he couldn't master tying his shoes.

"Jer, what's wrong?"

His son didn't answer but shut his eyes tight, the tears now squeezed from his eyes. He took a deep, noisy breath, forcing air through his plugged sinuses.

"Did something go wrong in the interview?" Howard raised and dropped his arms helplessly. "What? What is it? Tell me."

Jeremy struggled to speak, trying to breathe in enough air to talk. "I called Mom," he finally said, his lips deep red and swollen.

Howard was temporarily stunned. What did Bernice have to do with anything? "Your mother? Is she okay?"

Jeremy's legs buckled and he slid down against the wall until he was seated on the floor. Looking down at him, Howard wondered if there'd been an accident at home. Maybe someone was in the hospital?

With his hand bunched into a tight fist, Jeremy struck his knee. "The letter came today. I didn't get into Brown."

"Oh, is that all?" Howard laughed with relief and looked at the ceiling. He huskily patted Jeremy's shoulder. "Get back in the ring, kid. Brown's not the only school in town." He held out his hand so he could help Jeremy up, but his son remained seated. "Jeremy," he said curtly, "Get up. Stop playing around. Let's go have lunch and talk about your interview."

"You just don't get it!" Jeremy hid his face behind his knees.

Irritated, Howard said, "I get it. You really wanted to go to Brown and they turned you down. Life's tough, kid, but this will probably work out for the best, you'll see. A year from now you'll be thanking your lucky stars you didn't go to Brown. You're going to love it here. Trust me."

With a rough motion, Jeremy moved his palms across his eyes, blotting his tears. Pulling his hair back from his face, Jeremy looked up at his father. His face seemed to shrink so that all that was left were two enormous eyes boring through Howard. "Do you think I want to be so far away from Mom and Mike? Brown's only an hour from Boston!"

The corridor was quiet except for his son's sniffles echoing down the hallway. Howard stared at Jeremy's shoes, his new loafers bought especially for the trip and already scuffed at the toes. Jeremy had always been hard on shoes, ever since he learned to walk. Bernice had sent him dozens and dozens of receipts over the years for the endless supply of shoes for which she expected reimbursement.

Howard was a thin, lanky man, but he crouched with the grace of an athlete and laid his hand on Jeremy's head, lacing his fingers through his son's hair. Slowly, almost with reverence, he tousled it, aware that at any moment the hunched form might jerk his head in protest. But Jeremy didn't, and Howard continued to knead his son's soft hair. Blinking, he cleared his throat and said, "There are more than a few good schools in Boston." Now Howard threaded a strand of hair, lassoing it so it curled around and around his finger. Jeremy didn't look up, so Howard continued to crouch at his son's side.

A PROFESSOR'S HOUSE

Anyone watching us would think we were just another student and professor having lunch together. It happened all the time. The school encouraged it. Professors took their advisees and their honor students to lunch, and they invited classes over to their houses for dinner. Hancock is an elite college; individual attention is one of its selling points. So, sitting across the table from Mike, Professor Michael Ambers, in the main campus dining room was no big deal. We could have been discussing my paper on the socio-economic backgrounds of the suffragettes or the lack of primary documents in the college's library. Or, perhaps, my dilemma regarding whether to pursue a doctorate in history or a law degree after graduation. We could have been discussing any or all of those things but, of course, we weren't. After we settled our plates in front of us, I talked softly about accompanying Mike to a conference in New Orleans during spring break. I opened a book comparing the British and American suffragette movements and laid it on the table, pretending to question specific passages as Mike's eyes trailed my fingers over the page.

No one knew about us, thank God, but that was a drawback in some ways. I couldn't talk to my friends about Mike or explain to them why the guys we hung around with suddenly seemed like the sandbox set. I couldn't share with Dee Dee, my roommate, the fabulous panic I felt about being with someone twenty years older than me, a man who had a doctorate from Yale, a man who had published two acclaimed books, a man who had noticed me the minute I took a seat in his Twentieth Century American Social History class. I do stand out in a crowd; I'm not going to pretend I don't know that. But I wasn't the only pretty girl in class. There was Jennifer Selton with her perky personality and nipples to match, but she wasn't much in the brains department. And Susan Lambert, a stunningly beautiful redhead with freckles that on anyone else would have been a detraction, but on her were sexy. And she did have brains; her marks were as good as mine. Still, it was me Mike zeroed in on.

I had seen him around campus, his loafers moving in long strides up stone steps. He was always in a hurry, an invisible crown of importance hovering over his head. He dressed with impeccable taste in flannel slacks and brown tweed jackets flecked with a color that drew out his alarmingly green eyes, eyes the color of the well-manicured campus lawns. He wore one of those Irish caps with a brim that extended over his forehead. A lot of men wear hats to hide baldness, but Mike's hair was thick, waving back from his face in dark brown tufts, not a wisp of gray yet. He grew up in North Carolina and his accent was beyond charming. The whole package was one of sophistication and importance. It said: I've studied, I've traveled, I've published, I have a wine cellar. And this man, this glittering example of academic refinement had fallen for me.

Before Mike, I never would have guessed I'd get involved with a professor. It never crossed my mind. Professors were our teachers, our mentors, people to emulate and respect. They were out of our reach, and that was how it should be. Sure, I'd heard rumors about profs who were regularly on the prowl, and I'd been warned about not letting a certain teacher close his office door, but Mike wasn't in that category. Married to an elementary school teacher, he had two small children and was very much a family man, photos of his sons and their pre-school art covering every inch of his office walls. Just goes to show, you never can tell.

It started when I noticed him glancing at me in class, letting his gaze stay on me for a moment or two as he lectured. I'm an attentive student. I always look directly at the teacher, every teacher, nodding my head as they make their points, letting them know someone is listening. There was one day when our eyes locked and I felt embarrassed. He noticed it, and a rosy map spread over his neck, hugging his Adam's apple. He turned to face the blackboard and hurriedly picked up a piece of chalk to write down our next reading assignment.

It wasn't just physical attraction, although there was plenty of that. Mike was impressed with my research, my writing. When he handed back my short paper on the origins of the Temperance Movement, his comments read, "Miss Penfield, You show great insight and have a talent for exhaustive research." I loved that he called me 'Miss Penfield' instead of my first name,

Tara. He was old-fashioned, classy; he made me feel adult even if he wasn't using the politically correct "Ms."

Then I went to his office to discuss a topic for my second paper. Every student in the class was supposed to, but the paper was the last thing we talked about. The room hummed with a divine tension as we sized each other up. I wore a cropped navy blue jacket over a simple white shirt and my best jeans. My blonde hair, freshly washed, still held the scent of apple shampoo. Mike's jacket was draped over the back of his chair, and this unnerved me, excited me, as if he were one step toward nakedness. I was in his office several minutes before daring to stare directly into his eyes. Once I did, I never looked away. His stare was mesmerizing, and I sat in a trance, letting him do most of the talking until I was certain my voice wouldn't falter when I tried to speak.

Mostly, we complimented each other. He told me he appreciated my contributions in class and wished other students would learn the importance of participation by my example. I told him how much I was enjoying his class, that his lectures were so interesting. I wished I could have thought of something more original. He told me there weren't enough female historians and that he hoped I was considering graduate school. His respect for women stirred me. He made me feel good about myself and I wondered if that's what love is, being with a person who makes you re-evaluate yourself, sort of make you fall in love with yourself. I walked out of his office feeling like the college was lucky to have me as a student.

Not too long after that meeting, I was sick with the flu, feeling like hell and distraught over missing Mike's class. Sitting on my bed in my old bathrobe and floppy slippers, I was annoyed when the phone rang. I picked it up and a lyrical voice asked for "Miss Penfield." Mike was concerned that I had missed class and wanted to make sure I was well. I explained I had the flu and told him how sorry I was to have missed his class. He assured me I could make up the work, not to worry, to just concentrate on getting well.

I hung up and looked at the phone as if it could tell me what was going on, where all this was going to lead. That afternoon, an arrangement of daisies was delivered to my room with a card that said, "Hope you're better soon, M." I explained to Dee Dee that my mother sent them, and felt guilty when she exclaimed, "How pretty!" We had been roommates for three years, and I had never lied to her before. But when I looked at the flowers, I understood that what Mike and I were embarking on had to be protected, hidden, or it would never have a chance to bloom.

When I felt recovered enough, I went to Mike's office and thanked him for the flowers. I had pressed one in wax paper and was using it as a bookmark. He was pleasant, but he didn't want to talk about the flowers. He brushed my thanks aside and reminded me I had work to make up. I was startled. Maybe I had misread everything, maybe he sent flowers to all his sick students, but then he suggested we have lunch and discuss what I missed in class.

That was the first of many lunches. A few weeks later when he told me his wife was going out of town to visit her sister who had a new baby, I knew it wasn't idle information. The boys are in bed by eight, he told me, and we arranged that I would come over at nine.

What is it about a professor's house that makes you want to grow up, get married, and have a house of your own? Mike and Amy, his wife, lived in a two-story house not far from campus, just around the corner from the gym. From the outside, it wasn't that impressive, like any house you'd pass walking down a street. But inside, it was filled with bookshelves holding leather volumes on all kinds of subjects. There were framed, modern prints on the white walls, and a couple of Japanese scrolls. The furniture was eclectic, a lot of antiques that didn't match, but each was unique, possessing character. On the mantel over the fireplace, on the coffee table, on every flat surface, were beautiful objects. Every piece of pottery was colorful: small green vases with a yellowish sheen, a wine-colored bowl ornamented with huge blue leaves, enormous ceramic pots in shades of turquoise and indigo on the floor in various corners. It felt magical, so different from my parents' home where everything matched and blended like the showroom of a boring department store.

While Mike checked on the boys, I studied the photographs of Mike and his family, each picture encased in a brass or beautifully tarnished silver frame. On the edge of one of the bookshelves was Mike's wedding picture. I couldn't resist walking over to it so I could get a look at Amy. She was pretty in a simple, off-the-shoulder white dress with a peasant ruffle over the front and a heart locket around her neck. She had dark blond hair down to her shoulders, partly obscured by her veil.

My body felt like a cauldron, envy and jealousy bubbling up from my feet to my hair, but I told myself it was an old picture, about ten years old; maybe she wasn't that pretty any more? And no matter how attractive she was, something had to be wrong with her, terribly wrong, because why was her husband interested in me? During these last weeks of advance and retreat with Mike, I hadn't let myself think about Amy. I was interested in his sons, Matt and Michael Jr., because they obviously meant so much to him. But Amy was a factor I didn't want to consider. There was obviously serious trouble in their marriage, and it had to be her fault, because it couldn't possibly be Mike's. Mike hardly spoke of her, and when he did, it was in a perfectly normal manner. He said things like, "Amy wanted to live further away from campus, but I convinced her I had to be near my office." Looking at her wedding picture, I harbored a bizarre resentment that she had usurped me in the photo. I imagined Mike and me side by side in the picture. I'd be wearing a much more sophisticated dress, and Mike would be holding me more tightly than he'd held her. At that moment, he came up behind me and placed his hands on my shoulders. I set the photo down.

We walked quietly up the stairs and into the boys' room. Matt and Michael Jr. were asleep in bunk beds with a wooden frame painted bright red that Mike told me he had built. We stood there in the dark room listening to his children breathing. One of the boys slept with his mouth open, and there was the ragged whispering of air struggling through a tiny stuffed nose. I looked at Mike and was moved by how proud and protective he looked. He straightened the covers on each bed, pulling the bedspreads up to their chins, bending to drop a noiseless kiss on each forehead.

We tiptoed out. I was going to tell Mike how adorable the boys were, but as soon as we reached the hallway, he drew me to him, wrapping his arms around me tightly, and we kissed until I worried saliva was sliding down my chin. I don't know how long we stood in that narrow hallway. I almost believed I was in my own house with my own husband and children.

In the master bedroom, I was uncomfortable. How could I not be? The room, the bed! where Mike slept with his wife. And there was evidence of Amy everywhere: bottles of perfume on the dresser, a partially ajar closet door revealing dresses and skirts, a message next to the telephone on the night table written in an unmistakably female hand. I shut my eyes and let Mike take over. Every touch, every stroke of his hand, was a soft hammer chipping away at my doubts, my guilt. We rolled under the soft flannel comforter until we fell asleep, the warmth of his chest resting against my back. Just before dawn, he woke me up.

"The boys," he whispered. "They get up early."

I sat up and worried how I looked. My hair was a snarly tangle and my eyelids were sealed with the litter of sleep. I slid out of bed and felt embarrassed as I put my clothes on, balancing as I slipped my underwear up my thighs and rummaged on the floor for my bra. Once I was dressed, though, Mike came over and hugged me. I ran my arms up and down the back of his velour robe, drinking in the musky scent the night had left on him. We went downstairs and kissed for several minutes at the front door before I went outside and ran headlong into the dawn. Exhilarated, I raced all the way back to the dorms rejoicing in the marvel of it all, of Mike, of love coursing through my body until I thought I could fly.

I expected that I would sit through my history classes with Mike in a state of bliss, enthralled with our secret. Wrong. I was miserable. I sat there watching as he gave himself to everyone in the room and treated me like any other student.

A rash broke out on my chest and back, and I had to go to the campus doctor for a cortisone cream. I couldn't sleep through the night, waking up at three or four in the morning only to lie there in an agitated state until I could get up, dress, and look for Mike on campus. Whereas before I was an attentive, assured student, I was so distracted now that I barely took notes. The first time Mike called on me after our night together, I stammered through an answer, feeling like every word was a confession to the class that I had slept with the professor. Mike's face flickered with disappointment, and I felt the back of my throat stretch for something out of its reach.

Over lunch the following day, though, he reassured me. He told me I was brilliant, the best student he'd had in years, and that I should relax, calm down. My spirits soared and I worked at being detached and casual in class. My stomach was always doing flips, and I developed this nervous, dry cough, but I did a decent job of covering up, affecting an indifferent expression. And Mike stopped calling on me in class and that was fine with me.

Unfortunately, Amy didn't go away that often, so our relationship consisted of occasional lunches and eyeballing each other in class. But then, in late February, Amy took the boys to visit their grandparents for a weekend. Mike was supposed to go, but he begged off pleading too much work. That meant we had two nights together! With the boys gone, we wouldn't have to tiptoe around the house. We could relax fully with one another. Let our guard down.

Friday night was wonderful. Mike called my room as soon as Amy left, and I jogged over to his house a little after eight. We sent out for pizza, took a candle-lit bubble bath, and clung to each other the whole night. Every moment was filled with promise; my life seemed full of possibilities just beyond my fingertips, possibilities that would turn into realities with just a little time. But in the morning, Mike was nervous. The mailman chatted with him at the door and I think he worried about my being seen. Then Amy called, putting the boys on the phone one at a time to talk to their dad, and Mike looked stricken. It was my turn to reassure him; I jotted a note telling him that I was leaving and would come back after dark. I held it up to him and he nodded while talking to Mike Jr. I exited through their back door and crossed the field behind the house. I spent the rest of the day in my dorm room, too anxious to watch television or read. At mid-afternoon, Dee Dee swung open the door and seemed relieved to see me sprawled on my bed.

"Where were you last night?" she asked, and I scrambled for something to say.

"The library," I answered lamely, starting to laugh because it was such a dumb answer.

"Yeah, right. On Friday night, all night. It closes at, what? Ten?"

I swung my feet around and planted them on the floor, pulling my body up to sit at the edge of the bed. "Look, if I tell you something, do you promise not to tell anyone?"

Dee Dee bounced onto her own bed, eager to hear some gossip. "Tell me!"

"Do you promise?"

"Yeah, yeah. What is it?"

"Well, I met a Burrell guy." Burrell College was a couple miles from our campus.

Dee Dee looked perplexed. She pulled her eyebrows up under her long brown bangs and asked, "Why is that a secret?"

Why indeed. "Well," I started, looking down at my feet, stalling for time, "Tom, that's his name, is seeing someone else, an old girlfriend that he's trying to break up with, but they've been going out a long time and he has to let her down easy. We want to lay low until then."

I didn't look up, afraid to see Dee Dee's disbelieving face, but instead she asked, a girlish bounce in her voice, "So where'd you meet him? What does he look like?"

Relieved, I looked up and told boldface lies to my best friend. I told her we met at a party the weekend Dee Dee was home for her parents' twenty-fifth wedding anniversary. Tom was our age, a senior, and he drove an old Thunderbird. He was an English major and was moving to Taos to join a meditation community after graduation. We weren't going to get too serious because we knew we were going to separate soon.

"Wow," Dee Dee said, "he doesn't sound like your type at all."

I smiled deep inside myself. "What's my type?"

She leaned back on her elbows. "Oh, you know. Serious, smart, ambitious."

Pretending to pout, I said, "You don't think a person who drives a Thunderbird can be serious?"

She lifted her shoulders in a shrug. "Maybe. Hell, I don't know. When do I get to meet him?"

"Dee Dee," I said sternly, "you can't tell anyone about him. You can't meet him until he breaks up with his girlfriend. I don't know when that's going to be."

"Okay, okay. It's just all *so* mysterious!" she said in a kidding voice.

Late that afternoon, after Dee Dee had gone to an early movie with a bunch of other girls on the floor, Mike called from a pay phone and said Amy had come home early because the boys missed him. I held the phone against my ear, hearing his voice fade and lose its color. I didn't respond for several seconds, my eyes and nose feeling plugged because of tears. He kept telling me he had to get off the phone, but he couldn't hang up until I said something and I was too upset to talk. Then, out of the blue, he invited me to come with him to a conference in New Orleans the next month. A trip together! I could forget about a night together in Hancock if days together in another city, a romantic city, awaited us.

We continued to have lunch together about once a week, always in a campus dining room. I saw Mike eating with lots of students, male and female. I took a close look at the female ones, but it was obvious they were discussing schoolwork. When we dined together, we made plans for New

Orleans. My parents had sent me money to go to New York during spring break with my friends, an early graduation present, but they wouldn't be any wiser if I went someplace else. Dee Dee thought I was going camping with Tom, the mystery man, and she promised to keep my secret.

Mike and I were going to have four nights together in a luxurious hotel, dinners out every night, leisurely walks through the French Quarter, time to make love and just be together. It would change everything. We wouldn't be able to come back to business as usual. I imagined we would make plans to be together after I graduated, after we waited a respectable amount of time after Mike's separation and divorce. It pained me that Amy would undoubtedly get the boys, but I would be an understanding wife, the children welcome in our home at all times. The trip to New Orleans would be the magic that would put all of this in motion.

I bought elegant lingerie that I wrapped in tissue and put in my suitcase even though the trip was three weeks off. Soon, I thought, I'd be buying a whole wardrobe for my trousseau, and I fantasized about whether Mike and I would return, for sentimental reasons, to New Orleans for our honeymoon, or seek out a new, even more romantic place.

Then, as we had lunch one day in the main cafeteria, he looked at me, those emerald eyes cutting through me like green glass, and said, "Maybe you should go to New York with your friends."

I couldn't be angry with him, not after he explained it all. Mike told me he was worried he was falling in love with me. "I love you!" I whispered fervently over the cafeteria table, trying to make him see it wasn't a problem, it was a good thing, inevitable. He shook his head, closing his eyes as if I were too painful to look at me but not have me.

"My boys," he said, and he blinked his eyes several times, the electric green of his irises sparkling.

"We won't hurt them," I offered, desperate to make him see that I would accommodate any arrangement. My thoughts about being his wife evaporated in a single moment and I saw how desperate I was to have Mike in my life if only for a few moments each week. I would settle for anything.

He turned his head and looked out the cafeteria window. His expression showed him to be fighting something, and my love for him stabbed me; he was so good, so stoical.

He looked at me, or just to the left of me, and said, "I'm sorry. You're wonderful. I don't deserve you. But I can't risk it, I just can't."

Leaning over the table, I pleaded quietly, "You deserve me and I deserve you! We can still go to New Orleans. No one will know—"

He shook his head, lifting a book and pretending to be examining the index. "It's too painful," he said as he turned a page. "We've got to stop."

He stood and lifted his briefcase. "You can probably get the full text of that journal through interlibrary loan," he said loudly, conscious that a colleague of his had just sat down at the next table. I watched him leave the cafeteria and then pretended I was jotting notes on a legal pad, looking at the book every minute or so. Finally, I stuffed the book in my knapsack and headed for Mike's office. I knew he had office hours that afternoon from one to three, but when I got there, his office was empty. After about twenty minutes, I went back to my dorm room and flung myself down on my bed. I cried for a couple of hours, until I heard Dee Dee's key in the lock. Closing my eyes, I pretended to be asleep.

I went to my next history class eagerly. It had been torture not seeing Mike, and I convinced myself that the sight of me, confident and courageous in my seat, would cause him to feel the same, would move him to change his mind. I even raised my hand to speak, to force him to acknowledge me, but he didn't call on me. He managed to avoid my eyes the entire class. Worse, he seemed buoyed up by a manic energy, telling jokes and bantering with the usually droll guy who sat in the back of the room. During that first lecture, I felt my will leak out of me and spill all over the floor. I waited for him after class, joining a small group of students who stayed behind to ask him for extensions on papers. Standing just outside the circle, I was determined to accompany him to his office. Before he got to me, however, he threw up his hands and said, "That's all, folks. I'm late for a squash game."

A few of the students made disgruntled sounds but nothing matched the stun I felt at being so obviously snubbed. I walked to his office and slipped a folded piece of paper under the door. "Can we talk? T." the paper read. I went back to my room fairly certain he'd call, but when I was still waiting at five o'clock, I let Dee Dee talk me into going out for hamburgers.

"What's with you these days?" she asked me. "You seem like you're under some kind of a spell."

She had nailed it, but I didn't tell her anything. She asked if it was Tom, or his girlfriend, that was bothering me, but I shook my head no and talked about mid-semester stress as I forced myself to eat French fries. I couldn't tell her the truth; my privacy was all I had left.

If it weren't my senior year, I would've dropped the class. As it was, I needed it to graduate on time. I skipped a couple of classes, though, hoping that Mike would call me like he did that time I had the flu. He didn't, and I found that it was hard to stay away from class. It was the only time I saw him, and I lived to see him. With each lecture, however, I felt more and more humiliated, and I sat at my desk loathing myself because something had to be terribly wrong with me for Mike to have made such a swift and complete emotional recovery. As spring break approached, I found myself still fantasizing about that week in New Orleans, unwrapping the lingerie from the delicately folded pink tissues and fingering the satin and lace nightgown. I had chosen rose, a color the saleswoman told me would enhance my "youthful complexion." I should have taken the lingerie back to the store, but that would be irrefutable proof that the relationship was over, and it was the only evidence I had that it ever existed. Well, that and the daisy bookmark.

The Friday before spring break started, I took my seat as usual in Mike's class and kept my head down. Hearing his voice was agony enough, but I couldn't bear to see his green eyes. At one point during class, he called on Susan Lambert who was sitting to my right. Susan, who was usually so articulate, stuttered her way through a couple of sentences on domestic life in the fifties. I jerked my head up and looked at her, at her embarrassed confusion, and then I looked at Mike and saw that jagged flush spreading over his throat. Mike looked at me momentarily and I stared back at him in wide-eyed accusation. He dropped a piece of chalk and I felt a tiny stream of elation run through me. After days of feeling lovesick, I finally experienced a different sensation, a delicious, nourishing anger.

After class, I walked to the library and sat in a study carrel, trying to decide what to do. I could confront Mike or I could wise up Susan. More elaborate plans started to build in my mind. I could go to the Dean, or maybe to Helen Leep, a faculty member in the psychology department who wrote editorials in the school newspaper on the need for a sexual harassment policy. But then I thought about the publicity, the possibility of my parents finding out, the ordeal of being questioned by a panel of supposedly objective faculty, and my nerve failed. I decided that the only good thing about the affair with Mike was that no one knew about it. I was left with the problem of wanting to hurt Mike, to injure him in a way that wouldn't bounce back at me. How could I do that? The answer came to me in one word: Amy.

I knew that Mike was leaving for New Orleans early Saturday morning of spring break. Just before noon, I walked to his house and, after pausing at the doorstep for several seconds, rang his doorbell. I heard footsteps approaching and Amy opened the door. I think I half expected her to be wearing a wedding dress like she was in the picture, but she was dressed simply in jeans and a frayed blue blouse that wasn't tucked in. Her blonde hair was very short; there was a big puff of bangs in the front, but behind that, it was clipped very close to her head. She looked exhausted with violet circles under her eyes and crows' feet at the corners.

"Yes?" she said, waiting for me to speak.

My first prepared sentence was supposed to be, "Mrs. Ambers? Hi, I'm Tara Penfield, a student of your husband's, and a little *more* . . ." After her questioning gaze, I was going to tell her everything. But standing there, I felt sorry for this woman who didn't realize that her husband most likely was jetting to New Orleans with my classmate. When I started to speak, one of the children, a tiny boy with almost white hair, came up behind Amy and asked for juice.

"Excuse me," Amy said, bending down and hoisting the little boy onto her hip. She faced me again, "You were saying?"

"Tickets," I blurted loudly. "Would you like to buy tickets for the senior class dance?"

"Dance?" Puzzled, she wrinkled her nose and suddenly looked girlish; I could see that she was pretty despite her exhaustion. "I didn't hear about a dance," she continued.

Why can't you just say no and shut the door? I wanted to scream at her. Then she asked me, "How much are the tickets?" and I really panicked since there were no tickets, there was no dance!

"Twenty-five dollars," I said, hoping I put the price high enough. "A couple," I added tentatively.

She smiled and shook her head no.

"Thanks for your time," I said, hurrying down the walk and almost bumping into the mailman.

I was one of the few people in the dorm who hadn't gone away for spring break. The emptiness of the building closed in on me as I laid on my bed thinking about my situation. Dee Dee thought I was camping with a man who didn't exist and my parents thought I was in New York. How many lies had I told? I sat bolt upright and made a decision. Pulling my suitcase out of the closet, a plan started to take shape in my mind. I took a cab to the airport and within a couple of hours, I was looking out the window of a plane at vaporous clouds. I was headed to New Orleans.

I knew Mike was staying at The Bourbon Orleans Hotel. He had shown me the brochure, and it was easy to walk unobserved through the spacious lobby. I had been there forty-five minutes when I saw Susan Lambert enter through the revolving door. I recognized her bright red hair clear across the lobby. She was alone.

"Susan!" I called. "Susan!" I was practically running after her as she approached the elevator.

She turned around, looking back at me with a baffled, frightened, expression.

"Congratulations," I said, huffing as I caught my breath. "He brought you instead of me."

"Tara?" she said, as if she still didn't recognize me. "What are you doing here?"

"That's what I want to tell you. Can we grab a cup of coffee somewhere?" I gestured toward the doors.

She edged away from me slightly and said, "I'm kind of in a hurry."

"Oh, why's that? Mike waiting for you in the room?" I spoke matter-of-factly, my breath more even now.

"What?" She was nervous, her tawny-colored freckles becoming more prominent.

"Mike," I said simply. "Professor Ambers. Mike to you and me and God knows how many other female students."

She bent her head towards me and blinked her eyes slowly. "What did you say?"

"Did you get to see the master bedroom? Family photos on the wall, the adjoining bathroom with the green and yellow wallpaper? Oh, certainly you saw the bunk beds that Mike built." I spoke quickly, like I was ticking off symptoms of an illness.

"What are you saying?"

"You heard me. I was in his bedroom too. Now, what I want to know is what are you going to do about it?"

Susan walked away from me, taking wide steps out of the lobby and into the cocktail lounge. Once she got there, she clearly didn't know what to do, but I came up behind her and gently took her elbow, ushering her to a small table.

We drank two beers each while we compared notes, Susan's shock transforming into rage with each swallow. I complimented her. "It took me weeks to get to where you are now. You're a fast learner."

Susan swallowed the last of her beer and slammed the bottle onto the table. "Let's nail him," she said.

Susan told me Mike would be busy at the conference until that evening. We went up to the room and went through every article of clothing he brought. Within a couple of minutes, we found a Discovery card in the pocket of a pair of pants and almost three hundred dollars in cash. We called room service and ordered champagne. After we drank two-thirds of the bottle, I opened my suitcase and showed Susan my lingerie. We laid it out on the bed carefully and Susan produced a tube of bright red lipstick. She proceeded to write vertically down the length of the gown: "Love and Kisses, Amy, Tara, Susan." I took the lipstick and drew a pair of enormous eyes on the bathroom mirror, and wrote beneath them, "Helen Leep is watching you!!" As we finished the champagne, Susan and I discussed going to Helen and spilling our story. We weren't sure we'd have the nerve to do it, but we agreed that we could keep Mike guessing what we were going to do for a long time.

By then I was hiccupping pretty badly, laughing hard as I watched Susan hang Mike's boxer shorts from the railing of the little outdoor terrace. We went out to dinner at Antoine's and then went dancing at a crowded bar in the French Quarter. Around midnight, I found myself dancing with a man with a Cajun drawl as sweet and thick as pralines. "Hold tight, darlin'," he told me as we bobbed in and out of the crowd. And I did, clinging to him while the sound of the zydecko accordion thundered in my ear with such an instructive beat, I found I could two-step. We danced around and around the floor, moving so easily together I could tell when he was going to turn me and when he was going to bring me back close to him. As I leaned against his shoulder, I watched the lights above us seeming to swirl higher and higher into the ceiling, twinkling like silver stars against a big black night.

POST-DOCTORAL

"Really, Mother, I wish you wouldn't go on like that."

Louisa Smith sniffed at her daughter's remark and took a dainty bite of her croissant. Despite her large size, Louisa always aimed for the petite: small bites, little sips, diminutive gestures. Only her voice seemed suited for her ample frame.

"Margaret, don't be naive. The quality of this conference slips a little each year. By the time I retire, the speakers will be illiterate children with no sense of French literature whatsoever. This is hurting you, too. Don't doubt the power of context." She looked about the dining hall at the other conference attendees, in particular at a woman in a denim jumper and brown clogs seated at the next table. Louisa shuddered visibly, her shoulders lurching beneath her purple silk dress.

"Mother!" Margaret whispered, her large hazel eyes flickering in a horizontal zig zag, "this isn't a fashion show; this is an academic conference—"

"Don't be bowled over," Louisa interjected. She picked up her knife and dipped it into the plastic container of apricot jelly. She spread a generous amount on a tiny piece of croissant and took a minuscule bite. She looked at her daughter and said, "You look like a tired schoolgirl slumped over like that. You have a doctorate. Act like it."

Margaret kept her head bent over the table, lifting only her eyes. "Oh, what's that supposed to mean, Mother? That I should wear a hat during a meal, even if I'm eating in a cafeteria?"

Louisa daintily touched the tip of the periwinkle feather adorning her black beret and took another nibble of her croissant. "I don't lower my standards to suit the tastes of young people today. Perhaps this conference will help you to mature a bit."

Margaret narrowed her eyes until her mother appeared to be

enveloped in gauze.

"Stop squinting. It's unbecoming."

Crumpling her napkin and putting it on her tray, Margaret said, "I knew this was a terrible idea, rooming with you at the conference. I must have been out of my mind."

Louisa held up a shiny orange package. "Sanka? Can you believe this? Next, they'll be serving us Kool-Aid." Louisa glanced at her watch. It was so small she had to raise her wrist until it was directly in front of her eyes. "What time is our appointment?"

Margaret lifted her chin. "*My* appointment, Mother." The tips of her fingers hit her sternum. "*Mine.*"

Louisa dabbed each corner of her mouth with a napkin. "I'm only thinking of you. Let me have a few words with Dimitri and the post-doctoral position is yours. I guarantee it." Louisa hoped she sounded convincing; in truth she knew the outcome could go either way.

"If you think I'm going to bring you to the interview, you're crazy!"

Examining the coffee stirrer with distaste, Louisa answered, "You don't know the whole story, Margaret. I may as well tell you, since you may have an office down the hall from Dima, that's his *soubriquet*, next year."

Margaret pretended to pick lint off the cuffs of her blazer as she said idly, "Tell me what? That you and he were at Columbia together in the fifties? I've only heard that a million times."

"This is so bitter!" Louisa set down her Styrofoam cup and looked at it as if it were alive, deserving of upbraiding. She wiped her mouth with the napkin again, and said slowly, "No, dear, there's *more*. I should have told you earlier, but some subjects aren't suited to casual conversation."

Margaret swallowed the last bite of her bagel and said, "Out with it Mother. What's the big dark secret?"

Louisa cleared her throat and took out a compact from her purse. She could not see her entire face in the small mirror, so she waved the compact about, examining first her eyes, then her nose, and finally her mouth. "Dimitri and I weren't just classmates at Columbia," she said, clicking the compact shut. She waited for Margaret's response but when she saw that her daughter was stubbornly withholding any expression of interest, she continued. "I was his obsession for several years. I never—" she cleared her throat, "*dallied* with him as the other female graduate students did, and I'm afraid he never quite forgave me."

Margaret blinked. "This is your big news? That you never went out with the man? Call the press. This will make the front page for sure."

Examining the cuticles on her fingers, Louisa said, "Margaret, you're not *listening*. Why, the man has carried a torch for me for years. And perhaps a grudge. He may welcome the opportunity to hurt me in some way to pay me back for never—"

"Dallying with him?"

"Yes," Louisa said shortly with a defiant nod. "And don't think he wouldn't use you as a weapon to hurt me. Oh, he would love to cut me to the bone by denying you a brilliant start to your career. But, a few words face to face with me, well," she smiled, "that would soften him immediately."

Margaret pushed her forearms onto the table. "Mother, you were at Columbia, what? Thirty-five years ago? You married Dad, Dimitri Kalinov married someone else, many someone else's from what I've heard. I think this is all ancient history, no, make that prehistoric."

Louisa stiffened. "When your father died, Dimitri was the first to send me a sympathy card. The very first."

Smoothing her skirt over her lap, Margaret said easily, "Well, I should think that speaks well of him, of his sympathy for a former colleague."

"Sympathy," Louisa said briskly; "call it that if you'd like. I know," she held a hand over the amythyst brooch on her dress, "in my soul, *my soul,* that Dima picked me out as his true love years ago." Louisa looked at her daughter directly, saying, "He only entered into those ridiculous marriages, trite liaisons, out of desperation for not being able to have me."

"Mother, don't you ever get tired of talking about yourself?"

"Margaret, if you keep scowling like that, you'll get permanent frown lines. Now, listen. I talk about myself for *your* benefit. We're always wiser in hindsight. There are things I wish I'd done differently in my career."

Margaret stood. "And you want me to learn from your mistakes. That's just it, Mother, they're *your* mistakes. I have to go to the ladies room." She walked hastily away from the table as Louisa shook a container of Tic Tacs into her open palm. One by one, she slipped five mints into her mouth. Several minutes later, gazing at Margaret's empty chair, Louisa understood that her daughter had ditched her.

Well, Margaret was headstrong. She'd been so since a toddler, but that gave her fierce determination and discipline, traits that, along with her obvious intellect, would help her become a major scholar. Oh, what I could have done with her talent! Louisa thought. I could have had my pick of Ivy League schools, my books published by Yale University Press, paid research leaves in Paris. Stifling a yawn, she thought, I wouldn't be as tired as I am now, worn out by years of teaching a heavy course load to mediocre students. Hopefully her daughter would never feel this exhausted, this depleted.

Louisa had reason to worry about Margaret's interview skills. Her daughter had spent more time with a heavily annotated copy of *Madame Bovary* than she had dating or even socializing with peers. Outside of a classroom or library, she was a fish out of water. She became painfully shy and withdrawn. Who could have guessed, Louisa thought, that a daughter of mine would be a wallflower, so ill-prepared to play the games of academe to her best advantage? With just a little coaching, though, Louisa was sure Margaret could learn what to say and *how* to say it. If only her daughter's stubborn pride didn't keep her from admitting how badly she needed her mother's mentoring. Well, Louisa thought, resigned, let's see how she manages on her own today. Of course, if she failed the interview, Margaret wouldn't confess it. But Louisa would know; a mother always knows.

Was there a more beautiful campus anywhere? Margaret couldn't believe so as she strolled through the college green of Brown University. The morning sunlight seemed to stride directly behind her, guiding her past the historic buildings. She stopped in front of University Hall to admire the rows of white-paned windows set in the charming old bricks. I could be working here next year! she thought. What a coup that would be, a post-doc at one of the finest comparative literature departments in the country. How her classmates would envy her! And her dissertation adviser, the competitive Francine Perreault, would be crowing about her for years. It was all within her grasp. A favorite passage from *Madame Bovary* ran through her mind: *The memories of her past life, which till then had always been so clear and definite, vanished so completely in the splendours of the moment that she could hardly persuade herself they were not a dream. There she was.*

She looked over her shoulder to make sure her mother wasn't following her. After she got the post-doc, she was going to have to be very firm that her mother keep her distance. If her mother had any thoughts of visiting her at Brown and proclaiming to all, "I'm Margaret Smith's mother," she was in for a harsh awakening. The last thing I need, the very last, she thought, is Mother showing up here and waddling around campus, peacock feathers and all. She thinks I need advice about academic politics and womanizing professors? Ha! I didn't get to where I am without encountering a few lecherous profs. I can certainly handle one of mother's ancient admirers.

A few minutes later, she knocked on the door of the Chair of the Comparative Literature Department and slowly moved it open a few inches. "Dr. Kalinov?" she called. She pushed the door open the rest of the way.

A man with fluffy trails of white hair on each side of his head looked up from behind his desk. His exposed pate was nicely rounded with a smattering of freckles reaching down to his bluish-gray eyebrows. He wore glasses, thin lenses in simple gold frames that gave an unobstructed view of his alert eyes.

She said cheerfully, "I'm so eager to meet you."

Dr. Kalinov looked her up and down, and his quizzical expression immediately became animated. His eyebrows sailed up as he said, "And I *you.*"

The Russian accent she had heard so much about! There was a refined, musical lilt to his voice. "I'm not too early?" she said, knowing she wasn't.

"Nonsense," Dr. Kalinov said. "Why I've been waiting for you, hoping you'd come along any second." He shook her hand vigorously.

She smiled and seated herself in the rather small wooden chair in front of his desk. "Well, are you enjoying the conference?" she asked.

"Conference?"

"Yes. Is it nice having Brown host it?"

He tapped his cheek. "Da. A university has to have a lot of people running around acting important or it will be mistaken it for an asylum. Which, of course, it is."

She chuckled and crossed her legs, aware that her knee was showing through the partition in her skirt. "Yes, sometimes it's hard to tell the patients from the staff."

"Ah! You understand exactly! We should celebrate." He pushed himself back from his desk, his chair rolling on its wheels over the carpet. Stretching his arm to reach a file cabinet, he opened it and pulled out a bottle of Stoly.

"My goodness." She uncrossed her legs and brought her knees demurely together. "Isn't it a little early in the morning for vodka?"

Fishing deeper in the cabinet, Dr. Kalinov produced two shot glasses. "Nonsense. It's five o'clock somewhere." He smiled broadly as he poured the vodka. "You know, it *is* five o'clock in Paris! Right now, it is five o'clock there. If only we were clinking glasses on the Left Bank."

She hoped that she wasn't blushing as she was wont to do when feeling unsettled. *Relax*, she commanded herself. Think of Flaubert's words: *It was something like an initiation into the social world, a taste of forbidden fruit.* Yes, a little alcohol was no big deal.

"Dr. Kalinov—"

He reached across his desk and took her hand. "Dima. Please, call me Dima. And I should call you?"

Looking about the room, as if there was another person present, she answered, "Margaret. Margaret Smith. I had the ten o'clock appointment?" She was beginning to wonder if Dr. Kalinov had mistaken her for someone else.

"Of course, Margaret at ten o'clock. But, if you will permit me, I will call you *Masha*." He bared all of his teeth and smiled for several moments.

She was deeply stirred. She hadn't been in his office five minutes and already he had chosen a nickname for her. "How lovely," she said, "yes, please, call me Masha. Isn't that the name of the little girl in the Russian version of 'The Nutcracker?'"

Handing her the shot, Dima clinked her glass with his own and said, "It was the name of my first love. Let's toast. To love!" He downed his glass in a brief, fluid movement. Margaret hesitated and then threw back her head and swallowed as rapidly as she could. She immediately needed to cough but fought the air creeping up her throat.

"Your first love?" she asked.

"Da," Dima said sorrowfully, immediately refilling their glasses, "that was many years ago." He offered her the refill and said, "But there is something about your face that makes it seem like yesterday." He lifted his own glass high over his head and said, "To yesterday!"

Oh no! she thought, watching as Dima downed his shot and again picked up the bottle. She leaned forward and placed her glass on the edge of his desk. "Dr. Kalinov," she started, "I think—"

"*I* think you should call me Dima," he sang, pretending to admonish her with a reproving index finger.

She cleared her throat. "Yes, Dima. Don't you think we should discuss my work?"

The corners of his mouth sank. "Your work?" he said blankly.

She nodded firmly. "Yes, well, this is an interview and, as much as I appreciate your hospitality," she tilted her head towards her glass, "we should probably get on with business."

Clasping his hands, Dima wheeled his chair back up to his desk and said, "Yes, work must always come first. So, why should I give you the job?"

She was startled. After such a friendly, odd but friendly, start, Dima now seemed so terse that she regretted declining the second drink.

"Well, you've read my dissertation, of course—"

"Of course."

The lack of expression in his voice stung her, and she stumbled over her next statement: "Well, my chapters on the influence of then current medical practices on Flaubert are thought to be groundbreaking."

"Ground break? What is that? You break ground?" He made a chopping motion with his hand.

Oh, damn. He wasn't understanding her. "Yes, groundbreaking. It's an expression meaning new, original." When Dima's dour stare didn't change, Margaret added, "In the very best sense of the word. Like your own book on Gide," she added hurriedly. What should she say next? She made a noise that sounded more like a cough and then faltered. She looked down at her skirt and imagined having to face her mother after this meeting. What would she say? That she couldn't make herself articulate? And Francine? Francine would rather disown her than face her colleagues over an embarrassing protégée. Dear God! What if her first position after grad school weren't at Brown, but at some podunk little school hidden away in corn fields? Or worse? Inheriting her mother's position at Hancock College in a few years, a possibility both she and mother refused to contemplate. People would be shaking their heads, saying things like, "Poor Margaret. Never even got out of the starting gate."

There didn't seem to be enough air in the room to fill her lungs. Small black dots appeared before her eyes and her neck felt too weak to support her head. Margaret imagined her body turning to formless, weightless Jello. She had a peculiar recollection of her mother at a picnic once saying, "I *hate* jello. It's so . . . *pedestrian*."

But suddenly Dima was at her side. "Lean over," he said calmly. "Yes, like this. Take it easy, it's okay. Da, good. Breathe, but slowly. Don't be in such a rush. There you go, better, much better."

Lifting her head, she knew how flushed her face must appear. "Forgive me." Her voice failed; she could only whisper. She tried again, "Forgive me," she said more audibly. Exhaling, she lied, "I didn't eat breakfast. You know, all the commotion of the conference. I'm just a little light-headed."

Dima picked up her hand and squeezed her fingers. "Masha, my little Masha. And here I am making you drink vodka. Forgive me, will you?"

She nodded weakly, grasping at hope she could save face after all. She smiled hesitantly. "No, the vodka was fine. Really, it was fine."

"Can I get you a glass of water? I'll just go in the hall and bring you some water." Dima pronounced water as "vater." He left the room for a minute and returned with a large glass.

"Thank you." She took a sip and felt the cool fluid travel through her. She realized that she had begun to sweat, her upper lip was damp, and she took several swallows of water. She exhaled. "Thank you. I feel much better."

Dima sat on the edge of his desk. Quietly, looking down at her, he asked, "Why did you choose to study Flaubert?"

Margaret had answered this question a hundred times in grad school. She sat back fully and crossed her hands on her lap. "I visited Brown in 1980, the year the University had the Flaubert Symposium. Perhaps I was a bit impressionable," she said with a small laugh, "but I heard Dennis Porter's paper, 'Madame Bovary and the Question of Pleasure,' and I was entranced. My own research led me away from that topic, to philosophical discussions on the role of happiness in that novel and other European works, and I find there is enough research there to last a lifetime." She paused to take a deep breath. "Is happiness realistic? Is it a worthwhile goal? Flaubert knew that buried amidst the gritty realism of life, there is *immense* passion." She swung her head on her final words for what she hoped appeared as an involuntary poetic gesture.

Dima nodded enthusiastically and applauded. She pretended to be embarrassed. "Forgive me; I do feel rather strongly about my work," she told him.

"If only my colleagues did. You see, they have lost their passion. Their passion is long ago spent, used up, as you say here. To study the masters, you must have passion, *grand* passion." He raised his closed fists and brought them together, shaking them forcefully.

"Yes!" He's a kindred spirit, she thought joyfully. "Flaubert incites passion in me. I couldn't turn my back on it; I knew I had to respond to his indictment of the numbness of a life without passion." She paused for effect and quoted a favorite passage: *"And Emma tried hard to discover what, precisely, it was in life that was denoted by the words 'joy, passion, intoxication', which had always looked so fine in her books."*

A slow smile eased across Dima's jaw. "Your dissertation, Masha, brought tears to my eyes. Tears!" Dima said, steadily holding her gaze.

She leaned toward him. "It did? Well, would you like to know how I plan to serialize it? It will give me several articles for publication, and I'm hoping to follow-up with a book on the varying themes of Romanticism and Realism in nineteenth century European literature."

"Excellent. Your research plans are laid out. I admire that."

Margaret swung her head so her hair rested behind her shoulder. Her voice took on a deeper, more assured, resonance. "Oh, yes. I thoroughly recognize the importance of scholarship. And I have so much of it to do. I would make the most of this post-doc. It is so important to me, Dr. Kalinov, Dima, to publish a critically acclaimed book before I begin teaching full-time."

Dima nodded his head weightily and said, "You, Masha, will be a great, great scholar. And, no doubt, an, how do you say, an *ex-em-pla-ry* teacher. Academe needs scholars who are able to inspire passion in students. Without that, we are less than foolish, no?"

He is so insightful! she thought. And for someone mother's age, he's still so handsome. His eyes are so blue and so full of energy, of *passion!* Why, Mother missed a great opportunity by not *dallying* with him, she thought, suppressing a laugh. No wonder she's still talking about him after all these years. "Your confidence in me means ever so much, Dima."

"You will go far."

"Thank you. I can't thank you enough for your encouragement."

But then he raised his hands in a mock gesture of defeat. "Unfortunately, our post-doc pool is full of gifted scholars. And, of course, each of my colleagues has his favorite."

She pressed her lips together to hold in her disappointment. Finally she blurted, "But, but, but my passion. You said that I had the passion and, and—"

He leaned forward and placed his hands on hers. "And if it were up to me, darling Masha, you would have the position."

She coughed. Picking up her glass of water she said, "You, you don't understand. I have to get this post-doc. I have to. I, I, I—"

"Calm down, calm down. Have some more water. Now, you were saying?"

She raised the glass too high and with too much force, slugging it down like a shot. As she started coughing, Dima rose from his desk but she waved her hand to assure him she was all right. Finally, she managed to say, "My mother."

He scratched the side of his head. "Your mother?"

"Yes, my mother." Margaret felt as if she were flailing her words about, flinging them at Dima. "My mother. My mother is Louisa Smith." There, I've said it, she thought. I have no pride.

"Hmm. Louisa Smith you say? Ah, she has a cooking show on TV? I think I saw her make borscht once. A little light on the sour cream, but—"

"No, *Professor Louisa Smith!* She went to graduate school with you. I understood that you . . . well, that you admired her."

Clasping both his cheeks with his hands, Dima said, "Can it be? Louisa after all these years?" He looked at Margaret with bewilderment. "And can it be that you," he said, a single finger pointed at her, "are her daughter? Her little Margaret?"

"Yes! Yes, I'm her!"

Dima leapt up from his desk and went behind it. He picked up the vodka bottle and filled his glass. "Well, why didn't you say so!" He raised his glass and she lifted her own. He announced, "*Na Zdorovie!* To Louisa! Let's celebrate!"

Louisa scanned the listing of papers in her conference program. She had missed the early morning presentation of "The Translator as Moral Arbiter of Language" and was a bit late for "Contemporary German Literature: From Bad To Verse?" That only left "Dainty Feet and Cultural Fetish, References to Foot Binding in 19th Century Chinese Literature." "Ouch!" she said aloud, her own feet throbbing in the confines of her new stilettos. Reading a few more descriptions, she gave an abbreviated sigh, unwilling to waste her breath on boring summaries of papers, panels, discussion groups. Perhaps I should take early retirement in two years, she mused, get away from these ill-dressed people who forget to take their name tags off at five o'clock. All these years of relentless work to raise Hancock's standards has worn me out, she thought. There are even days when it's hard to meet my own standards. She slowly shook her head. Yes, it's time to say good-bye to all of it.

She was sitting on a bench in the college green near an arbor of white and pink roses. The rims of the outer petals were gently unfurled, but each flower's center was still tight. To her right was a sprawling lilac bush, delicate lavender blossoms nestled in a lush, green ocean. Ah, at least the conference has given me the chance to sit amongst beauty, she thought. Closing her eyes, she felt the warmth of the sun on her face.

"Louisa!" someone called. "Louisa! Is that you?"

Her eyelids opened at once. Behind some small hedges, she saw two men staring at her. Oh, no, she thought, two more conference attendees eager to chatter on and on about the last paper presented. She didn't feel up to it.

But then one of the men approached and her heart seemed to enlarge. Well, you knew you would see him, she told herself; it was just a question of when. She stood, wobbling a bit in her heels. A discerning eye would note that they matched the periwinkle feather in her beret perfectly.

"Louisa!" Dima said as he opened his arms and wrapped them tightly around her shoulders. "It's you, it's really you! Albert, come meet an old friend!"

Beaming up at Dima, she said, "Yes, it's me. I'm hiding out from the madding crowd."

"Good for you! Still the rebel, I see."

She was delighted that his voice was exactly as she remembered it, so cadenced, so charmingly Russian. His brown hair had turned gray, but it was as thick and curly as she remembered, not a hint of encroaching baldness. The other man approached shyly, smiling tentatively as he observed Dima and Louisa.

"Louisa, this is Albert Reems, resident philosopher. Albert, this is Louisa. I've told you about her."

Albert extended his arms and clasped both of her hands. "Yes, you've often spoken of her."

"All good, I hope," Louisa said as she smiled up at the man, trying to ignore the severe pinching she felt in her toes. The shoes hadn't been available in extra-wide. My, Albert was handsome, with a salt and pepper mustache and topaz-colored eyes. His mouth, when he smiled, was a valentine, a darling dip in the center of his upper lip.

"Yes," Albert said. "Dima has told me wonderful things about your years at Columbia."

Turning to Dima, she said, "Why, it's funny he should mention that, because I was just remembering our trip to The Cloisters. And the argument we had there about Sartre."

Dima raised his shoulders and laughed. "Which one?"

"Yes, well, there were many."

"Let's sit," she suggested, lowering herself into the center of the bench, her weight finally off of her feet. The men sat on either side of her.

Dima said, "You should have seen her in those days, Albert; Louisa cut a most dramatic figure."

She tapped Dima's arm lightly in protest, although she couldn't conceal her pleasure. He began to gesture grandly. "She wore a long black cape with a large hood," he raised his hands high above his head. "And she wore no makeup except for red lipstick, as red as a fire truck." Circling his lips with one finger, he winked at her.

"It was the color of cherries," she protested, disappointed that he had a different association for her trademark cosmetic.

"Whatever," Dima shrugged. I tell you, Albert, she was the only one who saw through my act."

Turning to face Albert, she said, "Yes, I knew he wasn't the angst-ridden soul he pretended to be."

"Of couse I was but you knew why. You knew I was gay even then." Dima turned sideways on the bench to address them both. "Albert knows that I played the womanizer to throw everybody off. Then I kept getting married and divorced because I worried each wife would suspect before long. Well, Louisa here," he tapped her hand approving, "she was the only woman in graduate school who refused to play along with my ruse."

Were there bells ringing on campus or was it an internal clanging in her ears? Louisa continued to smile because she didn't know what else to do. "Colette was very dismissive of conventional sex roles," she blurted, and then thought, *why did I say that?* She looked quickly at Albert and said, "Well, I'm so happy to meet you." She offered what she hoped was a warm smile to Dima and said, "And I'm so delighted to see you happy, Dima." She added, "At last." Not knowing what else to say, she commented, "I didn't expect it to be so hot. I would've brought lighter clothes had I known."

Dima nodded. "It is warm today. So much of the year it is like

Siberia." Closing his eyes, he rolled his head lazily back and smiled. "Some days in January, the wind is so strong, I think I've been sent to a gulag." He said to Louisa, "Those are the days I kick myself for not taking a job on the West Coast."

Smiling, she said, "I suppose I'll have to become accustomed to New England winters."

"Are you leaving Hancock?" Dima asked at once.

"No, not at this late date," Louisa sighed. "But there is a certain post-doc I have high hopes will be here next year, and I'll visit her from time to time." She wondered whether the interview had yet taken place, or, for that matter, if her daughter had even mentioned her. Knowing Margaret, she hadn't. But, no matter; Louisa had her opportunity now.

"Oh, no. Not another post-doc," Dima said more to Albert than to her.

Shaking his head, Albert teased Dima, "Now, now, you were a post-doc yourself once."

"A hundred years ago, I was." Waving his hand wearily, he said, "Now there's a new breed of grad students. They are all too young, too eager, too enthusiastic." He crossed his legs and leaned forward. "Such enthusiasm! How did they ever get through graduate school and retain all that optimism?"

Louisa tipped her head and smiled primly. "Well, I know a young woman who could impress even you, Dima. A young woman who has traveled widely, spent summers in Europe since she was six, speaks three foreign languages as if she were a native, and has respect, true *respect* I tell you, for literature."

Dima widened his eyes comically. "What a recommendation. And tell me, who is this miraculous creature? A former student of yours?"

Louisa cleared her throat, "You could say that. In a way, she's my most accomplished student." Leaning towards Dima, she said, "The student of whom I'm most proud."

Removing his hands from the pockets of his jacket, Dima looked directly at Louisa and said, "Don't keep us in suspense."

"Yes, tell us," Albert urged gently.

Louisa clapped her hands softly together and announced, "Yes, Dima, my daughter Margaret is applying for a post-doc here."

Dima lowered his head into his hands. Slowly, he lifted his face and smiled. "Your daughter is already out of college? Graduate school, too?" He sounded genuinely incredulous. He swallowed and said, "Oh, we are old, friends, very old. How did we get to be so old?"

Tucking her feet beneath the bench, Louisa said, "Well, Margaret is only twenty-five. She got her PhD quite young. It must run in the family," she finished, hoping Dima would remember that she got her degree a full two years before he did.

"You must be very proud," Albert told her.

Smiling, she answered, "I am. Having one's child follow in your footsteps is a supreme compliment. But, of course, I knew Margaret was destined for academia since she was a mere child. Why, when she was only two, she was already lecturing to her dolls."

Dima frowned and made a disapproving sucking noise with his tongue. "Louisa," he spoke harshly, "how could you let your daughter become an academic? It's a dying profession."

Louisa's eyebrows lifted. "Yes, well, we academics don't get the respect we once did, perhaps, but someone has to—" Louisa stopped when she realized Dima wasn't listening. He appeared to be speaking to the ground when he said, "You slave away teaching, researching, and for what?" He thrashed at the air as if shunning the campus. "It's a farce, all of it." Horrified, Louisa watched as he spit on the ground, his saliva almost hitting her new shoes.

"Dima! How did you become so bitter? So disillusioned?"

Albert whispered to her, "It's a long story." He shook his head, indicating she shouldn't pursue the matter.

Louisa watched as Dima rolled his hands into tight fists, his knuckles straining against taut skin. He shouted, "You spend thirty years in a department with colleagues. Oh, there's a word for you, *colleagues*!" he said loudly. "Blackmailers, connivers, liars, the lot of them." Dima ran his hands through his hair, causing it to stick up in pointed tufts. "Turn your back for one minute and they're off in the Dean's office telling tales of how badly you chaired a meeting or why you shouldn't get research status or why you should retire early!" He yelled so loudly that Louisa expected the shrubbery to shake.

Trying to appear calm, Louisa said, "Surely it's not that bad. I've had some difficult department members at Hancock, but I would never—"

"It's a charade, all of it!" Dima looked across campus and shook his head. "If it weren't for Ivan, I would retire."

"Ivan? Who's Ivan?" Louisa asked faintly.

"A peasant," Albert said contemptuously, "a drunken, opportunistic peasant."

"A brilliant man," Dima countered, striking his chest with a flat palm, "the best *colleague* a man could have."

"That's how you got into trouble!" Albert reproached. "Did you learn nothing from that little escapade? Nothing at all?"

"Ivan is better read than any of the poseurs teaching here!" Dima shouted, the vein in the center of his forehead standing at attention.

"Excuse me," Louisa said, "But just what, *who*, are you talking about?"

"You almost ruined your career!" Albert said softly to Dima. Louisa realized that he was trying to quiet Dima by example. Albert looked furtively about as he spoke.

"Some people have no sense of humor." Dima said to Louisa. "It was a joke, a simple joke." He smiled at her, flashing his teeth, and Louisa realized that one of his front teeth was longer than the other. Had they always been like that?

Albert shook his head and removed a silver cigarette case from his jacket pocket. "Some jokes are not so funny. The Dean, the trustees, Dima, *the trustees!* They did not think your little joke was so funny, did they? Ivan should have been fired. Why he's still allowed to meander around campus pretending to change light bulbs is beyond me."

"He's an electrician!" Dima fired back at Albert. "There's no shame in knowing a trade. He's a brilliant electrician, self-taught. And self-taught in literature too!"

Albert spoke in a reproachful voice, "He should stick to electricity! Leave literature to the professionals!"

"Professionals!" Dima sneered, "another absurd word."

Louisa felt she was getting whiplash turning her head back and forth between the two men. "Enough, both of you! You're making no sense. Now, tell me, just what did this Ivan do?"

The two men looked at each other, deciding who would speak. Albert lit a cigarette and turned his face away to exhale smoke. Dima shrugged and said "I made a bet with another professor that Ivan could deliver my lecture on the first day of class and none of the students would even notice." He raised his arms and dropped them at his side. "Some people want to kill me for having a sense of humor. So kill me." He chuckled. "Today he's interviewing the post-docs."

"What!" Albert roared, no longer concerned about attracting attention. "Oh, you are *out of your mind*, do you know that, Dima?" Albert said bitterly. "Out of your mind."

Why didn't we just take the elevator? Louisa thought as she raced up the stairs. "Slow down, please! I'm telling you there's no need to worry." She was out of breath and speaking was nearly impossible. "I'm telling you," she said, sweating profusely as she climbed the last few steps, "Margaret would never be fooled. She's too cultured, too cultivated, too—Wait! Wait for me!" Louisa shed decorum and removed her shoes. She ran a few steps in her stockinged feet to catch up with the men. The three of them then hurried down the long corridor.

"If this gets out, Dima, you're done for!" Albert said. "No ifs, ands, or buts this time."

"Nonsense," Dima said brusquely, stopping suddenly in front of his office door.

The three of them peered in. Dima smiled. Louisa gasped and dropped her shoes onto the floor where they hit with two sad thuds. Only Albert spoke, a single word over and over, "Shit. Shit. Shit. Shit."

Louisa saw the bottle of vodka on the desk and asked herself if the young woman licking the bottom of a shot glass could possibly be her daughter. When Margaret noticed her in the doorway, she hiccupped and sang out, "Mother! I got the post-doc! Dima says I'm everything you always wanted to be!"

Ivan said, "This is your mother? No! Why, she looks young enough to be your sister!"

And it was true. As Louisa and Margaret looked at each other, something shifted between the two women.

"*Mon semblable, ma soeur,*" Louisa murmured sadly.

Margaret, looking away from her mother to *her* Dima, laughed and thought: *Not in a million years.*

A GENTLEMANLY PROFESSION

Rudy will tell you anything about himself. In fact, he can't shut up. Since his second divorce two years ago, he has been entangled with, devoted to, so many women, often at the same time, that he has to talk to you, pour his heart out to you, make you see that he isn't a scoundrel; he simply loves women, all of them. And boy, do they love him, or so he thinks.

As he's confessing his undying ardor for his latest love, he'll suddenly become smitten with a student waitress in the faculty dining room, gazing at her significantly as she refills his water glass until she finally returns his stare. Then he rolls his eyes at me as if to say, *what can I do? They throw themselves at me.*

He is curious, of course, about your own life, and listens with such rapt attention that in the old days, before you caught on to what a gossip monger he is, you actually found yourself confessing that you found the reference librarian with the curly red hair hot. You didn't know that his attentiveness wasn't polite interest but dirt gathering. Later, another colleague slapped my back, laughing as he said, "Say, Len, hear you got a thing for the redhead. Isn't she a little young for you?" Or the time I stupidly told Rudy that I'd had an article rejected by a major journal and he managed to bring it up at a department meeting. Who couldn't justifiably kill a fellow faculty member who pronounced, "I'm *never* going to submit to *Politics and Society.* Since they turned Len down, I want absolutely nothing to do with that journal."

Today is fairly typical of how our lunches have gone these last few months. It all starts with an innocent enough remark, on the surface that is, but I can spot one of his torpedoes miles off. We're both eating our sandwiches and he says, "I'm really worried about Brad," in that way he has. Someone who didn't know Rudy would think he was genuinely worried. Because Brad is friendly, bright, and good-looking, I immediately know that Rudy's on a destroy mission.

I'm supposed to say "Why? What's wrong with Brad?" so Rudy can lower his head, shake it deliberately, make that sucking noise with his tongue if he's really going for it. But I'm not a rookie any more. I search for an evasive remark, one that combats Rudy's pending story.

"You know, I saw Brad jogging on the track the other day on his lunch hour. Looked fit as a fiddle." I take a big swallow of my lukewarm coffee. "I'd give anything to be in the kind of shape he's in."

Of course, he's not deterred by this little road obstacle. "Len, c'mon," he tells me, "you're in great shape, really great shape." This too is part of The Rudeman's act; he routinely flatters you to death so you'll really let down your guard and open up to him.

"Need to work off some of this," I say, patting my stomach, realizing that I just admitted my paunch to Rudy. I can just hear him at his next lunch with whomever: "I'm really worried about Len; he's carrying around *some extra weight* these days." And he'll say it in just that affected way, laden with innuendo, like he's not just talking about pounds, but problems with my teaching or my marriage.

But today he waves his hand like I'm crazy, like I'm a triathlon competitor. Rudy has other things on his mind and doesn't want to waste time talking about my waist line. "Brad," he says, tapping his manicured nails against the table "I'm afraid, well, I'm afraid he's a little *too* trusting of Susan, if you know what I mean."

There it is. A bomb dropped on the table and waiting to go off. Susan is Brad's long-time girlfriend and a new friend of my wife's. They teach at the same elementary school.

"Susan?" I say. "Wonderful girl. Top notch. Molly and I had dinner with her and Brad, when was it? A couple of weeks ago?" I butter my roll, smushing it in my hand, pretending it's Rudy's head. "She served us a fabulous paella. Can that girl cook."

"*I know,*" he tells me, sleaze just lapping over his voice, like he's had private cooking lessons in Susan's kitchen. I'm supposed to be impressed or shocked, I don't care any more. I pick up my coffee, I'm still on my first cup, although lush head here is guzzling his second glass of wine. I look Rudy square in the face, his annoyingly boyish face with the impossibly small nose and eyes with the alertness of an elf's. In my mind, he's Jack Frost, no matter how many women he's slept with.

"Okay, out with it," I say, giving in, already disgusted by whatever he's going to tell me. It's bound to be some fairy tale about Susan pursuing him and he gallantly putting her off and putting her off until it's too cruel to put her off any longer.

"We ran into each other at the supermarket," he tells me in what he thinks is a tantalizing manner, like he's a spy giving me coded information.

"And, don't tell me, you liked her tomatoes," I answer in the same James Bond voice.

Surprise, surprise. The elf is actually affronted by this, by my implying that the initial attraction was his. He puts his chin in his hand and rubs his index finger against his temple, losing the tip of it in that wiry mass of blonde curls. Then he grins, no, he smirks, that damningly toothy smile, all pearly panels in neat rows.

"No," he says, shortly, "I didn't even notice her tomatoes, but you might say she went for my zucchini."

I groan at the bad joke. "Sounds like a helluva salad, but I've got a meeting with an honors student." I motion for the check and we pay and leave. He's still talking now as we enter Blaine Hall where the political science department is ensconced on the fifth floor. Rudy tells me that Brad doesn't seem to be thinking marriage and Susan's beginning to wonder if he'll ever jump.

"Ah," I say, "And you're worried that Susan is asking you to push Brad into some kind of action. And you don't think he should be pushed. I can see why you're worried."

I watch him swallow a sigh as we amble down the corridor; he thinks his senior colleague is a moron for missing the obvious.

"No, no," he says quickly, waving his hands like he's swatting a fly away. "She's only been hanging onto Brad because I wasn't available, see?" He looks at me now with an expression of fake defeat that says you've done it again, you've dragged it out of me.

"I thought you were always available," I say, smiling so he can interpret it as a joke if he wants to.

"I'm seeing a real estate agent. Linda. She drives a red Miata. But Susan, well, I'd love to have her wrap those long legs around me. I have to admit that if it weren't for Brad, I'd be awfully tempted."

Standing side by side in front of the elevator, he leans into me (I am pleased to be almost a head taller than him and stand with unusual erectness whenever I am with Rudy) and says in a soft but lewd voice, "She's had fantasies about me."

The elevator door opens as the bell sounds and we step into the compartment paneled with artificial wood. As soon as we begin rising, Rudy says in a low, grainy voice, "*Fantasies,* man. Can you believe it?"

I wonder if Susan's fantasies about Rudy are similar to mine, if she also has the one about his hair falling out or his developing some tortuous skin rash that requires him to wear some kind of sticky orange ointment that attracts mosquitoes and other pests.

Susan is very nice, and this is one of Rudy's meaner stories. Oh, I'll admit Susan and he probably ran into each other at the supermarket and Rudy inevitably made some tactless remark about when Brad was going to make an honest woman out of her or some such nonsense. Susan probably laughed, embarrassed by Rudy's lack of tact, and said something like, "In my dreams." It wouldn't take a lot for Rudy to translate that into "*You're* in my dreams." He wishes.

The elevator stops and we walk down the narrow corridor to our offices. I punch Rudy's shoulder with harder force than I should for joking around and say, "Well, if you happen to run into my wife in frozen foods, stay the hell away from her."

Molly is in the back yard tending the grill when I get home. She's leaning forward, her khaki shorts sliding up and revealing the cellulite on the back of her thighs, a popcorn-like dimpling that's gotten worse lately. The air smells like lighter fluid and charcoal, the bluish-gray smoke spreading the scent with the westerly wind. Todd, our one-and-a-half year old, is watching the fire from a safe distance in his playpen. I walk over and pick him up, his legs immediately kicking my gut. Molly steps back from the flames blowing high now over the grill. She puts the lid on the Weber and walks over to us, kissing Todd on the nose.

"Tell Daddy what you said today," she tells him in a little girl voice. "Can you say it? Say mail man. Maaail Maaan," she emphasizes. "He said it," she tells me, "said it clear as a bell when Frank came on the porch this morning. He looked right at him and said, 'mail man.'"

If I don't exclaim over this in just the right way and for just the right amount of time, Molly will give me the cold shoulder, answering, "Nothing," in that clipped little voice when I ask her what's wrong.

"That's wonderful! Give me five, big guy," I say, trying to slap my son's hand against my own. Molly takes Todd and puts me to work getting the hamburgers ready while she sets the table on the patio. This division of labor is good; we get in each other's way otherwise. While we're eating, I bring Molly up to date on the latest Rudy fabrication.

"That's sick," Molly says. "That's the sickest thing I've ever heard."

Molly has never met Rudy, but I share his antics with her.

"Len, why do you even talk to him? He's a total idiot."

"He's the biggest asshole I know, but when he asks me to go to lunch twenty-five days in a row, I run out of excuses."

Molly starts spooning vanilla ice cream into little porcelain bowls. "But why Brad and Susan?" she asks. "Why does Rudy have to lie about people who wouldn't hurt a fly?" The napkins start to blow in the breeze so I anchor them with the salt and pepper shakers.

I swallow my first spoonful of ice cream. It's so cold it clears the area between my temples, and I realize in an instant something I've overlooked before. "Rudy and Brad are both going to come up for tenure next year. Brad wasn't supposed to come up until the year after, but the department just decided to bring him up early. Rudy's probably got his nose out of joint about it and is trying to submarine the competition." I chortle. "As if he could."

"Yeah?" Molly looks at me expectantly.

"Sure," I say, nodding, eating more ice cream, holding it in the center of my mouth so it doesn't touch my fillings. "Brad's a sure thing. The students think he's God and he was just awarded a big research grant from the Kitchell Foundation. Hancock College is going to make a bundle off him."

Todd is grunting for ice cream from his high chair. I lift my spoon to him, and he's so excited, he spits in it. Molly's not looking so I shove the spoon back in his mouth, saliva and all.

"And Rudy?" Molly asks.

"Hard to say. He kisses a lot of asses. Just a question of whether the old boys are falling for it."

Molly eats her ice cream, slowly skimming a spoonful between her lips over and over. "Well, it's awfully disrespectful to Susan. I feel like telling her."

My spoon hits the bowl heavily. "Don't! You don't want Brad and Susan thinking we give any credence to Rudy's bullshit. It would just make things messy at work."

Why did I even tell her? I could kick myself but Molly sighs and nods her head. "You're right." She sounds resigned. Turning in her chair, she offers Todd a spoonful of her ice cream. "But that jerk has got some nerve. I mean, I don't know that Susan even wants to get married. She's never said that to me. What the hell is Rudy talking about anyway?"

"Don't all women want to get married?" I ask, the teasing obvious, but I still put my hands over my head like I'm ducking an imagined blow. Molly gives me her reprimanding school teacher glare, eyebrows raised full mast.

"Well, Brad is a nice guy," I reason. "A lot of women would probably want to marry him."

Molly stands and begins to stack the dishes. "Suppose so. Like a lot of men would like to marry Susan." There's a challenge in her voice.

"Without question."

She carries the dishes into the house through the sliding glass doors. I reach over and pull the tray on Todd's high chair forward so I can lift him out. Holding him, I walk the perimeter of the yard, moving around the litter of toddler toys sprawled across the grass. I almost trip on a plastic pail and drop Todd. I set him down and let him wander on the grass.

Maybe after dinner, I'll get to take a dip in the pool. Gearing up for classes is always rough, and I need to unwind, forget about the wunderkind professors pushing their way up and the fact that I haven't had a decent merit raise in two years. I make the same salary as the new hires and pretty soon they'll be out-earning me. I just know it all started with Rudy blabbering about that journal rejection. Even Sarah, our department secretary, gives me pitying glances.

"Len, what is WRONG with you!" Surely every neighbor on the block heard Molly screaming at me from the kitchen window.

"Not so loud. What's the problem?"

With the volume not turned down even one notch, Molly shouts, "Your son is in the sandbox eating dirt! Do you *think* you could watch him while I finish the dishes? Do you think you're *capable* of that?"

I don't answer. I just lumber over to the sand box and scoop up Todd. "Mommy's a witch," I whisper to him in cooing baby talk. "Yes, she is, she's a witchy, witchy, bitch." Todd giggles, opening his mouth, and drops a stream of wet, chewed sand on my white shirt.

On Monday morning, I get a major windfall. Brad walks into my office with an embarrassed smile and tells me he and Susan are getting married in a couple months. An almost fatherly pride and excitement swims though me looking at Brad's happy face, but there's also a black thrill rising in my soul: Rudy's going to shit his pants when he hears the news.

The rims of Brad's ears are pulsing a vibrant pink. "We're going to keep it a secret for a week or so, just till we get in touch with both of our families and make sure we can get the church for the twenty-seventh of November." I'm touched that Brad has chosen to confide in me; no one else in the department knows. Susan, Brad tells me, is going to ask Molly to oversee the signing of the guest register. Knowing my wife, she'll privately sneer at such a minor responsibility, but nothing can dampen my spirits because I know that Mr. Obnoxious is going to get impaled on one of his own stories. A lightbulb goes on over my head and I say to Brad, "Say, Molly and I are going to have a barbecue the day before the semester starts. We haven't done the invites yet. What d'you say you and Susan make the announcement at the barbecue?"

Brad seems hesitant, his shoulders rising up into a doubtful shrug. I hurry to say, "You know, everyone will hear at once. It will be exciting. A way to really start off the semester with a bang!"

Now Brad's got an embarrassed grin on his face and he nods shyly. "I think Susan would go for that."

"Of course she will! Women love being the center of attention." I almost laugh out loud. No one loves being the center of anything more than Mr. Oompa Loompa.

That afternoon, at a departmental meeting on curricular issues, I watch Rudy watching Brad across the large rectangular table we're seated around. Brad is almost the exact opposite physical type from Rudy. His dark blonde hair is very straight and he has a long, but not too long, nose. Brad is lanky, too big for the straight-backed chair he's sitting in; he played basketball in high school. His expression, while not exactly serious, is at least thoughtful. You always get the feeling that Brad is really taking in your words and giving them due consideration. Rudy, with that upturned nose and perpetual grin, is the court jester in comparison.

Brad politely interjects a comment into the discussion about an assignment he's developed to help students learn to Shepardize cases on Lexis. Our department chair, Walt Emriss, obviously approves of this, his long jaw working itself up and down in a forceful nod. Walt's loaded, an heir to some shopping chain out in Minnesota. Teaching is just a gentlemanly profession for him, but he wields a lot of power and is always voted onto the important committees. "And that's for your Intro Constitutional Law class?" Emriss asks.

"Yes," Brad answers, almost stammering because he's nervous talking to Emriss, "but I'm also going to use it in my Supreme Court seminar next semester."

"Fine. That's fine," Emriss says. "We should all be doing more skill-specific assignments like that."

Rudy starts fidgeting in his chair, wondering no doubt how he can call some favorable attention to himself to outdo Brad. But he's too late. The meeting is winding down with the sound of pens being clipped and appointment books closed. I stay in my seat for a moment while I'm putting my laptop to sleep. On his way out, Rudy leans over me and says in a low, conspiratorial voice, "Brad's got more to worry about than Shepardizing cases."

I look up at Rudy and he winks at me, like this is just between us guys.

"Rudy," I say, "I need to talk to you." He turns around and comes back, sits on the table, his legs swinging a good six inches from the floor. I wait until we're the last two people in the room. "Say, Molly and I are having a barbecue a week from Saturday. Four o'clock. Can you make it?"

"Hey, wouldn't miss it. What's the occasion?"

"Oh, Molly wants to have one last outdoor party before the weather turns cool. Bring Linda. We'd love to meet her."

A smile eases across his face and he shakes his head. "Afraid I'm in the dog house there."

"Oh?"

"*Yeeaah*," he slows his speech. "She was getting too serious. Told her I needed a little hiatus."

I'm starting to wonder if this Linda even exists. Probably another one of Rudy's fantasies. Actually, this is better. Yeah, it's much better for Rudy to be standing alone when Brad and Susan announce the engagement.

I give the little man a wink and say, "So come stag. You might get lucky."

I'm getting the silent treatment from Molly tonight. She has no interest in having a barbecue and can't believe I invited people over without getting her okay first. Whatever. She's always got a bug up her ass about something. Her last words at dinner tonight were, "Fine. You clean the house and do the grocery shopping."

"I don't know what to buy," I protest. "I don't know where to find the stuff." It's true; I wouldn't know the produce aisle from the cereal aisle whereas Molly cuts coupons and knows every inch of the store. "C'mon, Mol. Do this for me. It's just shopping."

Molly looks up from scraping the plates and points the butter knife at me. "It's high time you learned! What good is a PhD if you can't even shop for a barbecue?"

I stand and untie Todd's bib. Clearing my throat, I speak slowly, "Did it ever occur to you that entertaining could help my standing in the department? The Shawns have that New Year's cocktail party every year and the Davidsons throw the commencement bash." I paused before saying, "I get the distinct impression people think we're anti-social. I don't think it's an accident that I haven't been chair of the department yet." I think Molly is going to give in when she sighs, but she just picks up the plates and says, "Make a grocery list, you idiot. It's not rocket science."

So after dinner I sit in my study and make a list of every possible thing people eat at parties, anything that can be thrown on a grill or tossed in a salad. And for all her bitching and moaning, Molly won't be able to resist making some fancy desserts. She's famous for them and loves the compliments.

I turn the paper over and start a different list. On the top of the page, I write "*Rudy.*" Lowering my head, I scribble furiously for the next several minutes, erasing some items, adding others. Finally, I set my pencil down and review the list:

Short - should be shorter
Lush - and how
Womanizer - so he thinks
Narcissist - needs everyone to love him

Competitive - it's not enough that he succeeds; those around him must fail
Tries to twinkle - what is that weird thing he does with his eyes?
Ass Kisser - enough said
Pretends to be concerned about everyone - only cares about himself
Gossip monger - makes up crap and tells everyone
Hair - tangled like Ramen noodles

I stare at the list so long that when I lift my eyes, I think I can still see the words on the white wall. When I get into bed that night, I'm whistling. Molly looks up from her magazine and asks, "What are you so happy about?"

When Rudy arrives at two on the dot on the Saturday afternoon of the party, the first thing I do is pour him a tall Long Island iced tea and he knocks it right down. I'd asked him to come an hour early to help me set up and he was all too happy to oblige. It's a ridiculously hot day and we both slip into the pool for a quick swim after we've set up all the TV trays in the back yard and pulled lounge chairs out of the garage and positioned them around the patio.

While Rudy's in the downstairs bathroom changing out of his wet swim suit, I pour another Long Island tea for him. Molly appears with Todd on her hip and surveys the work Rudy and I have done. When I told her earlier that I'd asked Rudy to help set up, she'd turned to me and said, "Why him?"

I'd shrugged my shoulders and said, "He loves to be at the center of things. I figured, why not put him to work? And remember, not a word about the engagement. Brad and Susan want to surprise everyone with an announcement."

Rudy comes out of the bathroom and goes right for Todd, raising him up in the air, then down, then up again. I'm over there in a second, ready to catch my son should the jerk drop him, but Todd is loving it, laughing and showing his latest tooth.

"Oh, I almost forgot," Rudy says, handing Todd back to Molly. He reaches into his khakis pocket and pulls out a tiny silver kaleidoscope decorated with bright geometric shapes.

"Like this," he says to Todd, demonstrating first with his own eye and then handing the silver tube to Todd. Todd looks through the cylinder and is amazed, his mouth a wondrous hole. He drops the pipe and Rudy catches it, handing it to Molly with a smile.

"Thank you," Molly says, smiling at Rudy. "That was so thoughtful of you." She turns to Todd and says, "Can you say thank you? Thank you?"

Todd says something that sounds like "ank oou," and Rudy slips his index finger into Todd's rolled fingers and makes like he's shaking his hand. "Well, your welcome little fella."

I'm about to be sick. Seeing this fraud play Uncle Rudy is too much. He tells us he's going to load the beer into the refrigerator and heads off briskly to the kitchen.

Molly leans in and whispers to me, "*That's Rudy*? He seems so nice."

"Seems," I remind her.

I find the elf in the kitchen rearranging the cheese in the fridge like it's his house. He's absolutely stuffing the thing with beer and I notice he's almost got his second drink finished off and he's left himself a beer on the counter.

The doorbell rings and I head for the front door but then stop like I just remembered something. "By the way, Rudy, can I ask you another favor?"

"Name it."

"Things will get kind of busy. If you hear the doorbell and we're running around getting drinks and stuff, would you mind letting folks in?"

"No problemo."

"I really appreciate it."

The first couple to arrive is Brad and Susan. No surprise since Brad is always punctual. Susan shouts hello to us and immediately goes off to find Molly. I greet Brad warmly, even more warmly than usual, and I can feel Rudy's radar go up a couple of inches. After being in the singular embrace of my thanks, he doesn't want to include Brad in our camaraderie.

"How about a drink, Brad? Ready for another one, Rudy?"

"Sure," Rudy says, and I lift the pitcher of Long Island tea and pour carefully so the elf gets just liquid, no ice.

"So," I say holding my glass out before both of them, "here's to the future of the department." I'm amazed at how generous I sound, as if I were really hoping that both of these guys were going to be with me at the college forever. We clink glasses and take a few swallows.

The doorbell starts to ring repeatedly and I'm very busy getting drinks, showing people the pool, and getting more ice from the refrigerator.

On one trip to the kitchen, I see Rudy answering the door, a beer in his hand, and greeting a couple of more faculty members. I'm standing near the picture window in the dining room when I spy Walt Emriss's mocha-colored Mercedes lumbering slowly down the street as he checks house numbers for the right address.

Right away, I tell Molly that Todd's crying for her from his crib. I want to make sure drunken Rudy is the one to greet Emriss at the door. Then I make myself scarce. I go into the back yard and pick up the video camera, getting good footage of Charles, the department's Marxist, getting pushed into the pool by Doug, the full professor who teaches modern European politics. I start moving around the yard, stopping in front of the guests and making them say something to the camera. People are having a good time. Everyone is drinking and the heat is intensifying the effect.

I stay in the yard maybe fifteen minutes. My body is so full of giddy energy and expectation about what's going on inside the house that it's hard to appear relaxed. I keep imagining a drunken Rudy greeting Walt Emriss and his wife, Elena, at the door. First, of course, Rudy will fawn all over Emriss who will have to take note of Rudy's flammable breath. Then, Rudy will turn to the lovely Elena and his career at Hancock College will crash and burn in a spectacular conflagration.

Rudy won't be able to help himself. Elena is stunning. She's twenty years or so younger than her husband, probably in her middle or late thirties, but she doesn't look it. She wears her honey-blonde hair shoulder length, and she has such a riveting saphire stare, it stops you in your tracks. And she's petite, probably only five five in heels, short enough for Rudy. My only question is whether he'll get Elena alone or try to pull off his debonair act in front of her husband. I'm hoping this will be one of Rudy's more reckless days.

I wish I could be there to eavesdrop on their conversation, but I don't think I could witness it and not give myself away. I can just picture Rudy blatantly staring at Elena, getting her to look back at him finally, and then laying some loser line on her like, "Did anyone tell you that you have the most beautiful nose?" She does, a beautiful, patrician nose, but Rudy will think he's being original by not commenting on Elena's eyes or smile like everyone else does. From there, he'll make several ingratiating comments about himself, maybe even spill his drink on her, and he's history. Emriss will either witness it all first hand or Elena will tell him about it. Oh, I know the Emrisses are too well-mannered to make a fuss today, but Walt has the memory of an elephant. He still remembers comments on my teaching evaluations from my rookie year. When Rudy comes up for tenure, he'll shoot him dead.

I walk into the house and hear the Beatles singing about twisting and shouting. Molly and Susan are having a ball turning each other around in some kind of modified twist. Molly stops dancing, running her hand over her forehead to wipe the sweat off, and picks up an appetizer tray. She sees me and calls, "Check everyone's drink." I nod as she walks off, but then she turns back and looks at me quizzically. "You heard Todd crying?" she asks. "He's sound asleep."

"Good, good."

I find the Emrisses in the dining room. It was bad form not greeting them in person when they arrived, and I apologize, explaining I was in the back yard. It's a real coup that the Emrisses have come; they don't often socialize with the faculty unless they're putting on the show.

"That's all right," Elena tells me after I apologize. "A nice young man let us in and got us drinks."

What's this? Detectable irony in her voice? And there's no mistaking that hint of a scowl that passed over Walt's face. It's a done deal. The rest of the day will just be the icing on the cake.

"Well, I hope you brought your suits, because it's a good day for a swim." I imagine Elena diving into the pool in a bikini that matches her eyes. If she does, Rudy will dive in right after her. "Let me know if I can get you anything," I say, and they nod their thanks at me.

Rudy is positively blotto when I discover him shooting pool in the basement with Betsy Sims, the department's old maid. She's much too old for him but she's the type who's grateful for any guy's attention. Rudy's talking loudly, though still coherently, complaining about his last shot and demanding, jokingly, that he get another turn. I call him away from the game for a moment and say, "*Rudy,*" like he's done something I'm impressed with. "What did you say to Elena Emriss? I've never seen her so charmed."

He looks up at me quickly, surprised, but in a moment starts shaking his head, all innocence, believing immediately that he's once again the inevitable object of someone's admiration.

"Why? What did she say?" he asks, trying for indifference and pretending to watch Betsy line up her next shot.

"Well," I say, taking a tantalizingly slow sip of my drink, "she inquired who the nice young man was who met them at the door. I assume that was you, Rudy boy."

"Yeah," he says with a modest chuckle. "That was me," he finishes with a drunken slur, pretending to be modest.

I give him an admiring nod, tap my knuckles against his, and move on.

By six-thirty, everyone is outside dining on ribs and various salads. I find Brad and Susan and suggest they make their announcement while everyone's in the same spot. They're jittery as I call out for everyone to be quiet. I look at Brad with a smile, extending my hand towards him to prompt him.

He and Susan step forward with their arms around each other. They look at each other, Brad starts to talk a few times, then Susan, but they keep breaking into laughter. Finally, Brad hollers, "We're getting married!"

Immediately there are high-pitched peals of surprise and everyone applauds. I open the first bottle of champagne, aiming it so the cork flies into the pool. Everyone is rushing up to Brad and Susan, hugging them and wishing them the best. Emriss shakes Brad's hand gravely and even kisses Susan on the cheek. He emits a dignified approval as he chats with them, almost smiling, which is something I've never seen.

Molly brings out the two-tired cake with white icing. She was so proud of thinking to make a miniature wedding cake for the dessert. Setting the cake on the main serving table, Molly picks up the video camera and waves at Brad and Susan to come over. "You need to practice for the big day!" she shouts. We all laugh and call out instructions to them as they cut the cake and feed it to each other. Someone yells out, "Kiss! Kiss!" and everyone picks up the chorus. Brad and Susan put down the cake and give each other a long kiss to raucous applause. Molly and I pass out slices of the cake and I open a couple more bottles of champagne.

I haven't felt this great in years. This is the best department party ever. The day has gone flawlessly, and it was all so easy, really. Rudy, wherever he is in the crowd, is reduced, no doubt, to a shell by this point. He'll have no choice but to seek Elena out and try to restore his ego, continue the drunken damage he started earlier in the day. But where is he? I scan the crowd, but there's no sign of him. I can't imagine Rudy would slip out without saying good-bye. Of course, if the wedding announcement absolutely devastated him, he might have fled to his car and driven off recklessly. I do have a moment's qualm; that drunk shouldn't be on the road. Damn. I had planned on slapping him on heartily on the back and saying something like, "Guess Susan prefers Brad's zuccini."

But then Molly's at my elbow, saying, "Where is Susan? Brad is looking everywhere for her. Check the house."

"She was just here. They were feeding the cake to each other."

Annoyed, Molly places her hand on my back and gives me a little shove. "And then she disappeared. Go find her. I'm going to make the coffee."

Despite the noise outside, the house is very still. But then I hear it, a strange sound that sounds like muffled hiccuping. The noise seems to echo from below, so I head for the basement.

Leaning against the pool table is Susan. Even if her mascara weren't smeared all over her cheeks, I could still tell she'd been crying by her glossy eyes.

"Susan? Are you all right?"

She nods, although a new round of sniffles starts. Finally, she says, "Just all the excitement. I needed to slip away for a few minutes."

I nod my head like I understand, but I don't. I thought brides-to-be liked being the center of attention. Molly did everything but take out a full-page ad.

"Brad's looking for you. Should I tell him you're here?"

"No," she says quickly, pressing her hands to her cheek to remove the last tears. "I'll come up." She opens her purse, removes a brush and sinks it into her lovely auburn hair. Almost nonchalantly, slipping the brush back into her purse, she asks, "Is Rudy around?"

When I don't answer, she glances at me and blinks her eyes. She snaps her purse shut and asks again, "Have you seen Rudy?"

I shake my head no. Susan walks past me, her footsteps on the stairs the only sound. My head hurts, a tight cluster of pain knotting itself just over my neck. Climbing the stairs, I try to remember how many drinks I had, but I don't want to think. In the kitchen I down a glass of water and then a second. Aspirin, I need aspirin. The thought of walking up another flight of stairs to the medicine cabinet in the bathroom is almost too much. But then the pain crawls from the back of my head up to my crown, and I head up for the Advil.

Outside the master bedroom, I start gulping air in cupfuls. I see them through the open door, both of them, Rudy and Elena. He's sitting on the bed, his head on his knees, and she's gently rubbing his back.

"I'm sorry. It's terrible of me to behave this way," he says. "It's just . . . they look so happy." Now he covers his head with his arms. He looks completely destroyed, humiliated at having to admit to himself that he was wrong about Brad and Susan. An image of Susan sniffling collides with my migraine and knocks it up in my head so my skull feels painfully lifted. My brain feels like it's contracting over and over to the merciless pulse of my blood.

"I really love women," Rudy says, in a strained, sickly voice, and I wonder if he's going to be sick on the carpet. "I don't know why it never works out."

Elena looks down at the collapsed form and smiles. She looks maternal, like this is her son weeping over a school yard slight. She moves her hand through his hair, one of her fingers coiling the inner spiral of a curl. "It's all right," she tells him. "You'll meet the right woman, you'll see."

Taking a few steps backwards, I turn and quietly walk down the hall. Finally I stop and lean my shoulder against the wall, wondering how I'm going to re-join the party. The days at work lay themselves out before me like a stack of blue books to be graded, endless, monotonous, relentless. I see Rudy and me at lunch together day after day. His ego is long gone, but a new, more dangerous person sits across the table, trying to arouse my sympathy about his job, about his failed relationships, about his terrible, terrible life.

THE ERINYES

"This is a list of our demands."

Dean Herb Shrilley tried to catch the piece of paper shoved across his desk, but it curled up at one side and flew into the air. He clapped it with both hands the way one might kill a mosquito and grimaced at the now crumpled paper. He tried to sound matter-of-fact as he said to the students, "Student input is always welcome on faculty searches. Generally each department invites students to come to a lecture of the visiting candidate—"

"That's too late in the process for our input!" one of the three young women shouted in a clearly rehearsed monotone, raising both her hands to her ears to deny his words passage. Her head was shaved and she wore an elaborate belt that circled her waist over and over like a writhing serpent. The Erinyes, Herb thought, those punishing mythic women had infiltrated his office. He would have to scold his secretary, Mrs. Tribble, for letting them in.

"Read our demands," said the one whose eyebrow, nose and lip flashed with silver earrings, "and you'll see that we want to make sure that you bring the *right* people to campus to interview."

Herb laid the paper flat on the desk and attempted to smooth it out. "Well, the History department will consult with me about bringing in the most qualified candidates in the field of British history—"

"Qualified doesn't cut it," the bald one said, karate chopping the edge of his desk to make her point. "The department needs a woman of color from a developing nation. Imperialist British history has been taught for far too long. We *must* hire someone who can address the history of the colonized, who can assess the impact of the classist, racist Empire on oppressed peoples."

Herb guessed she was the leader of the trio. She had the motivating forthrightness of a general giving orders to troops. While she spoke, the woman with the piercings raised a fisted hand over her head while the third, a girl with large brown eyes, gazed at the bald woman with adoration.

"We have affirmative action policies—" Herb offered.

"That don't apply to women from Africa or India or . . ."

"China or Latin America—"

"Or, or . . . Madagascar?" the brown-eyed girl said as she looked apologetically at the other two. She was the most reserved of the three, an Erinye in training, but Herb couldn't really distinguish one from the other. The three young women melted and merged into a single enormous and intensely irate person wearing dour black clothing. He knew to cut his losses and end the meeting.

He stood. "Ladies, thank you for taking time from your studies to provide me with your suggestions—"

"Demands." The leader also stood, prompting the others to do the same.

"Let's not quibble over vocabulary. I'll share this, er, this document with the search committee so they'll be aware of your concerns. Demands, I mean," he added when he saw he was about to be interrupted again. "And now, if you'll excuse me, I have an appointment across campus."

The women exited into the outer office noisily, one of them glancing at Mrs. Tribble and saying, "Are there any *male* secretaries on this campus?"

Herb closed the door and waited a minute before buzzing his secretary. "Mrs. Tribble, if they come back, don't let them in. I'm staying in for lunch. No interruptions. Please."

"I'll do my best," Mrs. Tribble said unconvincingly. She had come with the job and wasn't the gatekeeper a dean needed.

He felt his heart palpitate. Pressing his hand to his chest, he inhaled deeply until he felt a regular rhythm return. He closed the long curtains on the window behind his desk and crossed the carpet to turn off the lights. The room was now completely dark except for the glorious glow emanating from the fifteen gallon aquarium. He had always loved fish, ever since he was a boy and the only pet he'd been allowed was a single fish. This aquarium had been a present from his wife, Elizabeth, who had seen to every detail, from the simple but gleaming goldfish that swam in its waters, to the tiny but detailed structures with Greek columns and Roman arches assembled to resemble an ancient city state. There were only a half a dozen fish and they had plenty of space to move freely. He liked to think of it as Troy or the submerged world of Atlantis. The aquarium was the only tangible evidence in the office of his own past as a classics professor. It sat atop an old Formica kitchen table that he had brought from home.

Rolling his chair in front of the tank, he sat down to gaze at the aquarium. He relished the quiet in the room, the only sound the gentle suckling of the water filter. Mrs. Tribble, of course, was just behind the wall, but he imagined himself miles below the earth, cocooned in a kingdom under the sea that was unreachable to modern man. The goldfish, so luminous and quiet, moved about with peaceful purpose. With small movements of their fins, they traversed the tank, making shimmering turns when they reached a wall. Reaching in his inner breast pocket, Herb took out a cylinder of goldfish food and opened a partition in the roof of the tank. As the first flakes fell, one fish, then another, and finally all swam to the surface to partake. A minute later, having eaten their fill, they resumed their silent travels in the lower depths of the aquarium. Was there a more tranquil world anywhere? Poseidon, you were so wise, Herb thought, choosing the sea for your domain, away from the petty quibbles of man.

Sharing the events of the day with his wife was always precarious. Elizabeth insisted on knowing every event that transpired in his office, but Herb dreaded her lambasting him with, "Why didn't you speak up?" and "You're the Dean! Why do you put up with these things!" Still, he felt unburdened when he had admitted every last humiliating detail of his day. Elizabeth's pronouncing a certain faculty member "an insouciant blowhard" or describing Mrs. Tribble as "the queen of incompetence" had a restorative effect. At least he then felt able to chew and swallow his dinner. During the last year, his colitis had been torturous.

Predictably, Elizabeth was outraged by the visitation of the Erinyes and their list of demands. Her first exhortation upon examing the list, "Expel them! Get rid of them!" wasn't helpful, but he felt a rush of gratitude that his wife was so irked on his behalf.

"Even if I could do that, dear, that would only make them martyrs to the cause."

"Cause? What cause?"

Sighing, Herb answered, "Political correctness. Any time the administration makes a move of any kind, there's an outcry from the students that we're not being politically correct. And many faculty have jumped on the bandwagon."

"Oh, that." Elizabeth waved her hand dismissively. "These fads come and go. My uncle belonged to a hooligan fraternity that made the pledges swallow goldfish. That fad ended."

In an instant, Herb's appetite vanished. "Elizabeth, do you know why that fad ended? It was cruel to the fish! That *was* despicable behavior. This *fad*, as you call it, is about hiring with political awareness."

Elizabeth picked up the list and waved it at Herb. "*This* is political awareness?" She recited, "If a woman of color does not interview for the tenure track position in British history, be prepared for a student boycott of classes and continuous protest rallies at various campus locations. Local news agencies will be invited to cover events. A letter campaign to the Trustees will commence. Hancock College alumni will be urged to withhold donations until this matter is rectified." As if searching the heavens with her eyes, Elizabeth said, "Do you mean to tell me that *only* a woman of color can teach students *about* women of color? That's absurd! Why, with that kind of logic, only an ancient person could teach ancient history! Odysseus may have traveled a long way to get home, but he can't very well travel to Hancock in 1990 now, can he!"

Herb stood and pushed his chair to the table. "You make an excellent point, dear, although I suspect that the young women who came to my office today would tell you there'd be no need to hire a time traveler. You see, I'm considered obsolete, one of the useless perpetrators of a canon honoring dead white males. In fact, these modern day Erinyes can't wait for me to join their ranks. I should phone Hades and make my permanent reservation."

"Pooh. Herb, that's just nonsense and you know it." She picked up the list and read, "Following the interviews, two *female* history majors will meet with the search committee to assess candidates."

Suppressing a groan, he said, "Dear, I'm going to watch *Jeopardy!*. No interruptions. Please."

Herb generally liked meeting with the History department although they were a formidable lot. They almost always voted as a block at faculty meetings, and that gave them disproportionate influence on campus.

Herb thought of them as hammering out their differences ahead of time with Hephaestius's own mallet. When he finally returned to the Classics department, Herb hoped to instill this same discipline in his colleagues.

Today, however, he dreaded the discussion on which candidates to bring to campus to interview for the tenure track position in British history. It was a reminder that George Winston, one of his favorite faculty members, was retiring. Sure, George could be a curmudgeon, but he had taught at Hancock thirty-five years and had a much needed historical perspective. The new faculty hires showed little interest in college history other than breaking with its traditions. They thought staff attendance at commencement should be voluntary, that there was no need for faculty to be on campus during freshman orientation. George and his wife, Eleanor, were old school. They could be counted on to attend every college function, to come to every meet and greet, to stay in touch with students long after they graduated. Herb also appreciated that George never rushed into anything. He could be counted on as a voice of caution in campus faculty meetings. So many of the young whippersnappers went off half-cocked about changing this and changing that before they even knew the lay of the land.

Four members of the History department were present in the faculty conference room, three men and one woman. Gathered around the table, Herb noticed that each had a copy of the list of demands in front of them. He had sent a copy to the department and had heard back that the Erinyes had already paid several visits to the history faculty. Sighing, he reached for the roll of Tums in his pocket.

Affecting a business-as-usual tone, Herb began, "So, History Department, you very efficient people, have you agreed on your top three candidates?" He turned to Kathryn Rector, the medievalist and current chair, and said, "Who are your top choices?"

"Well, two of them are no-brainers," Kathryn began as Herb noticed the others nodding in agreement. She opened the top folder of a short stack on the table, saying, "There's Kenneth Bohland who's currently on a post-doc at Columbia, and there's Sarah Kramer who finished her PhD two years ago at Princeton. She's been teaching at Wellesley on a non-tenure track."

Relieved they were off to a consensual start, Herb said, "I thought those two looked top notch as well. How did the phone interviews go? Are they both interested in Hancock?"

"Kenneth is *very* interested," Kathryn answered. "His mother is a

Hancock grad and he definitely wants to teach at a liberal arts college."

George cleared his throat with a deep guttural sweep and asked, "What year was his mother?"

"I didn't ask," Kathryn replied briskly.

"Well, it would have to be, oh, 1940 or earlier," George said. "Those would have been the Hill years. Let's see, his administration began in the mid-thirties and Lee took over in 1943."

Herb noticed Kathryn blinking with impatience and knew he had to cut George off. He asked, "And the young lady at Wellesley, do you sense strong interest from her?"

"Ah, well, that's a different matter." Kathryn opened a notebook and scanned a page of notes. "Sarah seems to be very popular at Wellesley. She was hired as a sabbatical replacement and was able to stay on because of an unexpected maternity leave. She's officially on the job market but I've heard rumors that Wellesley is scrambling to come up with a position for her."

"I hope not," Dan Cotwell, the American historian, said; "She looks really good."

Mike Hogarth, new in Chinese history, said, "I think so too. She has a book on British aristocracy following World War I coming out from Oxford."

Kathryn took a moment to look at each person and said, "I got the feeling Sarah enjoys being at an all female college, but a permanent position for her at Wellesley isn't a sure thing. It depends on a number of factors, and things seem to be happening slowly. What we don't want to happen, of course, is a repeat of what we went through with Jill Petersen."

There were loud murmurs of agreement. George said, "That was a damn waste of time. She came here for a year and then went back to Hampshire when they advertised a new position. She was a hippie from a flake school and we never should have hired her. I said it then and I still say it."

With a soft tap of the table, Kathryn said, "George, that's water under the bridge." She looked at Herb and told him, "The whole department agreed that there's sufficient interest in Sarah to bring her to campus despite what might be brewing at Wellesley. Does that meet with the Dean's approval?"

Herb nodded with what he hoped appeared to be thoughtful gravity. "She merits a campus interview. Most definitely."

Kathryn said, "All right. I'll invite both of these candidates for interviews and get the schedules to everyone. Now," she said, lifting two folders from the bottom of the stack, "let's discuss our choices for the third interview."

The room went quiet and Herb sensed the calm before the storm. Removing her glasses, Kathryn set them on the table and said, "Herb, the department is split between two candidates, Joseph Gutierrez and Patricia O'Neil."

Herb felt a churning whirlpool in his stomach, Charybdis wreaking havoc on his lunch. "Yes, I've read the folders," he said. "Joseph hasn't defended his dissertation yet, has he? Has he even completed it?" Herb, of course, knew the answer but he had long ago learned the benefits of making others acknowledge weakness in a candidate, in a policy, in any stance.

Dan placed his forearms on the table and spoke quickly, "He has just one more chapter. I did his phone interview and he told me he's *sure* he'll be finished this summer. He's tentatively scheduled the defense for mid-November, right before Thanksgiving." With a nervous cough, Dan said quickly, "Oh, and he prefers to be called José. In fact, he's having his name legally changed to José."

No one said anything. Herb tried to read Kathryn's face, but she was pretending to compare her written notes with the candidate's resume, clearly a ruse not to look at Herb. Finally, Dan continued, a challenge in his voice, "We've brought in people who haven't finished their dissertations before. This wouldn't be a first."

"That's true," Herb said slowly, "but that's been the case when we didn't have another candidate who's further along. Ms. O'Neil has just defended her dissertation. As I recall, she wrote on the impact of England's penal laws on Irish Catholics. She's published an article in *The Journal of British Studies* and has another forthcoming in *European History Quarterly.* I would say Ms. O'Neil is well on her way to becoming a solid historian. Who conducted her phone interview?"

"Me," Mike said.

"And?"

"Well, she's good. Nice, I mean. She answered all the questions."

"She answered all the questions?" Herb repeated, hoping this junior faculty member noted the dissatisfaction in his voice. "You found her articulate? Highly intelligent?"

"Oh, sure. She's clearly very bright and she has a sense of humor.

And her letters of recommendation indicate that the students at Fordham really like her."

Herb addressed Dan, "And Joseph? Excuse me, José. How do the students at . . . is it Ithaca College? How are his evaluations there?"

"Top notch," Dan asserted, nodding. "His class on British Foreign Relations got rave reviews."

"Well," Herb began, "it sounds as if they both have their merits. What are their flaws?" When no one answered, he attempted humor with, "No flaws? None at all? C'mon, people, there's at least one crack in even the newest building and certainly so in young academics."

Mike coughed and placed his fingers on the edge of the table, looking down at them as he said, "Well, let's address the elephant in the room. We've been given these demands," he lifted the paper, "and the whole campus is watching us. We don't have a woman of color to bring in. I mean, there's not a qualified one in the pool and, ah, at least—" he closed his eyes and then said in a rush, "there's a man of color we can bring in."

Herb felt some sympathy for Mike, a young faculty member, clearly nervous speaking in front of George and Kathryn. George was retiring and would have no say in his tenure decision, but Kathryn might be mentally recording this moment to use against him in the future.

George shook his head, a flat smile on his face. "Nonsense. We bring in the most qualified candidates. This," he said, shaking the paper so it rattled, "is ridiculous. They want to demand something, let them go to the cafeteria and demand pizza. The students don't dictate to the faculty." He waved his hand as if he were throwing something. "Let them protest. So what? The ones who care about their grades will go to class and to hell with the rest of them."

Mike and Dan exchanged wide-eyed looks. They both started to speak, then stopped. Kathryn rose higher in her chair and took a deep breath, saying, "We do have to address the demands. The student paper will want a statement from the search committee. We have long-established procedures for bringing the most qualified candidates to campus. We would welcome a minority candidate, but he or she has to meet every criteria for hiring."

Sliding his arms forward on the table, Dan blurted, "Look, it's the third candidate. Chances are we're going to hire Kenneth or Sarah. Why can't we bring in José as our third? Make it look like we're at least trying."

"Trying to do what? George asked, "trying to meet the demands of foolish students? That makes us look foolish."

"Look, George, I don't think we should call them foolish, okay? I mean," Dan paused, and Herb wondered if he would back down, but the young man continued, "I don't want to be rude here, but we've taught British history forever, and, uh, always from the perspective of the Empire. I think we should give the students credit for wanting to learn history from the perspective of the oppressed classes."

Katherine clasped her hands and said quietly, "We don't know that Joseph, José, rather, Gutierrez teaches from the vantage of the oppressed. We shouldn't assume that from his name. Why, he might be insulted to know that *any* conclusion was being derived from his name."

Chuckling, George said, "If surnames are supposed to indicate that, why not bring in Patricia O'Neil? With a name like that, this woman might have a lot to say about British oppression." Lifting a yellow legal pad, he said, "Her dissertation is on the penal laws? Laws that prevented Catholics from owning land, going to school, earning a living. Who knows? Miss O'Neil's forebears may have starved to death during the potato famine. Isn't that oppression? The students throwing these demands around should recognize that."

"But, George," Dan said, "Patricia's not . . . you know, she's not . . . she's, well, she's—"

"*White*?" George laughed. "Well, why didn't you say so, Dan? Let's not beat around the bush. From what I've heard, the students behind these demands are also white. They've convinced themselves they've taken up some noble cause but they don't know their asses from their elbows."

Herb felt an involuntary smile tug at the corner of his mouth and pretended to cough. Was anyone here going to rescue Dan from George?

"This is a liberal arts college. We're supposed to encourage critical thinking," Dan said with more confidence. "Oppression is a major factor in the history of—"

"Wasn't oppression in its every possible form the reason for the Irish Diaspora?" George asked the room at large. "My forebears were English but, hell, I don't feel guilty eating potatoes."

Herb wrote down George's last remark so he'd remember to share it with Elizabeth. Kathryn made a point of looking at her watch. "My seminar meets in fifteen minutes. Let's wrap up. Patricia is more qualified but is she more deserving of a campus interview? In light of concerns brought to us by the student body, does José Gutierrez merit special consideration?" Kathryn looked about the group, saying, "When sensitive matters arise that question longstanding policies, as in this case, we look to the Dean for guidance. Kathryn sought his gaze and asked, "Herb, what do you direct us to do?"

Direct? When was he ever allowed to direct *anything?* The faculty normally rode herd over him. But now, now that they needed a scapegoat, suddenly they wanted his direction! The back of Herb's neck felt prickly and his suit jacket felt too heavy. He wanted to take it off but feared his underarms were stained with perspiration. *I didn't sign on for this!* he thought. *I was hired to manage the faculty, not to placate the students!* He felt hot, so hot. Water, he needed to feel it gliding down his throat. More than that, he wanted to plunge his whole body into cold water, to swim with complete absence of thought. Taking a deep breath, he announced, "Patricia O'Neil will be the third candidate. If none of the three are acceptable or available, we'll bring in Mr. Gutierrez. We're adjourned."

He walked briskly back to his office, stopping only to take a bunch of telephone messages from Mrs. Tribble. Closing his door, he dropped his briefcase and exhaled over and over. He felt unable to draw in one deep, long breath. He crouched in front of the aquarium. Opening his eyes as widely as possible, he felt himself becoming mesmerised by the tank's light, by the shimmering fish themselves. He took the entire lid off of the aquarium and set it carefully on the floor. Leaning over the tank, Herb whispered, "One, two, three," before plunging his face into the waiting water.

The front page of *The Hancock Herald* announced: *"Dean Shrilley Ignores Students' Demands!"* Miss Tribble had brought him the latest issue of the student paper as she did every Friday afternoon. The look on her face, her darting eyes and pressed lips, told him it was bad, very bad news. Scanning the front page, Herb first caught a highlighted quotation of the article in boldface print: *Professor Rector says the History department sought the Dean's guidance on the selection of candidates invited for campus interviews.* Damn, Kathryn! You sold me out! The story continued on the next page, and Herb found another highlighted passage, this one a quote from George: *I applaud Dean Shrilley for having the gumption to stand up to students who think they can kidnap academic freedom and hold it hostage.* Oh, no, Herb thought, his heart starting to bounce. This was much worse than he feared.

On the following page, students gave their reactions to Professor Winston's words. Herb's glasses slid down his nose and he poked them back into place. Surely one student, at least one, would show some understanding. Phrases leapt from the page: *Out of touch. Imperialist dinosaur. Old Guard.* But the worst was the last comment, the ominous, menacing statement: *I say we take Dean Shrilley hostage until he agrees to the wisdom of our demands!*

Herb felt swift, pulsing cramps in his lower abdomen. He had to go home. He needed the comfort of his own bathroom.

In the outer office, Mrs. Tribble asked, "Unscheduled meeting?" and he managed to nod. "Are you coming back this afternoon?" she called as he opened the door and fled into the corridor.

It was too bright when he left the building. It was after four o'clock, but the sun shone like it was noon. Herb wished he had a hat, sunglasses, anything to disguise himself. The students were lounging everywhere in Hancock Park, enjoying the warm weather. Herb stepped over a tangle of limbs, his head throbbing with whatever music was screaming through buzzing speakers. He took a large step sideways to avoid a crunch of students sitting on a blanket, and felt something other than grass beneath his foot.

"*Owww!* Hey, you stepped on me!"

Glancing at the speaker, Herb felt his heart constrict. He had stepped on the ankle of a bald girl. Was it her? "Sorry," he murmured and started to run. Mid-way through the park, he thought he spied the girl with the face piercings. Oh, merciless day! Sprinting, he didn't stop moving until he reached the edge of campus. His breath poured out of him over and over again. I'm never going back, he thought. Never.

Herb stayed inside his house the entire weekend despite Elizabeth's pleas to have dinner at the Hancock Inn on Saturday evening.

"Herb, you must show the students, the faculty, that you're not afraid of anything!"

But he was. On Sunday night, the thought of going to his office the next morning terrified him. He lay in bed with the covers over his head, not a moment's sleep the entire night. Elizabeth wanted to walk with him to the office but Herb refused. "You're not my mother taking me to school for the first day." But as he walked the three blocks to campus, Herb felt hopelessly alone. Most of the students were still asleep at this hour, but the quiet was eerie rather than comforting. The outer office was empty; Mrs. Tribble wouldn't be in for another twenty minutes. She was punctual, Herb had to admit that.

The fish! He'd abandoned them all weekend. Normally Herb was in the office every day, but it had been more than two days since he fed them. The robust goldfish seemed no worse for wear, although they ate now in a manic fashion, their fins pumping furiously as they gobbled the food. He watched them swim through and around the arches in their miniature buildings, and felt cheered. No matter what, he thought, the fish carry on. Sighing, he thought, so must we all.

He sat at his desk and commenced with the day's work. Reviewing his schedule, he was happy that he had no meetings scheduled this morning. Herb was behind in reviewing a proposal to add a faculty position to the Education department. He rummaged through his in-box and pulled the request out. Sighing, he grabbed his red pen and murmured, "That damn department is already over-staffed. Why do those people feel so entitled?"

When Mrs. Tribble brought in the first cup of coffee of the day, Herb was feeling positively gleeful about turning down this request which had clearly been thrown together at the last minute. He'd only have to read portions of it aloud to the Curriculum Committee to convince them that Education had no real need for more faculty. There! That was done. Now Herb could move on to composing a brief introduction for a speaker coming to campus later that week. Grabbing a legal pad, Herb felt energized; the morning was going well. Through the window, he could see that campus life looked as it should, students hurrying to classes as the bell in Hancock Tower chimed. His fears about student reprisals over the history interviews dissipated. They've probably already moved on to some other issue, he thought. Elizabeth was right; these things come and go.

Writing introductions for campus speakers was one of the few responsibilities Herb enjoyed. And what a gift that the woman's name was Thalia Bizo. Bizo! The Greek goddess who protected sea voyagers! Oh, this will be fun, Herb thought. He usually had to dig deep to find a connection with the classical world, but an environmentalist named Bizo? So easy. He picked up a pencil and began jotting notes about equating pollution to the sirens who lured sailors to their death.

A rumble of voices sounded through the window. Herb cocked his head to listen. A sentence was being repeated over and over by a chorus of voices. He thought he heard, *"Me, a seaman. Me, a seaman."* The chant grew louder and now sounded like, *"Me are seaman. Me are seaman."* Well, that's hardly grammatical, Herb thought. He swiveled in his chair and parted the curtains, astonished to see, how many? Fifty students? Seventy-five? They were crossing Hancock Park, their voices ringing and rising together, and Herb now understanding them to say, *"Meet our demands! Meet our demands! Meet our demands!"* Pulling the curtains shut, Herb swallowed and then pushed the button on the intercom.

"Yes?" Mrs. Tribble said as if nothing was amiss. Surely she heard the students. Was she deaf?

"Mrs. Tribble," Herb said and then stopped speaking because the distraction of *"Meet our demands! Meet our demands!"* was now pounding in his head. "Mrs. Tribble," he tried again, floundering for what to tell her. She should lock the outer office. Yes. And call campus security! But as he started to speak, the decible of the voices grew until the walls of his office resounded with *"MEET OUR DEMANDS! MEET OUR DEMANDS!"*

In her complacent voice, Mrs. Tribble said, "Dean Shrilley, there are students here to see you. Would you like to meet with them now or should I have them schedule an appointment?"

"Appointment!" Herb yelled into the intercom, "Appointment!"

"What did you say? I can't hear you, Dean. Oh, it seems the students would like to meet with you immediately. Is that all right?"

"MEET OUR DEMANDS! MEET OUR DEMANDS!"

There was no lock on Herb's door. How could he barricade himself? He could never move his oak desk across the floor. His chair was on wheels and therefore useless. What? What? His eyes fell on the aquarium.

He ran to the tank and put his hands on the edge of the Formica table. Positioning his feet behind his torso, he pushed until his lower back protested. "Herakles, give me strength!" It wouldn't budge. Well, if it won't push, then pull it, he thought, moving to the other side of the table, his hands gripping the underside of the table's edge. When he first tried to move, his feet slipped on the carpet. Finally, they found traction and the table began to inch across the floor.

He thought he heard a twist of the outer doorknob. Adrenaline rushed down and through him like a waterfall. With one last massive pull, he lodged the aquarium into place and took a step back. The fish were agitated;

they moved frenetically to the lowest depths of the tank and hid behind the buildings. The door to his office bumped against the tank, the metal knob hitting its back directly in its center. No! Kneeling in front of the tank, he whispered to his fish, "Achilles and his army are here. Our fate is one and the same." The water in the tank jumped as the doorknob slammed repeatedly against the aquarium in time to the syncopated chant: *"MEET O-UR DE-MANDS! MEET O-UR DE-MANDS!"*

He would later recall the sound as the doorknob shattered the back of the tank. It wasn't as loud as he had expected, and perhaps softer than his memory of breaking a neighbor's window with a ball when he was a child. But then came the fracturing sizzle of faultlines that rapidly traveled the panel of glass. Holding his breath, he watched as the entire back of the aquarium fell in jagged glass puzzle pieces to the floor between the skewed table and the now half-open door. The water gushed onto the carpet making a sound that reminded him of a toilet being flushed.

Students peered around the gaping door, stunned by the water and the glass, the table still restricting full entry. The chant softened, someone saying, "Hey, shut up back there! There's been an accident."

Accident? Herb thought. Accident? No, this wasn't an accident!

"Stop pushing!" a male voice yelled. "There's glass here! And a barricade."

Then Herb heard a female voice yell with disgust, "Ewwwww! I just stepped on a fish!"

Dropping to his knees, Herb crawled under the table and tried to locate his goldfish. "Water! Mrs. Tribble, get some water! Fill a coffee pot or something! Fill as many mugs as you can find. They're dying! They're dying!" Spying a tiny goldfish flopping, its gills desperately opening and closing, he scooped it up and set it in his cupped palm. The fish gave a final flip of its tail and lay still.

Lifting his head, he realized the bald Erinye was now at the head of the crowd. Wide-eyed, she had edged the door open farther and inched her way around it, slipping to her knees to be eye to eye with Herb under the table, like children playing house. She peered into his hand and asked, "Is it dead?"

"What do you *think!*" he hollered, moving his face so it was only an inch from hers. "Are you *happy* now? Now that you've destroyed private property? Now that you've taken a life!" He inhaled a mighty breath and blew each word into her face, "*Who* the *hell* do you people think you *are?*" He backed out from under the table and pulled it aside with a furious tug, leaving the bald girl scrabbling on her hands and knees amid the sharp glass.

With a roar, he lurched out the door toward the students. The crowd shifted backwards into the outer office.

"You think you have the right to ram down a door, destroy an expensive aquarium and *kill* fish?" He held up the goldfish by its tail. His stomach swelled as he took in a healthy raft of air. "Well, I've got news for you: *you don't!* If you don't like the way we hire around here," he slowed his speech, "get the helllll out!" He gestured with his thumb over his shoulder. "Leave! Transfer! Get the hell out of my office and the hell out of this school!"

A male voice at the back of the crowd said, "Hey, we have the right to protest."

"Who said that!" Herb walked until he was in the center of the crowd. "Who said that? You have the right to *peaceful* protest. There was nothing peaceful about this! You destroyed property! You killed fish! *Innocent* fish!" Recognizing a student directly in front of him, he said, "Mr. Morgan, isn't it? Aren't you on academic probation? And here you are busting into my office. I wonder what your parents would say about your *extracurricular* activities?"

The student lifted his arms and said, "Hey, man. I'm out of here. Just don't call my parents. Okay? I'm leaving."

"Hey, that's not fair," a boy in an maroon Oberlin College T-shirt said, "you're using intimidation to avoid addressing—"

"You don't like it? *Fine!* Go to Oberlin! In fact," Herb turned and waved his arm to take in the crowd, "why don't *all* of you go to Oberlin! Get out before I call the police and have you all arrested for vandalism."

Something flashed in the corner of his eye. Turning, he saw the girl with the pierced face, standing with her arms folded against her chest, a defiant gleam in her eyes. He pointed at her and said, "You're about as oppressed as the *queen of England!* Take your fake proletarianism and get lost!"

The door to the outer office opened and Mrs. Tribble entered with a glass vase filled with water. "It was the only thing I could find," she explained.

"Mrs. Tribble," he said as he took the vase and dropped the dead fish in the water, "if these students aren't out of here in sixty seconds, call the police." He walked back into his office and shut the door. Crawling on all fours on the soaked carpet and glass, he gathered three of the dead fish and put them in the vase. The other two he found motionless on the fake coral at the bottom of the tank. Staring at the dead fish floating on their sides in the vase, he couldn't deny that he was feeling something other than grief, something much more than sorrow for his little swimmers. In fact, he couldn't remember ever feeling better. He raised his fist over his head and thought, *You don't mess with Dean Shrilley!*

"All's well that ends well, that's what I always say."

"Indeed you do, Elizabeth. Do you want to see the article in the student paper?" Herb creased a page in the newspaper on his desk.

"No, I just stopped in to say hello. I'm meeting a couple friends for coffee at Bidwell's."

Herb nodded. "The ladies who lunch. It's a lovely day for a walk into town. I'm enjoying the breeze through the window."

Glancing at the paper, Elizabeth said, "Well, just tell me the gist of the article."

He cleared his throat and said, "Well, it's just a minor article tucked away on the fourth page. It says Kenneth Bohland has been hired following a series of campus interviews, et cetera. Oh, and the last sentence says, 'Students' plans to protest the hiring of any candidate not a woman of color were aborted.'"

"Aborted?" Elizabeth gave a laugh. "Well, that's an odd choice of words, isn't it?"

His eyebrows raised, Herb nodded. "I suppose so, but reporting in the student paper is uneven at best."

She shook her head with disapproval. "I still say those vandalizers should have been expelled. If there are no consequences, they might pillage again."

Smiling broadly, he said, "Not in this office." He laughed and shook his head.

"Well, aren't you in a good mood. Okay, dear, I'm off. Try not to be late tonight."

"I'll do my best. Say, I'd love something spicy for dinner."

"Spicy? It upsets your stomach so terribly."

Placing both palms on his abdomen, Herb said, "I feel great. How about chili?"

Elizabeth kissed his cheek and said doubtfully, "We'll see."

Alone in the office, Herb stared at the freshly washed carpet. There was no battle stain to mark the dead fish that he had buried in his backyard along with their minature world. And soon, Herb thought, there'll be no trace of me in this office. He had told no one, not even Elizabeth, that he planned to leave the Deanship and return to full-time teaching the next academic year. He would leave on a high note, in many ways, the highest of his career. He lifted his arms over his head and yawned happily. There was a knock at the door and he said, "Come in."

He looked up to see Mrs. Tribble in the doorway. She was smiling in an odd way, her hands behind her back.

"Well, Mrs. Tribble, don't you look like the cat who ate the canary."

She strode into the room as if she were walking in a processional. Reaching his desk, she said, "I have something for you." One of her arms came around and Herb saw a large glass paperweight containing a vivid turquoise fish. It's long, diaphonous fins were caught in a series of lovely angles.

"I know it's not much," Mrs. Tribble said, "but I thought it might help." She waited at his desk expectantly.

"Thank you, Mrs. Tribble. What a kind gesture."

"It's a beta. It was real. Well, it wasn't when they put the fish in the glass, but I mean, before that. It was real then."

Tilting his head, Herb looked at the paperweight, at the vibrant fish lodged dead center in the glass and said, "Yes. It really looks like it's swimming."

A LONELY VIRTUE

No matter what anyone says, it's the wives who run this town. I suspect this is true of most college towns, but it's definitely the lay of the land in Hancock. I should know. I'm the Dean's wife.

When we first came to Hancock in 1958, Herb was fresh out of Michigan with a PhD in classics and I was his bride. Twenty years later, he was pulled from the ranks to become Dean of Arts and Sciences. So I've been the Dean's wife for going on twelve years now. Herb is going to step down next year, return to teaching classics, and the town is buzzing as to who will replace him, as if anybody could. If I had my way, my husband would remain the Dean until he retired, but Herb misses teaching and writing, so what can I do?

Herb is a wonderful scholar and no one works harder than he does. When he was a faculty member, he served on every committee, attended every meeting, got his grades in early. He edited an important collection of papers on Herodotus (his introductory essay is widely cited), and had a hoard of student advisees. There's only one thing wrong with Herb, and that's Herb himself. He's a bit on the stiff side, not exactly a people person.

That's where I come in. I tease my husband that for all the entertaining I've done during the last twelve years, I should be a paid employee of the college. Who welcomes the new faculty members every year with a barbecue? Who plans a monthly faculty dinner with a rotating guest list everyone's dying to be on? Who greets people in the receiving line at homecoming, making enough chit chat to fill an ocean so no one notices Herb's silence? It's me, but that's not all I do. Not by a long shot.

Every speech Herb gives to the faculty is reviewed (and improved) by me. Well, I am a Radcliffe graduate with a degree in English. My writing skills are more honed than those of the composition professors, I assure you.

I also look over the agenda for each faculty meeting and anticipate who's going to say what and who's going to oppose what. I coach Herb, get him ready: "When you talk about faculty evaluations, don't let that windbag Sanders digress about the good old days when everyone was a family. Oh, and if Joe Koczyk tries to hold court about how they do merit raises at other institutions, suggest he go teach someplace else for a few years and then report back. That ought to get a few chuckles." Yes, it's a tremendous amount of work, but Hancock College is worth the effort.

A minor influence some might call me, but if they knew the full story, they'd be shocked. And impressed. Ask Sheila Martins, who had me to lunch seven times the year her husband, Ted, was up for tenure. That was cruel of me, I know, dipping my spoon into her sumptuous lobster bisque, all the while knowing I wasn't going to put in a good word to Herb. The thing was, Sheila was just too eager to be settled in Hancock, to preen around town as the wife of a tenured faculty member. You have to understand, in a college town such wives are the equivalent of homecoming queens. After they ascend the throne, they review and make judgments about the educational pedigrees of the incoming faculty men and their over-educated, unemployed wives. Compassion is a lonely virtue among the academic.

Now, Anne Siddons will be grateful to me for the rest of her days. Her husband's tenure case was wildly controversial. Ned had been refused tenure at Amherst before coming to Hancock, and it appeared as if the same thing were likely to happen here. It was his own fault. You can hardly get mediocre teaching evaluations year after year and think no one's going to notice. And there was talk about a tête-á-tête with a student that semester Anne was nursing her mother back east.

But I couldn't abandon Anne. After dining with us, she always wrote me a note thanking me for such a lovely evening. She complimented me on my outfits, remembered to get my son a gift when he graduated from high school. She would die before she missed my annual women's tea, always offering to write the place cards with her elegant script. Mind you, Anne had no illusions about her husband; she knew he wasn't top drawer, but she was determined not to have to move again, not to uproot Justin and Jason, her twin sons who were still in elementary school.

Anne never came right out and asked me to speak to Herb, but one dismal morning we met for coffee and she confessed to me that the Psychology department had split six to five on the tenure decision. She lamented that

Ned hadn't slept in two weeks. Well, what could I do? I placed my hand on hers and said, "People can be so cruel." She nodded, sniffling into a tissue, and continued, "I don't know what I'd do if I didn't have you to talk to. You're such a comfort, Liz." Unlike Sheila, Anne wasn't coming to me out of desperation, as a last ditch effort for a dying cause. Anne knew I had the power to get the job done. Getting her unexceptional husband tenure could be my final and greatest achievement as the Dean's wife.

When I first approached Herb about Ned's tenure, he said flatly, "Elizabeth, there's nothing I can do. I cannot tell the Tenure Committee to overlook the Psychology department's recommendation."

"But you can influence them!" I protested. "As soon as the committee realizes what you want, they'll do it. They always do."

"Elizabeth, personnel matters are confidential. Confidential." He went into the den and turned on the television. When Herb is watching *Jeopardy!*, anticipating questions on antiquities, even the threat of the faculty unionizing couldn't get him out of his easy chair.

Well, I had my work cut out for me. It was easy enough to find out who was on the Tenure Committee; lists of committee members are distributed each fall semester, and Herb keeps a copy in his study. The members of that year's committee appeared to be largely from the sciences, a pretty no-nonsense bunch, but, thankfully, Simon Rupple from the French department was included. His wife Elise and I were close friends, having arrived in Hancock the same year.

I called her one afternoon before Herb was home on the pretense of asking about her daughter, Ginny, a sophomore at Smith and about to celebrate her twentieth birthday.

"Oh, you don't have to send her anything," Elise said, "it's awfully considerate of you, but really—"

"But I want to! She's such a dear. I thought perhaps a cashmere sweater or a new purse. And of course, I want to send her a goody box full of cookies and brownies."

Elise was moved. "Liz, you're an angel. Ginny will be delighted with whatever you send. This is so kind of you."

Now, the tricky part, to segue into the real matter. "Well, it's nice to be involved with something pleasant. I've been trying to cheer up poor Anne Siddons but I'm afraid I'm not doing a very good job."

There was momentary silence on the other end but I knew Elise was dying to launch into the subject, to act concerned about someone having a bad time of it. "Oh?" she said. "Is Anne ill?"

I walked with the phone and looked out our front window for any sign of Herb. The coast was clear. "This whole tenure mess with Ned, it's just about killed Anne."

"Ohh," Elise said, "Ned's not going to get tenure? I forgot this was the year he was up." This was probably true. Her husband was not an important figure on campus; Simon's appointment on the Tenure Committee was no doubt as the token humanities person. I was always filling Elise in on campus politics.

"Yes, Ned's up this year. But his department has decided not to recommend him for tenure, and poor Anne can't bear the thought of starting over somewhere else. You know, this is Ned's second turn-down."

"Right. I remember now. Was it Williams that turned him down the first time?"

"Amherst."

"Amherst, that's right."

I could hear a bit of clanging in the background and I guessed that Elise was cooking while we chatted. I asked, "The little Siddons boys, do you know them? Justin and Jason?"

"Yes, they're so adorable. Ten years old and they still dress alike."

I wondered if Elise really did find them adorable; I remembered them as screaming brats at the Memorial Day college picnic. Still I said, "They're cherubs, both of them. And so happy in Hancock. It would be a shame if Ned had to drag them off to God knows where. No one's going to be clamoring to get him after two negative tenure decisions."

"Thank God we got to raise our children here, huh, Liz? Of course, there was never any doubt that Simon and Herb were going to get tenure."

I tapped my fingernail against the phone. "Yes. But times were different then. There wasn't as much . . . backstabbing."

"Backstabbing?"

"Yes." I lowered my voice although I was alone in the house. There was absolute quiet on the other end of the phone as Elise anticipated my next remarks. "From what I understand, there's someone in the Psychology department. A woman. Anne thinks, well, I can't say for sure, but I gather Ned told her that this woman is poisoning everyone against him."

I heard Elise's quick intake of breath, one of her trademarks. "That's terrible!" she cried.

"Yes, her name is Helen Leep. Do you know her?"

"Helen Leep, Helen Leep. That doesn't sound familiar. Who's her husband? Do they have the same last name?"

Vaguely, I heard a car motor pass our house, but when I looked out the window, it was just our neighbor down the street. "She's not married," I told Elise.

"Oh, one of *those*."

"Yes, the number's up to nine now."

Elise sighed impatiently. "Can you imagine coming to this little town alone? I mean, what do those women do when they're not teaching?"

"Steal husbands. Ask Cindy Harper," I answered breezily, referring to last year's scandal. Ken Harper hasn't been invited to our house since.

"Is Helen Leep on the prowl?" Elise asked quickly.

"I've heard that she wants the department to hire another woman, and the only way that can happen is if Ned's bounced."

"*Ahh*, so she wants more single women in town."

"Strength in numbers. And it seems the ends justify the means."

"What do you mean?"

I swallowed, wondering whether I had the nerve to say what I'd deduced from Anne's conversation. It was reading between the lines, yes, but it couldn't be far from the truth. "Well, mind you, this is all rumor so take it with a *huge* grain of salt."

"I understand. Tell me," Elise implored.

Pausing for emphasis, I whispered, "Well, I know you're the soul of discretion Elise, so I'll tell you. The word is she made some . . . overtures to Ned that were rejected."

Holding the phone an inch away from my head to protect it from the small scream at the other end, I continued, "And then this Helen Leep attacked Ned on every front; she criticized his collegiality, his teaching, his research, his committee work. By the time she was done, the department surrendered."

Stunned silence is one thing, but Elise was wordless for so long I worried. Finally, she said, "This is an outrage. An outrage. *Who* does this woman think she is?"

Relaxing, I joked, "Helen of Troy. Able to get the Psychology department to take up arms for her."

"Well, it's the most despicable thing I've ever heard."

"Now remember, you didn't hear this from me, Elise. In fact, I can't even remember who first told me about all this, but apparently it's all over town."

"Oh, don't worry. I won't say a word. But it's just the most awful thing."

I heard a car door slam and this time it was Herb. "I agree. But let's talk about happier things. Now, what size sweater is Ginny?"

Elise couldn't keep a secret if her life depended on it, thank God. By the time she was done spreading the news, every faculty wife in Hancock wanted to take out a contract on Helen Leep's life. Their husbands got an earful and I wasn't surprised when I heard that the Tenure Committee asked the Psychology department to reconsider their recommendation, and they voted to give Ned tenure after all.

I couldn't talk openly about it, but I had brought the whole thing off. Anne and I never discussed Ned's tenure again, but she sent me a five-pound box of Godiva chocolates with a little note that said, "To the sweetest woman I know. Enjoy!"

Helen Leep. Yes, I did feel some small needling of guilt, but then I asked myself why? The woman already had tenure; no real harm was done to her. And besides, I detested the woman.

She had arrived in Hancock with a huge chip on her shoulder, letting everybody know that she would have preferred to be at a university instead of a liberal arts college. At the new faculty barbecue, you could hear her voice over all the others droning, "The library here is pitiful. It's positively rinky dink. I don't know how anyone expects us to do research. And to think I had Stanford's libraries at my fingertips."

Clearly, the woman was not the team player Hancock College needs. She ambled around our backyard, flicking her cigarette ashes on my tulip beds, a flume of smoke trailing her. Yes, she was attractive in a certain bohemian sense, with her sandals and paisley skirt. Like most of the female professors, she didn't wear makeup, but her eyes were arresting, alarming actually, those turquoise ovals outlined with black lashes that whipped back almost to her eyebrows. She scanned the trays of my famous marinated shish-kebobs with disapproval and asked, "No vegetarian entrée?" Who knew smokers were vegetarians?

In the receiving line at homecoming that year, she told Herb that she was going to make an appointment with him to discuss concerns of the junior women faculty. "I'm their designated representative," she informed him while the line behind her lengthened. "We have a number of issues we'd like to address."

Poor Herb. He just nodded and smiled and said something like, "Call my secretary." I was prepared to simply shake the woman's hand and mumble a brief, "Good evening," but she didn't even bother to stop in front of me. As far as she was concerned, I was just window dressing.

Over the next years, I observed Helen Leep making inroads on campus. She chaired the Women's Studies committee and was brought up for tenure a year early. "A shoe-in," Herb told me one night at dinner while I grilled him about that year's nominees. "Her research is cutting edge. She's a real star."

Not in my book. We dutifully invited her to the dinner honoring the newly tenured faculty, a Hancock tradition, but she couldn't make it. She didn't call or drop me a note; she simply emailed Herb that she'd be out of town presenting a paper at some conference. In the years since, she's never shown me the slightest consideration.

I hoped that Ned's tenure would rile Helen enough that she'd leave Hancock, go be a star on some other campus. But, truth to tell, I don't even know if she voted for or against Ned. Anyway, she stayed in town, which probably meant that the gossip about her overtures hadn't reached her. Unfortunately, Ned proved all of his detractors correct. Psychology students knocked on Herb's door and complained about their professor who was always unprepared for class and unavailable during his posted office hours.

One night as Herb and I ate dinner at the Hancock Inn, we were approached by Phil Epstein, chair of the Student Life committee of which Ned was a member. He sat down at our table and proceeded to rant at Herb: "How the hell did Siddons get tenure? That guy was bad news from day one."

Herb set his knife on his plate and dabbed at his mouth with his napkin. "Phil, everyone's got their opinions—"

"We haven't gotten a damn thing done on Student Life this year because Siddons gets everyone off track with the stupidest, most irrelevant garbage. He's a loose cannon. You never know what he's going to come up with. Last Wednesday, we had a two hour meeting and got nothing accomplished because he kept trying to convince us to suspend meetings during the summer." Phil wiped his brow with his hand and exhaled like he had just finished some excruciating physical labor. "Everyone's complaining to me, like it's my fault the guy's still around."

Phil's voice rose louder and I noticed some of the other diners surreptitiously glancing our way. Debbie Mazur, wife of Ben Mazur in Sociology, was all but taking notes.

"I don't think this is the time or place—" I began, but Phil slapped his hand heavily on the table, causing the ice in our water glasses to rattle. "Either Siddons gets taken off the committee or I'm resigning as chair."

A fool's statement. I won't let Herb take ultimatums from anybody, except me. Phil didn't know he had shot himself in the foot, but I was already mentally erasing him and his wife, Edith, from the bridge club that met at our house on the first Friday of every month. And I would talk to my husband about reappointing a more suitable chair for the committee before Phil had a chance to grandstand by resigning.

Herb said, "Phil, why don't you drop in my office on Monday and we can discuss your concerns?"

"I've said everything I want to say. It's Siddons or me." As Phil walked back to his table, I smiled and beckoned to the waitress for coffee. I didn't want any but it was important to let the gawkers know that we hadn't been affected by Phil's bad manners, not one little bit.

But I watched as Herb looked forlornly at his half-eaten cheesecake. That little encounter had taken away his appetite.

"Eat up, honey. You don't want the chef to think you didn't like it." After the waitress filled my cup and left the table, I said, "You know, Herb, I'm glad you only have a few more months as Dean. Let someone else know what it's like to try and please all of the people all of the time."

He picked up his fork and dove it into his dessert. "You're right. It is going to be such a pleasure to just teach, to just be a regular faculty member."

I poured cream into my coffee, but it curdled, nasty little islands of white marring the black liquid. Pushing the cup and saucer away from me, I asked, "So who's the latest favorite for the job?"

"Could be Phil," Herb said simply, glancing across the dining room.

My fingers involuntarily began to claw the napkin on my lap. "You're not serious!"

Herb chuckled, pleased to have fooled me. "Nah," he said, eating the cheesecake more vigorously. "Helen Leep's the lead runner."

There was nothing I could do, nothing at all. Oh, I did try to caution Herb one night as we lay side by side in bed reading our books. As I turned a page, I said as nonchalantly as I could, "Isn't Helen Leep the one who tried to sabotage poor Ned Siddons a while back? You'd think the search committee would be concerned about that."

Herb grunted something incoherent and kept reading some new translation of Homer.

"Herb? Are you listening?"

Slapping his book shut, he took off his glasses and set them on his nightstand. "That's probably why everybody likes Helen. Siddons is such an asshole." He slumped down beneath the covers and within a minute was asleep, snoring with that little whistle that would be endearing if it weren't so jolting. As I wedged each earplug into place and fastened my mask over my eyes, I wondered if it wasn't too late to start singing the praises of another faculty member, a more appropriate person for the job of Dean. I owed the college that, to ensure that all of Herb's hard work wasn't squandered by Helen and her radical ideas.

Yawning, I mentally reviewed the faculty roster with an eye for Herb's worthiest successor. Why, Jeff Hogarty in Philosophy was a peach, very open to suggestions. And he was married; the Deanship was a two-person job to be sure. His wife was this timid little thing with a stammer who always deferred to me at meetings of the Hancock Women's Association. She would see the importance of continuing all the traditions I'd begun. Why, the Hogartys would be perfect, just perfect.

The next day I tried to come up with a plan but spent the day staring at a blank sheet of paper. Then Herb came home and announced, "Well, it's all but official. The trustees were bowled over by Helen Leep. As of July first, I'm out of that office for good."

"They've decided already?" I asked.

"Yup."

"Isn't this a bit rash? There might be other worthy candidates—"

"Who cares! It's over." Grinning like a bobcat, Herb poured himself a double Scotch and retreated to his study.

Two days later, I stared at a large picture of Helen Leep on the front page of the campus newspaper. The caption read, "Dean Leep has plans to revitalize the faculty." It was the end of an era.

I knew it was time to cut my losses, take a new perspective on things. Resilience is my middle name. Poor Helen was going to need a lot of help, a lot of advice and support. She had no spouse with whom to share responsibilities. Helen was a lamb in the wilderness with no idea of the scope of her job, and I was the one who could *best* brief her. Yes, Herb could orient her regarding academic responsibilities, but I would take her under my wing and explain all of the social obligations she would be performing. I would see her through her first homecoming reception, advise her on guest lists for her monthly faculty dinners, and, perhaps, give her a word or two about whom to listen to and whom to avoid when it came to significant college matters.

The next morning, filled with an almost beatific resolve to assist Helen, I cut a bountiful bouquet of azaleas from the garden and walked to campus. The Psychology department was on the second floor of Elsford Hall; I followed the wide corridor along until I found the door with her name. I knocked and heard the ungracious reply, "Yes?" Be nice, I reminded myself, and opened the door.

There I was stepping into her office with my hands full of flowers. Something momentous was taking place, a changing of the guard so to speak, and I felt myself become excited with my new role of mentor. I seated myself in front of Helen's desk and opened with, "Hard at work, I see."

She glanced down at the papers on her desk and nodded.

"Oh," I said, placing the flowers gently on her desk, "these are for you. Congratulations on the new job."

She stared at the flowers, a puzzled look on her face. "Thank you," she said slowly. She looked at me in such an odd way that I couldn't bring myself to say, "You're welcome." I searched her eyes, those alarming turquoise eyes, but I couldn't find the slightest hint of jest or sarcasm when she said, with more sincerity than I could bear, "Excuse me, but do I know you?"

What? I stood and extended my hand, "Elizabeth Shrilley, Dean Shrilley's wife."

Raising her hand, Helen stopped short of shaking mine, saying, "Ahhh. Herb's wife." She let her hand drop to her desk. "I've been expecting you. Please sit down."

At least the woman had a modicum of decorum. She glanced at the azaleas and said, "The flowers threw me. The wife doesn't usually bring the other woman flowers. And such lovely ones at that. I don't know much about flowers. What kind are these?"

How could any person be so stupid as to not recognize azaleas? And what nonsense was she spouting? My mind raced as I tried to review her words. "Azaleas! They're azaleas!" I said.

Nodding, she repeated, "Azaleas. Herb has brought me roses but never azaleas."

Did she say Herb brought her roses? "Roses!" Admittedly, my voice had risen.

I realized too late that her window was open, that anyone passing by might hear me. This woman with her impossible eyes lasering right through me was laughing, laughing at me. I jumped to my feet.

Rising slowly, still laughing, Helen said, "Kidding. Kidding. I'm just joking. Please, sit. It's time we talked."

Why, this creature wasn't fit to be Dean of Hancock or any other college! Helen needed more than social mentoring; she needed lessons in human decency. I placed both of my hands flat on her desk and said, "Why ever would you *joke* about a person's *marriage?* Why would you make that innuendo? Not that I believed you, not for a moment." I smoothed the front of my skirt and rested my hands on my knees.

Tilting her head, Helen chuckled inwardly. "I was surprised at how seriously you *did* take me. Rest assured, Herb's not my type." She set down her pen and said quietly, "And Ned Siddons's not my type either."

Pushing back my shoulders, I sat up taller in the chair. "I'm sure I don't know what you're talking about." So, the future Dean was a woman who listened to hearsay. Well, let's be honest, all administrators do but they should never disclose that.

Helen picked up her pen and began to tap it against her mug of coffee. In an absent tone, she said, "You don't know what I'm talking about." *Tap, tap, tap* with her pen.

I took in a quick breath of air and answered, "I assure you, I do not." *Tap, tap, tap, tap.* The sound was too annoying. *Tap, tap, tap.* I would have to scream if she didn't stop. As if reading my mind, Helen set the pen down. I exhaled with relief and felt ready for her next statement. But she picked up her pen again and the stop-start noise resumed but this time more loudly: *TAP—TAP—TAP—TAP—TAP.*

"It isn't easy being the Dean's wife, you know!" The tapping stopped. Feeling my eyes begin to mist, I searched my purse for a handkerchief but didn't find one. "Everyone expects something of you. You never know if someone really likes you, if she wants to be your friend, or if she just wants something out of you." I erupted into tears, so many tears. I hadn't cried like this since I was in college myself and kept out of Phi Beta Kappa on a technicality. "It's so tiring!" I said. "Oh, sure, the status is nice, but there are times, I assure you, there are times when I've wondered if it's worth it." Lifting my hands, I let them drop to my lap. "I'm just so tired. So very tired." And I was. I ached for my bed, to crawl between the sheets and sleep for eternity.

Standing, Helen produced a batch of tissues from a drawer and handed them to me. She said quietly, "I'm sure you are tired. You've been the Dean's wife for a very long time."

I nodded. "That's true." Looking at Helen, did I see a glimmer of understanding in her eyes? "Herb is the longest serving dean in the history of Hancock College."

Helen closed her eyes briefly and said, "I'm sure I'll learn that there are unsavory aspects to the job." She paused and waited for me to return her gaze. I rested my eyes on hers and she said, "There may be times when I have to do something that pains me but I have to do it for the good of the college."

I lowered my eyes and swallowed. "Yes. That's true." I clasped my hands together to keep them from trembling. Looking up, I said, "Herb has gone through some, well, some very difficult times." I spoke very softly, saying, "On occasion, the rarest of occasion, mind you, one has to engage in, well, in activities that one is not proud of."

"I know." She paused for a few seconds and said, "I imagine you've given him a lot of . . . help. I imagine you've given him quite a bit of help."

"Oh, if you knew the *half* of it! I've written speeches for Herb and made him rehearse them until he memorized them. *And,* I taught him how to make his words sound spontaneous, like he was just pulling brilliant thoughts out of the air. And Herb's not a thespian, believe me. That took work."

"Is that so?" Helen asked in such a way that made me think I'd revealed too much. But then she said, "You know, his address to the trustees last October was terrific. It struck just the right tone between modesty and sanctimony."

"Did you like it?" I moved to the edge of the chair. "I came up with the idea of using a star to illustrate the five goals for the coming year."

Nodding, Helen said, "That was very effective. And the way he shot down their proposal to allow Burrell College students to take classes at Hancock. The Trojan horse analogy, you came up with that?"

I bit my lip and admitted, "That was all Herb. I try to keep his classic metaphors to a minimum, but he can be impossible. Herb sees everything in terms of antiquities."

Nodding, Helen said, "I've noticed that. Say, let me ask you something, Elizabeth."

"Anything." She was being so kind. Yes, I would do anything I could for her.

Helen looked at the flowers as if she were seeing them for the first time. "I'm already hearing word of a grounds renewal program. The trustees want to spruce up the place. It's the type of thing I have no talent for." She actually giggled and said, "And I really don't care what the place looks like as long as Hancock moves up in the academic ratings. Before the grounds crew goes crazy planting shrubs and flowers with abandon, I'd like them to speak with people who have lived in Hancock a while. Get their opinions on what and where to plant, how to play up the college's history in the landscape, that type of thing. Would you be interested in heading up a committee?"

"Oh, I have so many ideas!" I had walked this campus, every inch of it, for years. I knew where the direct sunlight fell, what corners were always in shadow. "You know, for a brief time in the 1890's, Hancock published a literary quarterly called *The Daffodil*. Our school colors, the yellow and blue? Well, the yellow dates back to that. Students used to have an annual picnic in the lower grove when the daffodils were in bloom."

Helen stood and walked around her desk. "That's *exactly* the type of thing I'm talking about. Clearly you're the perfect person for the job."

"The day of the picnic was known as Daffodil Day. In fact, several students became engaged on Daffodil Day. Graduating seniors, the men, popped the question to their sweethearts at the picnic."

Helen offered her hand to guide me up from my chair. "Fascinating," she said. "So it's a yes? You'll head the committee?"

I set my hand on hers and gave it a reassuring squeeze. "You can count on me. I won't let you down."

"Great. Don't mention this to anyone just yet. I have to get the funding in order."

As we walked to the door, I told Helen, "I love a challenge. I'll start drawing up plans tonight." We said our good-byes and I stepped into the corridor, hearing the click of the lock being turned behind me. No doubt Helen needed to call the relevant people to tell them of my assignment, and wanted privacy. Good. She was showing discretion. No doubt, a formal announcement of my heading up the landscape project would be made at a future faculty meeting. Walking down the hall, my mind was positively buzzing with ideas. I would make the campus come alive in a rainbow of blossoms, turn the upper grove into an enchanted forest, plant daffodils completely around the clock tower. It would all be photographed and documented in a commemorative book that could be sold in the campus store. My first publication! Oh, I couldn't wait to tell Herb all about it. This new Dean, well, she really had her head on straight.

EMERITUS

For more than two weeks Professor William Harris had failed to finish his scholarly reading by mid-afternoon. Today, he slapped shut the current issue of *Daedalus* and pushed his chair back from his carefully arranged desk. The time has come, he told himself, to have a little chat with the students about all that racket.

Walking to the window in his study, William separated the old lace curtains and peered into the yard of the neighboring house, a large, dilapidated Victorian rented by college students.

"One, two, three, four, five, six," William said aloud, counting the students jumping and shouting on an old trampoline that Hancock College had probably sold for a song at last month's auction. Although it was late October, the students were barefoot. Now they joined hands and began to circle the interlocked canvas, singing, "Ring around the rosie . . ." William chuckled. College students are just children after all, he concluded, easy enough to handle. Some of those young whippersnappers teaching nowadays ought to realize that.

Although retired for five years, William faithfully attended biweekly faculty meetings. He composed speeches beforehand on any number of academic issues: the honor code, proficiency requirements, student retention, and lack of parking spaces on campus. He strived for eloquence, rehearsing and rehearsing in a way he hadn't had time to when he was still employed by the college. The silence, the profound silence that seized the room after he spoke pleased him. He felt himself an elder statesman, worthy of the title, *Professor Emeritus*.

He let the curtains fall and readied himself to go next door. As he slipped a scarf around his neck, he recalled that whenever his wife Lila, dead now for eight years, went to talk to the students about keeping the noise down, she brought them freshly baked muffins. Opening the door with a swift movement, William said aloud, "It's not necessary to bribe students. Just show them the consequences of their actions and they'll come around." Occasionally Professor Harris admitted to himself that he didn't miss Lila so much as he did her ear. She was his audience when he wasn't in front of the classroom. Professors, *real* professors, William believed, had a need to lecture. During those long summer months when school wasn't in session, William might have gone mad were it not for Lila. She nodded and smiled at him as he strode about the yard discussing his plans to create a true English garden and she listened attentively as he instructed her on gastronomic matters over dinner.

The students didn't see him as William approached. "I didn't know there were off-campus physical education classes," he quipped as he placed his hands on the frame of the trampoline.

One of the girls stopped bouncing and looked at him. "Oh, hi Professor Harris!" She wore what appeared to be a man's undershirt, the sleeves rolled high to reveal a rose tattoo just beneath her shoulder. "You guys," she said, lightly hitting the boy on her right who was still bouncing, "quit it! Professor Harris is here."

Satisfied he had the group's attention, William repeated, "I didn't know there were off-campus physical education classes." He didn't hear one of the boys grumble, "Well, now you know."

The girl who had greeted him laughed, as he expected they all would, and said, "I wish we could get academic credit for this. But we're just horsing around." She began to jump, pointing her toes downwards as she lifted herself into the air. "It's so much fun. Want to give it a try?"

"No, Miss, no. Thank you for the offer—"

"You're as young as you feel!" A young man wearing a purple bandanna on his head threw his legs out from under him and bounced in a seated position. "This is totally awesome!"

William nodded, a tight smile all he could muster. "Yes, I'm sure that's true. But my time is best spent improving my mind. As I've mentioned to you on previous occasions," he said, turning towards his house, "my study faces—"

"Pete Stirwell jumped with us for half an hour yesterday," the boy continued.

"He even did a flip!" The girl speaking had a large silver earring pierced through her lower lip. William recoiled, lowering his eyes to his hands.

"Yeah, come on up and try it Professor Harris," the boy in the bandanna said. "Don't let Pete show you up."

Now William looked at the taut canvas and wondered if it could support yet another person. "Professor Stirwell is a younger man than I am," he tried to joke, but it sounded like a protest.

"We'll help you up," the girl with the lip ring said, and before he knew it, William was stomach down on the trampoline, his pocket watch pressed uncomfortably into his ribs. He managed to get himself onto all fours, waiting until the canvas seemed steady, before he stood up. Once on his feet, he immediately upset himself and several of the students. As they fell on him, they laughed and he pretended to be amused.

"Isn't it fun?" a girl with a bare midriff asked him, one of her legs wrapped over his knee.

"In my day, a brisk game of rugby was the thing," he said, wondering how he could untangle himself from the co-ed.

The boy in the bandanna crawled from the heap and said, "Thank God those days are gone."

Managing to sit up, William said, "Gone, but not forgotten. Now, if one of you young men will kindly assist me, I'll make my exit."

Professor Harris was thankful that there was still one establishment in town where he could order a civilized cup of tea. Most of the eateries were over-run with students drinking harshly fragrant coffee from green and white plastic "earth mugs." At Bidwell's, you could still order a cup of Earl Gray and be served your tea in a stoneware cup and saucer; it wasn't china, but at least it wasn't plastic or, God forbid, a Styrofoam cup. The raisin scones had been prepared the same way since William could remember, and he didn't object that they were occasionally stale as long as the butter was fresh and the jam preserves abundant. Lila used to acknowledge his sweet tooth with all sorts of cakes and cookies, but now he made do with a daily stop at Bidwell's.

He put a single scoop of sugar into his tea, stirring the demi-tasse spoon quietly. This was his usual table, a small one by the front window that allowed him to watch the parade of college town life. Blowing the steam over his cup, he peered out the glass with approval as he watched the students walking past with backpacks on their way to class. The bell from Hancock Tower chimed twice, signaling the start of second period. Two male students shuffled along the sidewalk. One wore a set of headphones that he removed and offered to his companion who slipped them under his chin and over his ears. The lad closed his eyes and nodded his head rhythmically. He didn't hear when Professor Harris tapped the glass, but his friend did, looking quizzically at the older man. The Professor pointed at his watch and then to the main classroom building which sat in the southwest quadrant of Hancock Park. "Don't be late for class!" he shouted to be heard through the window and felt satisfied when the two appeared to walk quickly away from the window.

William always sorted his mail while drinking his morning tea. He removed it from his ever-present briefcase, a Coach bag in their lovely British tan leather. Today's bundle of envelopes was mostly bills: utilities, telephone, sewer. He sighed mightily. Such mundane matters shouldn't consume the scholar's time, and he again thought, Lila, dear Lila, these were your responsibilities, not mine.

He looked about for his waitress. His tea was getting cold and he wanted his hot water replenished. But then he saw that she was opening the door for a hunched, emaciated form moving with agonizing caution.

"Professor Vecchio!" the waitress exclaimed, "how nice to see you! Come in, come in." She slipped her arm through his and walked with him to the table nearest the door. "Give me your hat and cane and I'll put them right here for you." She hung both items on the wooden hooks behind his table. The older gentleman murmured thanks, William supposed; he could barely hear the older man's voice across the few feet from where he sat.

"Cappuccino?" the waitress asked, expecting an affirmative response. She walked quickly to the kitchen, ignoring William's outstretched finger. *Cappuccino,* he thought disdainfully. Old Vecchio will never let the world forget that he's Italian, the Dante scholar who directed the study abroad program in Florence. Although the tiny man was in his mid-eighties and, it was said with great pathos, rapidly declining health, he still commanded the greatest respect from not only college employees, but from the town residents as well. He had been awarded the "Professor of the Year" award more than any other teacher at Hancock College, and an alumna had established an enormous scholarship in his name.

All a bit much, William believed, for a man who had done so little for the college after he retired. Instead of remaining in the mainstream of college life, offering the benefit of his history with the institution to younger faculty members, Professor Vecchio had moved to Florence for ten years before returning to Hancock where his homecoming merited a special issue of the campus newspaper, *The Hancock Herald*. Previous students wrote letters of welcome filled with classroom anecdotes about inspired, often hilarious, discussions on *The Divine Comedy*. A colleague in Romance Languages recounted Professor Vecchio pouring half a cup of coffee back into the pot in the faculty lounge when he discovered he only had half the cost to drop into the "honor cup." He was honest, humane, a scholar of the highest caliber, the letters touted, a kind, modest man who often pronounced how lucky he was to make a living at what he simply loved to do: teach. He remained a bachelor all his days, eating every meal in town where the proprietors remarked on his friendliness, his generosity with tips, his invitations to them to attend his public lectures.

And now here was Emma Bidwell herself, rarely seen out of the restaurant's kitchen, bringing the old man his cappuccino, stating in a booming voice so he could hear her, "I MADE THESE AMARETTO COOKIES HOPING YOU WOULD STOP IN AND SEE US THIS WEEK, PROFESSOR. WE'VE MISSED YOU." She stood next to him chatting for several minutes, pretending not to notice when his upper dentures slipped and he had to cup his hand over his mouth.

When William finally got his waitress's attention, she abruptly asked, "Something else?" When she returned with the small pewter pot of water, he said, "I'm Professor William Harris. And you are?" He inclined his head.

"Bunny. Bunny Rafferty."

"Well, Bunny, it's a pleasure to meet you. Have you worked here long?"

She gave him an incredulous look and finally answered, "Three years."

"Oh, that long? And tell me, how do you like it?" He fixed his eyes directly on hers so that she could see she had his full attention, only then realizing that her right eye was badly crossed, rolling towards her nose like a heavy marble.

"It's a living," she answered as she left him at his table.

He glanced over at Vecchio, the old man gnawing at a small cookie with all the grace of a gerbil.

Was the college really in such dire financial straits that it could no longer afford refreshments at faculty meetings? Not even an urn of coffee was set up at the back of the room. In the old days, a variety of beverages and sweet rolls were always present. William debated whether this would be an appropriate topic for discussion as he took his seat in the front row of the lecture hall. And whatever happened to the faculty sherry hour on Friday afternoons? Another casualty to faulty fiscal planning, no doubt. How would I discuss that? William mused. "If refined customs are lost, all is lost," he imagined himself saying. Perhaps he would include something about fine spirits easing the free exchange of ideas amongst the faculty.

Herb Shrilley, Dean of Arts and Sciences, was seated at the center of the long table at the front of the room. Next to him, Alan Shilton, the secretary of the college, was thumbing through a worn copy of *Robert's Rules of Order*. The president of the college, Wyatt Reynolds, was on a fund raising trip out of town. William heard the murmurs behind him as more faculty members entered the room. Repeatedly, he glanced at his watch, and tried to make eye contact with Herb. Faculty meetings were supposed to begin promptly at four o'clock regardless of who was present or absent. William discreetly turned to survey the seats behind him; there were so many faces he didn't recognize, faculty on visiting appointments, junior faculty, even tenured faculty he couldn't name. He was disappointed that so few senior members of the faculty bothered to attend meetings. Their historical perspective was invaluable. Vision and leadership, William thought, that's what's lacking here.

At nine minutes after four, Herb said, "Let's come to order." The conversational din behind William subsided until the room was silent except for the shuffling of paper and occasional coughs. Herb continued, "Any questions or comments regarding the minutes of our last meeting?" After a brief silent pause, he said, "I move the minutes be approved. Seconded?"

"Seconded," William answered loudly and slowly, out of unison with those who also responded.

"Any announcements?" asked Herb. "Yes, Joan?"

William heard a strident female voice directly behind him fairly shout, "The Multicultural Curricular Committee is holding a faculty sensitivity workshop on Saturday, November 9th. At present, only six people have signed up. This is a travesty given the importance of this issue. The committee urges each academic department to send at least *one*," she raised her finger, "designated representative to the workshop. That person should then report back to his or her department on what was covered." The woman stopped speaking, but then added hurriedly, "Registration forms are available from each departmental secretary."

Herb nodded and scanned the audience. "Any other announcements?"

Surely someone will stand and question the merits of a sensitivity workshop? William was reminded of a strange movement towards openness and candor that took place on campus in 1970 or so. People sat in a circle at faculty meetings and "rapped" about whatever was on their minds. There was no formal agenda and nothing ever got accomplished. Well, that didn't last, William thought, and no doubt this multicultural stuff wouldn't either.

"We have only one agenda item today," Herb said, "and that is whether to cancel classes next year and the following years on Yom Kippur. We've had some discussion on this in the past, but several of you have asked that we address it again. In particular, Ben Jackson in the English department would like to speak to this." Herb looked into the middle of the audience and said, "Ben, the floor is yours."

Craning his neck to see the man, William gave up and turned to sit sideways in his chair. Ben Jackson, Ben Jackson, he thought; no, never heard of him. Obviously Ben was one of the new recruits, William decided, after noting that the speaker was wearing khaki slacks and a solid bright blue shirt. There was a time when no one, not even the newest faculty member, dared enter this room without a jacket and tie.

"Here's the thing," Ben said, both his hands plunged into his pockets, "every year students complain that we hold classes on Yom Kippur. Many students would like to go home and observe this holy day with their families or simply have the opportunity to observe it on campus. There have been two articles about it in the student newspaper in the last month. I don't think this issue is going to go away. I think we have to deal with it." The speaker shrugged his shoulders as if to say, "that's all," and sat down.

"Thank you, Ben," Herb said. "Let's open the issue for discussion. Yes, Peter Fallin, I thought you'd have something to say."

There were a few chuckles as Peter Fallin, a member of the Physics department stood. He was a bone-thin man with wispy gray hair combed back from his forehead. His face was empty of color except for his heavy black-framed glasses. The knot of his thin brown tie was pulled into a tight triangle.

"We've been through this over and over," Peter said wearily, "and I see no need to drag old stuff out of the closet just because a few students are making a lot of noise. The science departments simply cannot give up any more lab time. We're down one lab already because we're off the Friday after Thanksgiving. At this rate, we'll be shutting down for Groundhog's Day, Valentine's Day, who knows what else." He lifted his hands up and down in front of his chest, an imploring gesture. "Once and for all," he spoke with more volume, "we simply can't afford to lose another lab."

The discussion continued for thirty-five minutes. The scientists were accused of not understanding the religious significance of Yom Kippur, while they countered that the humanities faculty couldn't fathom the importance of biology, chemistry and physics labs.

William was forlorn. In his day, no one discussed a person's religion, and certainly it was not considered an academic matter. He listened carefully, hoping that someone's remarks would give him an opening for a witty response, something to make the group laugh, make them realize that this was hardly an appropriate matter for discussion. But in the end, Herb referred the issue to the Religious Life committee. "Bring us a recommendation as soon as possible," he said.

Herb looked hopefully at his audience. "Unless there's any new business, we can adjourn." Sighing audibly, his hand covering his forehead, he said, "Yes, Ned, what is it?"

Ned Siddons, a member of the Psychology department, rose from his seat and stepped into the aisle that divided the room. He was a red-faced man with a crew-cut and goatee of indiscernible color. "Something's got to be done about the students!"

Herb rested his jaw on his hand and closed his eyes. "Whaaat is it this time, Ned?" he asked, dragging his words.

"They're walking out into traffic all over town! It's a wonder they're not getting run over right and left. They don't look where they're going, they're jaywalking, they're crossing against the light. They have no respect for the law, no respect for anything. They think they own the town, that they can run through the streets and let the traffic be damned."

"Anything else, Ned?" the Dean asked. William noted that Herb still appeared to have his eyes closed. Herb continued, "I mean, are you making a motion here or just letting off steam?"

Laughter jettisoned from the back of the room down to the front. Ned turned to face the faculty members seated behind him and said, "Don't even get me started about students on bicycles. They ride those things like horses in an open field. You're driving along and all of a sudden, BOOM! From out of nowhere comes some kid like a bat out of hell—"

"Ned, is this really an issue for the faculty? After all, we have a police force in town to deal with these matters." Herb made an obvious show of looking at the large clock on a pillar at the side of the room.

"It's a town-gown issue!" Ned roared. "The townspeople get a bad impression of the students and then they get a bad impression of the whole lot of us. Well, something's got to be done about it, I say." He started to sit down, but then yelled so his voice echoed through the chamber, "Anybody with me?"

Ned remained standing, but the Dean waved at him to be seated. "Well," he said simply, looking out at those seated, "Anybody . . . with Ned?" He bit his lower lip trying not to smile.

William stood immediately.

"Yes, Professor Harris," Herb said, surprise in his voice. "You're concerned about town traffic?"

William cleared his throat for several seconds before speaking. "I think it would behoove Professor Siddons to remember that students are just that, *students.*" William perceived his voice to be calming, soothing. He said even more slowly, "If they're somewhat distracted when walking or cycling about town, is it really so surprising?" Now he punctuated his speech with enthusiasm, "They are at the most exciting juncture of their lives!" He raised his hands over his head as if he were announcing a football touchdown. "Their heads are filled with a myriad of thoughts. They possess an excitement for the ideas and concepts we're instilling in them. Remember whom we teach, my learned colleagues. After all, we were once students ourselves." As he spoke his last sentence, William tilted his head in what he fashioned a philosophical pose and waved his index finger softly in the air.

As he expected, the room was perfectly still as he sat. William looked down at his lap, aware that it would appear vain to look about for responses after such a well-spoken statement.

After several moments of silence, Herb finally asked, "Any response,

Ned?"

"Forget it," William heard the man say in a dejected voice. Well, that's another matter I put to rest, he thought with satisfaction.

"Fine," Herb said. "Our next meeting is scheduled for two weeks from today. We're adjourned."

William was disappointed that most faculty members immediately dispersed from the lecture hall. Why, the best part of a meeting was the debriefing afterward, the clusters of people talking animatedly about what had just taken place. He purposefully lingered at his desk, taking his time fastening the buckles on his briefcase, in case Herb wanted to thank him for putting an end to Ned Siddon's tirade. But when William stood, affecting a nonchalant look towards the front of the room, he saw that Herb was listening to a female faculty member who appeared not to be able to say anything without dramatic gestures. At one point, Herb stepped backwards, bumping into the blackboard, making more room for the woman to billow her arms about.

William started up the middle aisle of steps. He was almost to the door when he spied a book on one of the desks. Setting his briefcase on the floor, he picked up *The Decline and Fall of the Roman Empire.* Checking the spine of the fragile volume, he saw that it was the second volume of the six-volume set. The college library's call number had been taped and re-taped over the leather spine of the book. Well, at least someone's still reading the classics, he thought. But to whom did the book belong? Someone in history or classics, William guessed, but he scarcely knew anyone still teaching in those departments. He looked inside the back cover of the book for the card bearing the borrower's signature, but found an empty pocket. Turning the book over, he saw the striped black and white barcode in an upper corner. Then he remembered that when the library automated, borrowers' signatures on cards were a thing of the past. Exhaling, William whispered, "Ah, we must endure progress." I'll return it to the library and they can deal with it, he decided.

He opened his briefcase, intending to place the book inside it, but instead dropped the volume onto the floor, a small mound of dust erupting from the pages. As he was about to retrieve it, Herb and the gesturing woman walked past. "I understand your point, Joan," Herb said, "but there's no way we can force people to attend a workshop if they don't want to." They left the room and William heard their voices gradually diminish as they walked down the hallway.

William was alone in the room. Leaning over, he at last picked the book up and examined it for damage. The pages were so brittle, eager to crack with the slightest handling. What's this? William studied the pencil markings on both sides of the inside front cover. The script on the left page was difficult to read; the letters were small, dark, and scribbled upright. The writing on the right page, however, was flawless; curled but even letters tilted gracefully to the right. A delicate, feminine hand.

He read the first entry on the left page: "These faculty meetings are getting worse all the time!"

The response to this comment was on the facing page: "Don't take it seriously. Just think of it as Theater of the Absurd."

William smiled fully. Perhaps the young faculty today weren't so alienated after all. He had a mental picture of a young man and woman sitting side by side at the back of the room, the book open between them, perhaps the same pencil handed back and forth.

He read further: "I vote yes for having Yom Kippur off because it's one less day of teaching." And the woman's response: "So much for your religious convictions." William reverted to the page with poor penmanship and read: "I'm an atheist. Didn't you know?" The reply, written in such lovely letters puzzled him: "I suspected." Just who is the college hiring these days? For a moment, William questioned whether it was improper of him to read these remarks, this stealthy conversation between two people whose faces he probably wouldn't recognize. But he persuaded himself to read on, reasoning that if he didn't know the authors, it was harmless.

A few sentences on the left of the page could not be deciphered, although William gathered, based on the replies on the right side of the page, that they were about Ned Siddons. The female author had written: "I'm going to start laughing if he doesn't calm down," and "Speak up! You know you're *with him*." She had underlined the last two words of this sentence three times.

Remembering Ned Siddons calling on the faculty to rage with him about the students on their bicycles, William stifled a laugh but then realized he was alone and didn't need to hide his amusement. But the next sentence on the left of the page caught his attention: "Old windbag Harris is at it again."

He blinked and read the sentence again. Slowly William lowered himself into a chair and read the remaining entries:

"How long has he been retired?"

"Forever."

"Why does he still show up for meetings?"

"Bad case of 'Emerititus.' Old professors never die; they just go to faculty meetings."

"Why doesn't someone tell him to stay home?"

"Maybe the college is hoping he'll leave all his money to them."

The next and final sentence was such a non-sequitur, it struck William as surreal. Gently rolling letters composed the question: "Want to grab a pizza?"

William drove repeatedly around the rectangular pedestrians' park that was located in the heart of Hancock. Money, he thought, what money? "People don't go into academic work for the money, young man!" he shouted, not caring that the driver's window was rolled down half-way.

The book sat on the passenger seat. William imagined himself erasing the conversation, perhaps gluing new pages over the old. He would not return it to the library. Whoever had written such falsehoods about him would get a bill, hopefully a hefty one, for losing the volume.

He began his progression around the square again. As he stopped at the light on the northwest corner, his stomach bellowed loudly. William flinched. He disliked unfastidious noises. It's time for dinner, he thought, and decided to drive home. As the traffic light turned green, he stepped on the accelerator but then immediately stomped on the brake to avoid hitting a shirtless young man on a skateboard shooting by in front of his car. He finished rolling across the street and entered the park.

William fought for his breath for several seconds before he shouted, "You *imbecile!* What do you think you're doing!" He jerked the steering wheel hard to the left and drove over the curb, the wheels of his car bumping violently before he sped into the park. He could see the naked back of the student on the skateboard, one of his legs pushing against the ground to pick up speed.

William pressed his hand on the horn, a continuous siren ripping through the park. A family eating a picnic dinner looked shocked as he drove past, too disoriented to move. William didn't hear the older man raking leaves yell, "Hey! Cars aren't allowed in the park!" He drove on, determined to catch the impudent student.

Looking behind him, the student seemed confused by the ancient Buick barreling across the brick path. He picked up his skateboard and ran onto the grass. William swung the steering wheel to follow the student, but the front wheels of the car struck a park bench. William rocked forward, his head hitting the windshield, before he stopped the car. He sat in the motionless vehicle and watched as the student continued running, his long limbs carrying him through the shrubbery, past the swings and the rock garden, and over the newly planted flower beds. William roared, "Run, you bastard! *Rrr—uuu—nnn!*"

When the student was no longer visible, William looked around and blinked. Cars weren't allowed in the park, and a small group of incredulous looking students were gathered several feet away. One of them, a young woman, smiled and waved. "It's Professor Harris!" she yelled to the others as she ran over to the car. William thought she looked familiar; she must be one of his neighbors.

William opened the car door and stepped out slowly. Still shaken, he wanted to make sure his legs could hold him before he stood fully.

"That was *awesome*, Professor Harris!" the young woman said.

Her speaking prompted the other students to join her. A young man in denim overalls and no shirt extended his arm and shook William's hand. "Epic," he said, "really epic, Professor."

Startled but managing to stand taller, William said, "You think so?"

The student nodded and said, "Totally. You ruled that encounter, most definitely."

"Say, Professor Harris?" the young woman said. "You should come with us to the bonfire."

"Bonfire?" William asked.

She hopped with excitement. "Yeah, we're going to roast marshmallows and other stuff."

William gently shook his head. "Oh, thank you, dear, but I'm going to have to do something about my car. It will have to be towed—"

"Do it later, man, I mean, Professor," the young man said. "We can come back and push it after the bonfire. Right, guys?" The young man looked at the other students. One of them nodded and said, "Sure. Come with us, Professor." He gave William a hearty thump on his back.

When William said, "Well, all right," the group cheered, the student in overalls giving him an approving thumbs up. He walked through the park with the students, buoyed by their harmless banter and high spirits. He didn't know where he was going but the air held the scent of burning charcoal. Wherever they were going, they were getting closer.

ACKNOWLEDGEMENTS

Many of these stories appeared, in slightly different form, in literary magazines.

"A Lonely Virtue" originally appeared in *The Antigonish Review* under the title, "The Dean's Wife."

"Oracle House" originally appeared in *StoryQuarterly*.

"No Cost or Obligation" originally appeared in *American Literary Review*.

"Compromise" originally appeared in *Yuan Yang: A Journal of Hong Kong and International Writing* under the title, "Compromise House."

"Bag Head" originally appeared in *XX Eccentric, Stories About the Eccentricities of Women*.

"Live Your Life" originally appeared in *Other Voices*.

"The History of Prejudice" originally appeared in *The Iconoclast* under the title, "More Like Animals."

"Emeritus" originally appeared in *Thema*.

This book would not have been possible without the guidance, patience, and wisdom of Heather Tosteson, editor extrordinaire and an ever precious member of "the we of me." The author also thanks those writers and friends who read early drafts of these stories: June Goodwin, Barbara Savage Huff, Judy Kuns, and Nina Jaffee.

AUTHOR

Kerry Langan was born in Buffalo, New York, and completed her undergraduate and graduate education there. She had a career as an academic librarian before becoming a fiction writer. Prior to the publication of her first book, *Only Beautiful & Other Stories* (2009), her short fiction had appeared in more than forty literary journals published in the United States, Canada, and Asia, including *Other Voices, StoryQuarterly, American Literary Review, The Antigonish Review, Rosebud, Thema, The Seattle Review, The Cimarron Review, Fireweed,* and *Yuan Yang,* as well as in on-line journals. She is a co-editor of the recent Wising Up Anthology, *Shifting Balance Sheets: Women's Stories of Naturalized Citizenship & Cultural Attachment* (2011). She lives in Oberlin, Ohio, with her husband and daughters.

www.ingramcontent.com/pod-product-compliance
Lightning Source LLC
Chambersburg PA
CBHW030323020726
47493CB00004B/1136